slanderous tongue

slanderous tongue

A SUMACH MYSTERY BY

JILL CULINER

LIBARAY AND ARCHIVES CANADA CATALOGUING IN PUBLICATION

Culiner, Jill

Slanderous tongue : a Sumach mystery / Jill Culiner.
ISBN 978-1-894549-64-6
I. Title.

PS8605.U425S53 2007   C813'.6   C2007-900797-X

Edited by Cheryl Freedman
Copy-edited by Jennifer Day
Cover and design by Elizabeth Martin
Cover photo by Jill Culiner with Bernard Tisserand

*Sumach Press acknowledges the support of the Canada Council
for the Arts and the Ontario Arts Council for our publishing program.
We acknowledge the financial support of the Government of Canada
through the Book Publishing Industry Development Program
(BPIDP) for our publishing activities.*

ONTARIO ARTS COUNCIL
CONSEIL DES ARTS DE L'ONTARIO

Printed and bound in Canada

Published by
SUMACH PRESS
1415 Bathurst Street #202
Toronto Canada
M5R 3H8
info@sumachpress.com
www.sumachpress.com

ACKNOWLEDGEMENTS

It was on a wild and sodden night that I sat in an isolated sixteenth century French farmhouse and complained. About life in general. About the myriad frustrations of small village life and vicious village gossip. About hedges chewed up by machines, glorious trees ground into supermarket flyers, hideous housing developments gobbling up the countryside, and murdered chickens. Aloisia Bischof and Gilles Moëlo, owners of the farmhouse, listened — but with amusement. Don't bother complaining to us, one of them said (with a smile). Write about it. I will, I answered sourly. I'll turn all this stuff into an evil mystery. Good idea, they said (both smiling now).

Other people are also responsible for this book: Andrée Maugoussin, Pierrette Feuprier, Jean Borgogno, Rodolphe Bourdais — all villagers who tolerated my impertinent questions and invited me in to hear juicy stories about the old days, to learn about traditions long forgotten. Serge Paillard rummaged through libraries, finding me books on rural France. Josette Bonsard, Guillaume Le Comte and Pierre Fraboulet permitted me to lean over their country bars for months on end, listening to their fascinating tales.

Some gave me remarkably good information — the mystery writer Valerie Mazeau, Dr. Jean-Michel David, Dr. Ty Culiner, Danièle Thibault, Yves Besnard, ex-patriots Chris and David Ayress, Brian and Ann Gilbert, the gendarmes of Vaiges and Sainte Suzanne. For great patience, excellent suggestions and support, I thank Bernard "Bien-Aymé" Tisserand, Penny-Lynn Cookson and Roxanne O'Brien. Thanks to Lois Pike and Liz Martin at Sumach, to Jennifer Day whose discipline and determination caught out imperfections. And many thanks to my fabulous editor, Cheryl Freedman; her great knowledge of how mystery works, her humour and kindness helped shape *Slanderous Tongue*.

I am grateful, also, for the wisdom of my one and only true-to-life character: Werewolf.

1

Everyone in Épineux-le-Rainsouin knows that Madame Houdusse's spare change vanished on the same day Didier did — on Monday — although none of us are foolish enough to connect the two events. Didier, a grown man, strong and muscular, would certainly protest if anyone tried to steal him, whereas cash and other objects quietly disappear all the time. The church collection box was emptied in March, and two gold-plated chalices were removed in April; Madame Sauvebœuf now keeps the church doors firmly locked. On the night of April 28th, parked cars on the village square were divested of their radios. One week later, Monsieur Pateau's stock of wood was stolen from his outlying farm (he was absent at the time). The baker's black and white cat went missing on May 5th, a disappearance not necessarily attributed to crime, although some mumble the word vivisection, evoke the spectre of laboratories greedy for passive, trusting pets.

Madame Houdusse is understandably upset about the disappearance of her money, once sitting pretty in a decorated bowl on the sideboard in her dining room, right next to the baby photos sent by a second cousin once removed. Leaving her front door open to air the house (the weather has now turned very fine), she went to answer a ringing telephone in the kitchen. And in the winking of an eye, the coins were gone.

"I don't know how much was in there," her voice is distressed. "Perhaps twenty-five euros altogether. Not a fortune, perhaps. But the idea of people — probably foreigners — coming into my house, helping themselves to what belongs to me, well, that's what's so annoying. Letting too many of them into the country, they are. Not the way it used to be. English are the worst, coming here, jacking house prices up so high we can't afford them any more. Call it what you like, I say that's robbery, too."

With each retelling, she becomes increasingly indignant. We, the other residents, are sympathetic, of course. But we do not all agree as to the identity of the perpetrator (or perpetrators) of the various robberies. There are those who attribute them to gypsies — they are always the first to be accused in such cases — but no one has seen a gypsy here for well over a year, although Monsieur Vadepied claims their mobile homes were parked fifteen kilometres away along the Derval road. Madame Filoche, however, talks of a white Renault cruising through the village.

"The two men in it were looking at the buildings. Just driving slowly and looking. As if they were trying to find out which houses are occupied and which aren't."

Of course, we (and the police) demanded a description of the men.

"Darkish, I think," she said. "Maybe one of them had a black moustache, but I can't be sure. I wasn't paying attention, not all that much. But they were going slowly. Driving a Renault. I saw them several times. The man with the moustache, he was driving. Unless it was the other one who had the moustache. But two men, that's for certain. And I'm also certain it was a Renault. I don't know a lot about cars, of course. We women don't, do we? No, it was my late husband who was interested in details like that. Men always are, when it comes to cars. I would ask him, 'Now, what kind of car was that that just passed?' and he would always know. Always. But I can't tell one from the other myself."

There are others who mention, *sotto voce*, the local bad boy, Gilles. Perpetually jobless, living on welfare with his wife and three grown sons, Gilles has been held responsible for the "evaporation" of many objects: a pair of wooden shutters leaning against a wall (and destined for the rubbish pile), a few tools unwatched by their owners. He had given a party for thirty in the village restaurant, but left the bill unpaid. And he has borrowed quite a bit of money over the years — from Monsieur Douspis, from Monsieur Beauducel (since deceased), from Monsieur Filoche (also deceased), from the former baker Monsieur Viellepeau (now retired), from Monsieur Hautbois (roofer), from Monsieur Berthereau (cabinetmaker) — but neglected to return any of it. These days, Gilles keeps himself to himself. He has, indeed, been doing so for the last five years; since no one now greets him with anything other than a scowl when he crosses the square, he avoids us all.

Didier's absence is, as I said, rather a different matter. In fact, few of us ascribed any immediate importance to it. On Monday evening, he was seen going into his house, an eighteenth-century café modified by an American hand grenade during the war (retreating German soldiers said doors should be left open to indicate there were no hidden snipers, but the café owner ignored the suggestion), later renovated by Lemasson Enterprises into a modern structure in pink textured cement with PVC windows and PVC roll-down shutters. Certainly, Didier had gone out again that evening; he is said to have a very active social life, especially amongst the ladies. But where he went — or to whom — no one knows. And why hasn't he come back?

2

THIS INLAND *DÉPARTEMENT* OF FRANCE HAS NOTHING IN PARTICULAR TO offer the tourist. The landscape, agreeable enough, is not remarkable; gently sloping fields are hidden behind ancient hedges that farmers continue to rip out (some twenty-five thousand kilometres have disappeared since 1972). There are no gastronomic specialities, no fine wines, not many buildings of note for most have been drastically modernized since the late 1970s, an inauspicious era for architecture.

Our own village, Épineux-le-Rainsouin, cupped into a little scoop of a valley, snuggled against a low limestone cliff, was once hidden from pre-Roman invaders bent on pillage, destruction and doom. This modest situation should render it lovely, but lovely it isn't, and modern life renders modesty useless. The walls of the slate-roofed stone houses crouching around a thirteenth-century church are nowadays smothered under a thick layer of bright yellow or pink cement; their wooden framed windows have been replaced by the newest models in white PVC; wooden shutters have been rejected for white, electric PVC roll-downs. All improvements are orchestrated by our mayor's company, Lemasson Enterprises. Only crocheted curtains testify to tradition, as if inhabitants still wish to signal a certain pride in their ancestors' talents. These modern hangings, however, are not handmade; they come in cellophane packets, are purchased in hypermarkets.

As far as historical interest goes, there are few dates worthy of note. Three hundred thousand years ago, mammoth and woolly rhinoceros dwelt in Reuy's Cave before lumbering into extinction and being replaced by humans; yet even Reuy's Cave has vanished, filled in by the debris of most recent centuries. The French Revolution saw this village stoutly Catholic, defiantly Royalist; nonplussed by the rejection of liberty and equal rights, the new administration dubbed Épineux "a den of assassins and cannibals." Cannibals? Finally something intriguing! But supplementary information to support the appellation is lacking. Then, on January 15th, 1871, the limestone cliff above the village was a rather meek scene of battle during the Franco-Prussian War. The clash lasted mere hours; the armies moved on.

After 1918, when war widows were encouraged to run cafés to support themselves and their large families, five businesses opened their doors on the main square; here people met, talked, passed on news. There were various shops: a shoe shop, a dress shop, a hatter's, a household goods shop, a grocer's; there was a weekly *marché* with fruits, vegetables, clothes, live fowl, the occasional pig. My own house, a rather dilapidated building these days, was once a busy hotel, restaurant and café. But the bustle only lasted until the late 1970s. After that, young people began leaving, heading for towns and cities. Large supermarkets elsewhere fascinated villagers who would drive to them for an afternoon's sortie. Television replaced conversation. The hotel eventually closed its doors; the market, the cafés, the little village shops — aside from the baker's — all ceased to exist.

Today the main square has little to recommend it: it is not attractive, there are no trees, there is no grass. There is no longer horse manure on the road. There are no bumpy cobblestones, no chicken coops lining the sidewalks, no benches, as there once were, pushed against house walls, on which people would sit and analyze subjects of great interest: who was sleeping with whom, who was pregnant with whose baby. Perhaps to instil some modicum of beauty, three cement planters, created by Lemasson Enterprises, have been installed, and tidy geraniums and other domesticated forms of vegetation are permitted to grow in them under the watchful supervision of Didier, our presently absent *garde champêtre*. The square has now become a stretch of tidy, clean, empty pavement, dominated by the church, surrounded on all sides by two-storey, austere houses whose rows of windows are aligned, in almost martial determination, with those of their neighbour's. Perhaps I am the only villager to complain of this modern sterility? No doubt. These days, sterility is mistaken for good character.

Concentration has shifted to the new housing development in a former apple orchard east of the village: the pet project of our mayor,

Aimable Lemasson, president of Lemasson Enterprises. Mayor Lemasson says that we must keep up with the times, that the influx of new people into the development will bring fresh and vibrant life to the area, that little cement block houses, side by side on treeless streets, will add beauty and prestige. Most residents agree on all these points. Only a few of us are opposed; development adds nothing, we argue. Those who reside in such places work elsewhere, shop elsewhere, refuse to participate in village life, thinking it rustic, backward, not an adequate setting for their upwardly mobile ambitions. A housing development reduces a village to a bedroom community. But to the majority, we opponents of modernity are tired crocks, people of the old school, folk who cannot be taken seriously. Times are changing. We must keep up with the times!

So these days, Épineux-le-Rainsouin is the sort of village one drives through on the way to somewhere else. And driving through, one asks, "Who, in heaven's name, would want to live in a place like this? In a dead end like this?"

There's no definite answer. People live here because they are born here and are unable, forever after, to escape the sticky flypaper attraction of the place. Or, expecting a modicum of quaint village neighbourliness, outsiders — especially the British — buy houses here, then come to realize it isn't too awfully neighbourly, after all.

But neighbourly or not, a village is a microcosm. Although we make no great history, the mettle of greater places — Washington, Toronto, Beirut, London, Paris or Berlin — can be measured by the small events taking place in Épineux-le-Rainsouin. Here, too, is domestic violence, theft, corruption, adultery and even murder. Accuse us of being small-time? Why, the great of the world could not exist without us, the villagers. We point the way.

3

FROM HER LEAF-GREEN, FAKE LEATHER ARMCHAIR PLACED AT THE FRONT
window of her house (once a café and shop for household items)
Madame Douspis keeps watch over the village square, direction east.
She can see the road that passes the former branch line train station,
renovated into an oddly shaped, yellow cement village hall by Lemasson
Enterprises in 1996; the ancient stone bridge, reconstructed in steel and
cement by Lemasson Enterprises in 1964; the only remaining café-res-
taurant, an ancient building modified to resemble, oddly enough, a pink
beauty parlour; and, most important, the entire village square just in
front of the church. Pretty well nothing escapes the scrutiny of Madame
Douspis's faded blue but insistent eagle eye. Monsieur Douspis, less interested in comings and goings, sits at the dining room table, staring
straight ahead at the television high on the sideboard, watching well-
loved game show hosts award expensive consumer goods to guests with
knowledge of sports triumphs, soap opera melodramas, movie star scan-
dals and pop group successes. Does Monsieur Douspis listen to his wife
when she recounts the events happening right here, right on the square?
Whether he's listening or not, he has no excuse for not knowing what
is going on.

"Monsieur Vadepied is on his way to his garage — that's the fifth time
this morning. He has a hammer in his hand. And Madame Sauvebœuf
is going to get something from the shop — I can't imagine what. She
was there, at the shop, twice yesterday. But don't tell me that she goes
there because she needs something. I know better than that. She goes to
see if there's anything anyone's gossiping about. That's what she's like.
Nosy and prying."

From her house on the corner, just across the narrow road, to the left
of the church and village square, Madame Filoche keeps watch, direction

south, through large windows installed in 1920 by a clever cobbler who, foreseeing the popularity of straw-stuffed wooden clogs coming to a close, copied and displayed chic Parisian models. Madame Filoche's windows, however, are covered with semi-transparent curtains; she rarely lights a lamp. We never know, therefore, when she is at her post. Only when something of particular interest takes place on the square — if I appear with a guest, for example — does Madame Filoche pop, quite suddenly, out of her front door. Unwilling to give the impression she is nosy and prying, Madame Filoche always has an excuse for these appearances: "I'm just waiting for the postman because I need stamps. And you have a visitor. I thought so. I said to myself that you did." Unabashedly, she will poke her copper dyed, impeccably coiffed head forward, and peer short-sightedly at the object of immediate interest. Madame Filoche firmly believes that respectable folk should hide nothing.

Madame Beauducel controls the western view of the square from her house, once a thirteenth-century tithe barn tastefully renovated into a house in the nineteenth century, more dubiously modernized by her late husband in the 1960s. It stands slightly behind and to one side of our church, created in 1296, enlarged in 1412, hit by lightning in 1674, enlarged again in 1856, tastelessly renovated in 1972 by Lemasson Enterprises. Due to the position of her house, Madame Beauducel has a limited view: only half the village square, my house, the Douspis's house, Christelle's house, Didier's house. Because of this, she is often outside in winter as well as summer, tending to and watering the great many potted plants set against her walls.

Madame Sauvebœuf, on the southern corner of the square, has one great advantage over the other ladies. Her house, once the Catholic school and now neatly renovated into a yellow cement structure, is perched between two narrow roads: one climbs up past the cemetery and comes to a dead end at Malabry's intensive chicken farm; the second wanders its lazy way past damp fields and on to the next village. Perched thus between two roads, Madame Sauvebœuf's house has two doors. Depending on what or whom she wishes to observe, she will exit out of either opening. Rumour has it she writes down her observations in little notebooks, but this could be mere calumny, for Mesdames Beauducel, Douspis and Filoche do not like Madame Sauvebœuf; they consider her a gossipmonger and are not in the least averse to blackening her already miserable reputation.

One thing is certain: Madame Sauvebœuf's mother, who ran a brisk and materially satisfying black market trade in butter, eggs and meat during the Second World War, really did note down details: who crossed the square when, who visited whom, tidbits from overheard conversations. Perhaps she thought this was her duty? She was often heard to say, "Someone must attend to the order of things," and as others were apparently too lackadaisical or too untrustworthy for the task, she took it up. But Madame Sauvebœuf's mother has been dead these many years; impossible to know if her daughter, a woman in her late seventies, has continued on in the travail. Once, I asked Madame Sauvebœuf if her mother's old notebooks still existed. She was evidently embarrassed; perhaps she did not like the idea that I, a foreigner, one from faraway Canada, knew of them. She stared at me, flushed a fairly unattractive, bruised pink, and mumbled, "I don't know what happened to the notebooks. Even if they did exist once, they don't now because my four brothers burnt them along with my mother's other old papers when she died. And I never heard about the notebooks anyway. No one told me about them."

But if Madame Sauvebœuf doesn't continue on in the scrupulous ways of her mother, her husband, Monsieur Sauvebœuf, does. Several times a day, he appears on the village square and notes down licence plate numbers of cars parked there. I haven't seen him do this myself, but Christelle has. Or so she says. You never know with Christelle, though. She deeply dislikes the Sauvebœufs, claiming that they, her close neighbours, are always observing her. And what's more, Christelle is a liar. She can't tell the truth to save her life.

4

THE VILLAGE IS DIVIDED INTO TWO GROUPS: THOSE WITH WINDOWS, those with windows. The traditionalists, the folk without the Internet, gather information by observation and pass it on *en direct*. Thus, every morning at ten-thirty, Mesdames Beauducel and Filoche gather at Madame Douspis's to drink coffee, to consort (Madame Sauvebœuf is excluded from these rendezvous for the ladies claim to dislike gossip-mongers). Of course, Madame Douspis, a crabby, sarcastic old lady, often complains about the ritual; she doesn't like sharp-tongued Madame Filoche very much, nor is she fond of Madame Beauducel, a hatchet-faced, almost lipless woman of remarkably few words. "When the two of them are here, drinking my coffee and sitting pretty, you just can't get rid of them. They're capable of staying glued to their seats the whole morning!"

But Madame Douspis's house is the only logical place for all to meet, for Madame Douspis has legs that are so swollen, she never goes outside, except for occasional Sunday forays to restaurants for extended lunches. And since Mesdames Filoche and Beauducel are widows, they are not at all loath to leave the silence of their now too-roomy dwellings and linger there.

I also go to see the Douspis's, for both she and her husband are fond of me. Their horizon has shrunk to prune-size, and when we are together, I ask them questions about their younger days, about the old traditions that have vanished; I am an amateur ethnologist, and they possess exactly the sort of information I need. They are more than happy to please me, are satisfied to see me jot down their words. I promise them eternity of a sort; because of me, their stories will not be forgotten. And for me, it is necessary to have such contacts in the village: my life as a single woman, my work as a collector of almost forgotten traditions, can be a solitary one. I gather, go home, turn on my computer, fit together bits and bobs. I need the immediacy of contact, the co-operation of all. Perhaps because I am considered to be shamefully nosy (and, to a certain extent, this is true), some regard me with suspicion. "Why does she want to know so much? Times have changed; we have moved on. Why is it important to know what was discussed around the village pump or in the village wash house all those long years ago? We are not like that anymore. We mind our own business these days. We stay home; we watch the televised game shows. What is she doing, *l'étrangère?* But it is exactly this nosiness that allows me, a foreigner, to have doors opened, to be accepted as a quaint part of the scenery, part of the community.

So this sunny, mild Wednesday morning, I abandon my scruffy black and white dog, Werewolf, on the sidewalk, go into the Douspis's house, which is, in fact, attached to mine on the left by a party wall, sit down at the grey melamine table (a beauty in cherrywood is now, mysteriously, exiled to the attic) on an uncomfortable chair of aluminum tubes and grey melamine (the six that match the cherrywood table also dwell in the attic) in this room with its redone fireplace (once big enough to grill a whole hog and now reduced to uselessness by new zigzag slabs of false granite). I accept a little cup of acidic coffee, submit to a conversation spiked with nationalistic interjections.

"Life is good in France, isn't it?" says Madame Filoche. "You have to admit that life is better in France than anywhere else. And we have the best food in the world, don't we? Everyone has to admit that. All the foreigners. You don't eat at all well in your country, in Québec, do you? Everyone knows that. In Québec, where you come from."

"Not Québec. Ontario," I say, although I have — quite uselessly — made this correction many times over.

"Ontario? Well, maybe. But you still come from the country of Québec."

"Québec is a province like Ontario. Canada is the country."

"Call it what you like. We call it Québec." And all nod in agreement.

There are also the daily, enthusiastic discussions of illness.

"I've just taken six pills," Madame Douspis announces with pride, for she glories in the fact that medical science makes great strides with the express purpose of keeping her alive.

Monsieur Douspis, until now entranced by prancing comedians and raucous laughter on the television screen, shifts a bleary gaze towards his wife. "And me?" he asks plaintively. "What about me? My legs hurt. Me, what am I to take? What does the doctor prescribe for me? No pills, no pills at all. Just a powder to take three times a day. And I take it, this powder. But I still have the same pains in my legs. Nothing works at all anyway, not pills, not powders. So what's the point, I want to know? What's the point?"

"Twenty pills a day, it adds up to," continues Madame Douspis, pointedly ignoring her husband. "What kind of a life is this, I ask you? What kind of a life?"

"And the ringing in my ears never stops," counters Monsieur Douspis. "Especially when the church bells chime, twice every hour, once every half-hour. And then the church chimes stop, but you tell me, does the ringing in my ears stop, too? No, no. On and on it goes. On and on. I never have a minute of silence, never. I suffer. All the time, I suffer."

"And I have to take my pills every hour of the day for the rest of my life. Every single hour. Here are the ones I have to take at eleven sharp," Madame Douspis taps her pink, hooked fingernail on one compartment of a long plastic pill holder ever present on the table. "At noon, there are five more. Five!" She taps again. "This afternoon, there will be eight more. Eight."

"And I don't sleep well either," says Monsieur Douspis, who has to get up three times a night to help his wife to the bathroom.

"That's easy enough to cure," says Madame Beauducel, determined to show her loyalty for Madame Douspis. "If you sleep badly, that means there's an underground stream passing just under your bed. You have to move it and make sure it's standing in a northerly direction."

"And you know what the doctor has told you," says Madame Douspis. "He said you should get out, walk, lose weight. If you did that, you'd be in better shape. You'd stop complaining." Madame Douspis looks as chuffed as a boa digesting a tasty crocodile. She, of course, never walks anywhere, has refused to do so for years. And she does love her food. But as far as diets and walks go, well, somebody ought to be doing those. Why not her husband?

"And if I do get out and walk, then my back starts to hurt. So what's the point?" Monsieur Douspis sends me a look that begs for commiseration. But we all well know he doesn't want to be in better health. Illness has become a competitive game between husband and wife; it lends purpose to their life now that their four children live far away and rarely come to see them. Illness is excitement, it is tension, it's the glue that holds the marriage together. Madame has all maladies known to the animal world; Monsieur has pain.

Madame Douspis turns her beady eyes to me. "Of course, *you* are in good health, aren't you?"

"Yes, I am," I say rather guiltily and shrug my shoulders in dutiful apology.

"And so you can get out and about. See what's going on. See what's happening in the village." Madame Douspis pauses for a second, looks triumphantly at the others, turns back to me with sly and poorly hidden glee. "So tell us. What's new? What have you heard?"

All stare at me, bright-eyed, hoping I'll finally play the game, open my mouth, come up with a real pearl. "Nothing is new," I say, as I pretty well always do.

"And what about that no-good next-door neighbour of yours? That Christelle?"

"What about Christelle?" I ask innocently enough.

"What's she up to now?"

"No idea."

The anticipation in the eyes of Mesdames Beauducel, Filoche and Douspis dims. They are annoyed, for they are absolutely convinced I know something — some secret, some glorious, scandalously vile tidbit of information. But what? And how to get it?

"Who was in the café?" Madame Douspis prompts, for I am the only woman who goes in there each morning to talk with the owner, Pierre.

"Michel, the postman, came in very briefly. Then Philippe, the truck driver who hauls off dead animals, stopped for a coffee."

"And what did everyone talk about?"

"Not a lot. Pierre and Philippe talked about the football match. I read the paper."

And so, without my confidences, without news, as poor as they were before my arrival, they are obliged to conjure up other topics of immediate interest.

"The hairdresser was ten minutes late in getting her bread this morning," says Madame Filoche. "Probably has a lot of clients. She does well for herself." She makes a disagreeable little moue. Madame Filoche doesn't like anyone doing too well. She also doesn't like people who don't do well — people like Christelle, my neighbour. Christelle certainly doesn't do well for herself.

"And Didier, no one has seen him yet this morning. Not this morning, not yesterday either," says Madame Douspis. "He should have brought me my eggs yesterday at nine o'clock. He said he would bring them Tuesday." She looks out the window, looks out at the village square. Nothing much to see out there, only Monsieur Vadepied crossing as usual, back and forth, back and forth. Fifty metres down is his garage; he goes there to get wood for his stove in the house, to fetch a hammer, a nail, a screwdriver, a screw or a wheelbarrow. He brings a hammer, a screwdriver, a wheelbarrow from his house back to his garage. He inspects his car; he admires his woodpile. He is ever a man with a mission.

"I want eggs, too," says Madame Filoche. "When you see Didier, tell him I want a dozen eggs."

"Just as soon as he shows up here," says Madame Douspis, who makes a little egg money taking orders for Didier, who keeps chickens in a large, grassy field just outside the village. He is remarkably sentimental about the birds, Didier is, letting them grow fat and confident on good corn, wheat, bugs and worms, keeping them until they die of old age, breeding the best. To preserve the genetic material of the sturdier, more rustic chickens for future generations, he keeps various races: the round, miniature Java hens that are ferocious, protective mothers; orange Orpingtons, the best layers in cold winter months; Meusiennes with miniscule heads perched on their substantial bodies. There are others, too — those nearly extinct since the Second World War: black La Flèche, Gauloise dorée, elegant white Gâtinaise. Because his chickens are genetically diverse, they are more resistant to disease, to the mutation of viruses. He is quite adamant about this. He also believes that when birds survive infection, they pass resistant genes on to their young.

Perhaps to encourage good luck even further, Didier follows the old local custom of placing a horseshoe in the nest of brooding hens to ward off the evil eye. Whether or not this bit of quaint superstition is influential, we are all more than happy to buy the eggs his hens produce, even if they are somewhat dearer than those in the village shop. Thanks to Didier, we know those other eggs come from genetically modified chickens living in overcrowded sheds under artificial lights. Like all battery hens, their beaks have been sliced off so they don't peck each other to death; unable to forage, they feed on growth stimulants and chemical mush. When avian flu breaks out, it does so in confined battery flocks, certainly not amongst Didier's free-range creatures.

"Didier will definitely be coming here this morning," says Madame Douspis. She looks out onto the village square again, but now there is no one to see, not even Monsieur Vadepied. Just a car on its way to somewhere else. "It's strange," she muses. "I didn't see Didier at all yesterday. No one saw him. He should have been out watering the flowers. But he wasn't. You also want eggs?" she asks me.

"Sure. Why not? But I only need six."

"Me, too," says Madame Beauducel. "I want eggs, too. My son is coming on the weekend with his children. I'll need eggs for a cake. A dozen."

Madame Douspis nods. "I'll tell Didier when he comes."

"If he comes," says Madame Filoche with a triumphant note of dissatisfaction. It gives her great pleasure to say something bad about someone if she can possibly manage it. "You haven't seen him since Monday evening. I haven't seen him. No one has seen him. He's probably slacking off. That would be typical. You can't trust young people these days. They're always slacking off. Don't want to work, not like we used to, up every morning at dawn and out in the fields. And Didier, he's too handsome for his own good. A man for the ladies, that's what he is. He's probably in bed at this very moment. In bed and having a nice time, if you ask me."

"Not Didier," retorts Madame Douspis. "Didier wouldn't slack off. He always does his job correctly. He's dependable. Of course, he has women friends. He's a bachelor. But he wouldn't stay in bed the whole day."

"A young buck like that," sneers Madame Filoche, happily hacking

Didier's reputation to shreds. "A young buck always has a dozen women somewhere. That's where Didier is. Holed up with a dozen women."

"A dozen?" I ask. "A dozen all at once? Dear me. Madame Filoche, how do you know about such things?"

Madame Douspis snickers, but Madame Filoche throws me a look that could kill. "I don't know at all about things like that," she spits. "But I know how to listen, all right, and I know what some people get up to. Like *La Belle de Nuit*, for example. That's what people like *La Belle de Nuit* get up to. You can defend her if you want to, but there's no point. Can't trust her, can't believe a word she says. The one time she went to Madame Beaupied to have her hair cut, she claimed she was a distant relative of Maurice Chevalier and that he died owing her money. As if we were all going to believe that. As if she thought we were stupid enough to fall for lies. Who does she think we are? She has a nerve!"

All three women give a communal grunt of concurrence. Then they look over at me, hoping I will chip in, finally, with a good bit of malicious gossip. Finally. But I don't, of course. For despite her quirks, her lies, Christelle (called by the ladies *"La Belle de Nuit"* because she often goes out at night and doesn't return until the early hours of the morning, and because she entertains a considerable number of male visitors in her home), is a friend of mine. Sort of. Besides, I rarely give out information, at least never the vicious, slanderous, juicy sort the ladies crave.

"Well," Madame Filoche continues, "even if you don't want to know what is going on, there was a little white van parked in front of her house last night, and on Sunday night there was a green van. There is also someone who comes with a red car, but I only saw him once, that one. And they always come late at night. Just at the very moment that I close the shutters in my bedroom. That's when I see them, all those cars parked outside of her house." Her piercing little eyes prod from behind her metal-rimmed spectacles. "Do you know who they are, those men?"

"I never look out the window to check cars, to see who is afoot in the village and who is visiting whom," I answer, mildly enough. "I couldn't care less what Christelle does with her evenings or what she does once the door is closed and the curtains drawn. It's none of my business."

But Madame Filoche, she considers that sort of thing her business. She is eighty-four years old; her husband has been dead for many years. She has to pass the time doing something in an agreeable enough way, and observing Christelle's house, the comings and goings of her callers, is certainly an interesting hobby. And with Christelle, there are quite a few comings and goings.

But at the same time, I am thinking of something else. I am thinking of the nights when Madame Filoche is looking out of her window in the direction of Christelle's house. Perhaps on some of those nights, it is not only Christelle's visitors she sees? Perhaps she sees someone else — someone who comes to visit me? Someone who would rather not be seen. Perhaps her question is a veiled accusation? Perhaps she knows more than I think she does? But no, I tell myself. They are not very subtle, these ladies. They believe that because I am a foreigner, I am less intelligent than they. Were they suspicious, they would also be more blatant. So I ignore Madame Filoche and her little, shining eyes.

"You know she receives, don't you?" she asks me.

"Receives?" I say, innocently. "Receives what?"

Madame Filoche's expression changes to one of disgust. She knows I'm only faking. "Men! She receives men all night long. She receives! Doesn't she tell you that?"

I shrug. "I don't ask her if she 'receives,' do I? And anyway, she is a single woman. Why shouldn't she have boyfriends? She is young, only in her mid-thirties. So she has men who visit her. How do you know what she's doing when they come? Just because they are in her house, that doesn't mean she goes to bed with all of them, does it?"

There is a little pause. All shift their gaze away from me, look at each other, and shrug (except for Monsieur Douspis whose eyes have returned to the dancing comedians in drag). They are frustrated, to be sure, these ladies. I give them no satisfaction.

5

THE HOUSE WHERE CHRISTELLE LIVES ALSO SHARES A PARTY WALL WITH
mine on the right, for it was once part of my old hotel; her main room
was the ladies' café. Sold off in the early nineteenth century, her section
became a grocer's in the good old days when such shops sold pretty well
everything: thread, needles, rope, screws, buttons, gift items, local cheese,
farm-made cider. Older villagers still remember, with great nostalgia,
enormous mounds of creamy butter on the shop counter; cuts were tak-
en with a thin piece of wire strung between two wooden pegs. Now the
grocery is merely a badly renovated, rented house, easily accessible from
mine. To visit Christelle, I simply go out of my unlocked back door,
walk through my courtyard, open the unlocked wooden gate that leads
to her courtyard, go to her side door and knock: three staccato taps,
then two — a code we have agreed upon, for normally Christelle never
comes to the door or answers her phone; too many people are dunning
her for unpaid bills. Because I take this back route, prying eyes can't see
how often I come to talk to her. For, I must admit, I'm not proud of this
relationship; I don't really want my name associated with hers.

So why go to see her at all? Partly because I'm nosy, partly because
I purchase the occasional cigarette from her (I never buy a pack in case
I smoke them all, one after the other). And partly because we are both
single women and, as such, have constructed a sort of friendship, have
exchanged a few tales. Like me, Christelle is ever searching for the perfect
mate, for another crack at true love, although she has decided that any
permanent future spouse will provide her with a baby or two, a nice new
house, a big screen television, lots of new, expensive clothes and many
other consumer goods to which she feels entitled.

But as I mentioned, Christelle is a liar. When she first arrived in
the village, she told me she was a clothing designer but as things were,

at the moment, bad for design, she was taking a well-deserved break from that rat race. She had once been a student of the *beaux arts*, she said, and she is also an artist (the badly filled-in paint-by-numbers, cardboard Van Goghs, Monets and Cézannes hanging on her walls are meant to justify that tale). Later, having forgotten the stories of art and design, she claimed to have been a top-level salesperson; this would, at least, be believable, for she is a fast talker, a fantasy spinner. She also maintains she is unbeatable at the pool table, has earned considerable sums playing in the bars at night. She is waiting for a large inheritance from her deceased father who lived in the Caribbean, but her uncle's lawyers are conspiring against her. She is plagued by debt; she always has a big deal on the hob. She worked in an art gallery and was brilliant with both painters and clients, but the job came to a nasty end when she disagreed with her greedy boss.

She often talks about her family, the big house she grew up in near Poitiers, the family manufacturing business. But those, too, are lies like all the rest. She sometimes claims her family is in international transport, sometimes in the cement business. Or they are all in real estate, or in the travel industry. And as far as the big house goes, I've seen pictures of it: it is nothing more than an ugly yellow cement villa in a housing development — the modern defeat of French aesthetics. The two real facts I know are that the family she so often mentions will have nothing to do with her, and she has had two children removed from her care by social services. That's the real reason she's here in this drowsy village. She thinks that if she gives the appearance of living a good, clean, quiet life, her two kids will be given back to her. She doesn't have the vaguest idea that she hasn't fooled anyone.

In fact, Christelle is a born loser. She moves house every few years because she makes trouble for landlords. She drinks, drives, staggers home on unsteady legs that, far too often, don't carry her as far as her front door. She lives off welfare, refuses to find a job. Even when social workers insist she make an effort, Christelle, a wily character, manages to be unqualified for all prospects. If, nonetheless, she is placed in a company, she shows up late for work on a daily basis, does the job badly enough, takes off weeks for sick leave; no one has the slightest qualm about firing her as quickly as possible. Then, with great satisfaction, she sits herself down, turns on her television, pours out a glass of wine, lights a cigarette, talks about what jerks all bosses are. Her life is in order once again.

Basically, give Christelle a normal opportunity and she'll screw it up.

Today, when Werewolf and I enter her house, the television is on and blaring, as usual. It's a game show she's watching, and she shouts out the correct answers with triumph. As ever, she is smoking a cigarette and drinking a glass of wine. She's happy to see me, though. I'm pretty well the only person in the village with whom she has contact, and that in a strange way gives me an obligation to keep on being her friend. It's a character quirk of mine; I hate the idea of people being discriminated against — even if it's their own fault. And Christelle really does all the things that put people's backs up; she even avoids Pierre's café, thinking it too close to home, and instead picks up admirers in more anonymous town bars, in distant discotheques.

It is, of course, not hard to see why men are attracted to her: she is dark-haired, handsome, with large, brown, slanting eyes and the golden skin of a southerner. To her great advantage, she doesn't care a fig about her reputation; if the village gossips note the comings and goings of her beaux, what is it to her?

"You were at the Douspis's this morning?" shouts Christelle as she hands me a cigarette and I pass over the usual thirty *centimes* to pay for it. I can't miss the little note of jealousy tacked on to her question.

"Of course."

"They hate me," she yells. Even if the television wasn't blaring away, she'd be yelling. She always does. Christelle hasn't the vaguest idea what a mild tone of voice is.

"It's not that they hate you," I say with a little inner sigh. "It's just that you never say 'hello' to anyone when you see them on the street. People don't like that very much. They get offended. Yet it's an easy thing to do, you know. In a village, elementary politeness is required if you want people to be nice to you."

She ignores my words as if they are in a foreign tongue, one she can neither assimilate nor apply. It's so much easier to complain. People like Christelle prefer to feel persecuted. Victims don't need to change. They need their well-cultivated victim image to feel good about themselves and bad about everyone else.

"So what did they have to say, all those frustrated, dried up, unscrewed old bags who haven't had it in years and've forgotten what their cunts are made for. Never knew in the first place that you could have a good time with them." She chortles loudly at her own wit.

Once more, I sigh inwardly. "Nothing special. Just that no one has seen Didier either yesterday or today. He was supposed to bring eggs to Madame Douspis and he didn't."

"Didier!" shouts Christelle with a grimace. "That asshole."

"Asshole? Why is he an asshole? He's pretty good-looking. More or less friendly." And also around Christelle's age. Certainly, she must find him attractive as a male. Or perhaps that's exactly the problem: Didier doesn't show any interest in her.

"Not to me, he's not good-looking," says Christelle. "And I don't think he's so friendly. Not to me anyway. He's selfish, if you ask me. One day I asked him to come over here, repair the tap in the kitchen. It was leaking and the dripping sound was driving me crazy. I mean, in principle a *garde champêtre* knows how to repair things, right? I don't have money to go calling up Paillard, the plumber, right? And you know what he said to me, Didier? He said no. He wasn't a plumber. That he wasn't going to come and fix taps. That I could just call Paillard like everyone else does when they have a problem."

"Well, it's true," I say. "Why should Didier come to your house and do plumbing? And if he did, his name would be mud here in the village. Paillard would claim he was taking away work that should be his. You know how people are here. Jealous."

"I wasn't going to pay him," says Christelle with a look of sly astonishment. "I don't have money for that kind of shit."

"Oh, right. So Didier should have been thrilled to bits to be allowed to come over here and do some work." Of course, Christelle doesn't recognize sarcasm. And she never hesitates to ask for favours from any male who crosses her path, thinking that all in the big wide whirling world owe her a living. On the rare occasions when she really does have to call in a repair man (a car mechanic, for example), there's no way she's actually going to pay cash. A flirt, a kiss, a bit of sex — those

things are right up her alley. But not good cash that could be better
spent on booze, fags and clothes. And as far as Didier is concerned, a
roll in the hay with Christelle wouldn't interest him; she just isn't rich or
respectable enough. Those two things are important to him; I happen
to know that.

"Doesn't matter." Christelle lights up another cigarette. "He's still
an asshole, Didier. But I don't want to talk about him anyway. There's
something else I want to tell you. I have a big deal going. Big money will
be rolling in. Finally."

I shift in my seat. I'm always miserably uncomfortable when
Christelle starts in on her bullshit. "How's that?"

"The Internet. The Internet's the answer. I'm setting myself up as
a freelance secretary. People will contact me on the Net, give me their
business. I'll write out their letters, send them off. Big money in that."

Here we go again, I think. What does Christelle know about
secretarial work? Or the Internet? "How are you going to get an Internet
connection?" I ask. "You told me you can't even get a telephone hookup
because of your outstanding telephone bill. You only have a mobile."

"Don't need a normal telephone hookup. I'm getting high-speed
satellite Internet. Social services arranged it all. I asked them for money
to equip myself to work out of my home as a secretary. Told them
months ago I needed it all to set myself up in business. That I have to
do business from here because I'm not healthy enough to get out all the
time. That I suffer from bad migraines and that working from home
is just the right solution for me. So all the stuff arrived last week — a
gorgeous new laptop, a scanner, a printer. I get the Internet connection
tomorrow."

This time, I believe her. The one thing she doesn't screw up is
getting something for free from social services. That, she's brilliant at,
Christelle.

"I don't think you should count on making a lot of money," I say.
"Lots of people think they're going to get rich with the Internet, but
it doesn't work out that way. How are you going to find clients, for a
start?"

"No problem," she shouts with her usual smugness. "People will
hear about me, then use my service because I'm a lot better than other

Internet secretaries. Don't forget I've been to law school. Have a degree in law."

"You do? When did this happen? When did you get a law degree?"

She looks away, stares at the television where a gleaming Citroën is roaring across a prairie in some roadless Third World country, takes a long deep drag of her cigarette. "Been doing it for the last four years." Lying never fazes her. "Been going to night school. That's why I'm out all the time at night. I know that everyone says I just go hang around the bars, but it's not true. Got my law degree in the mail last week. Remind me to dig it out when I have some time, show it to you."

"I will. And secretarial work, what do you know about that? You'll have a lot of competition if you want to do it."

The Citroën commercial ends, and we are back to the game show and the sparkling teeth of the game show moderator. "Competition doesn't scare me. You've got to move with the times if you want to get ahead in the world." She drops her smoked-out butt into the ashtray, lights up the next cigarette. "I've also been doing a computer course in Derval for the last few months. Social services paid for the whole thing. How to set up your own business, how to use Word, Excel, Power Point. How Explorer works. I'm good at it now, really good. Good enough to make a bundle."

"You've really been doing a computer course?" I ask doubting, as usual, everything she says. I just can't see Christelle actually applying herself to anything serious.

But she isn't in the mood to continue the conversation. She's busy concentrating on the question being asked up on the television screen. She shakes her head in disapproval. "Julia Roberts," she answers promptly. "That one was easy. Too easy. But it's worth a thousand euros just the same. I'm the one should be up there on the show. Going to put my name in to be a contestant. Win some cash. Was already asked to do that a few years ago, but I was too busy back then."

"Oh yeah?" I say. Yeah, right.

6

Thursday morning, Werewolf and I cross the village square that is pleasingly rinsed in spring yellow sun. Monsieur Vadepied, a needle-thin figure ever topped by headgear of indefinable shape and matter, is on his way between house and garage, wrench in hand.

"You hear about the horrible accident on the road to Derval a few days ago?" he asks me. Monsieur Vadepied's conversation is always punctuated by violent death and suffering. "Funeral's today. One of the men in the fire department. Went home after work. Boss asked him if he wanted to go with him and some of the guys to the match in the city. Said no, he was going home, going to take a shower, have a meal, then going to see his girlfriend. Went home, took a shower, had a meal, then drove to Derval to see the girlfriend. On the way was a van parked by the side of the road, but didn't see it. Drove right into it. Smack, just like that. Drove right into it. Didn't have any lights on, the van didn't."

"Oh," I say.

"Head cut right off. Right off. Neat. Just like that." He makes an executioner's gesture, finger slicing neatly across throat.

"Oh," I say.

"Big funeral today. Won't be able to get in, so many people. In the cemetery in Derval."

"Oh," I say.

"Wet," he adds mysteriously.

"Wet? What's wet?"

"Dug graves there for years, in Derval. People say no water under the ground here, that everything's run dry. But not true. Water in the cemetery in Derval. Poisoned water. Used to work there, used to dig graves. We'd begin with shovels. After that, had to use pails. But the families, when the hole was done, they didn't see any water. Took it all out with pails first. If they saw water, they wouldn't have liked that."

"I suppose not," I say, while attempting to look thoughtful and concerned.

He waves cheerily, continues on his way. I walk over the little bridge near the *lavoir* (the old wash house), pass the mayor's house, go into the pink, frilly café and sit down on a stool at the plastic, marble-look bar.

"So how're the ethnologists of the world doing?" Pierre scoffs as he gets the espresso machine into action. He's a good-looking man in his early forties, with curly hair and bad teeth. I consider him a friend, despite the regularity of his sarcastic comments about my occupation, an activity he considers utterly futile. What's important in life, as far as Pierre is concerned, are the results of the match, the eventual purchase of a new car, the number of clients eating in his restaurant, the daily struggle to keep the last village café open.

"The ethnologists are doing just fine last time I looked," I answer somewhat testily. I'm not in the mood to defend myself again; doing it just gets too boring after a while.

"Good to hear," he mocks. "Good to hear you're all doing fine. Except the old days are over and done with. This is the twenty-first century."

I shrug. "You know what Einstein said: 'Great spirits have always encountered violent opposition from mediocre minds.'"

Pierre ignores this, but looks sour suddenly. Stick in a reference, any reference that might have come from a book, and he feels threatened. Gets huffy.

The door of the café opens and in rushes Michel, the postman. "Either of you seen Didier this morning?" he asks as he slaps down a pile of envelopes (probably bills) on the fake marble.

Pierre merely shrugs his negative, deliberately ignores the mail (he probably knows the envelopes contain only bills) and looks over at me with a faintly knowing expression. "How about you?"

"Why should I have seen Didier?" I ask defensively. "I don't keep tabs on the guy."

"It's just that everyone's been asking where he is," says Michel.

"Got the mayor pissed off, too, Didier has," says Pierre. "Was here this morning for a coffee. Talking about Didier. About how he didn't work on Tuesday or yesterday. Which isn't like Didier at all. If he's one thing, he's dependable."

"Well, he didn't deliver eggs to Madame Douspis either," I say. "And that's bound to cause a revolution on the village square."

"Probably attending some animal rights protest," says Michel with a snicker. Pierre snickers back. For both, animal rights are a big joke; to them, the word "farm" means battery chickens, intensive pig units where sows pass their lives strapped into place, or barns where cattle live in the dark and never see a blade of grass. Those of us opposed to such conditions are backward sentimentalists.

Michel heads back out the door with a weary grimace. "Can't stay to chat. Duty to our new postal administration calls." We watch him leap into his yellow postal van and roar away. He wasn't always in a hurry. Just a year ago, Michel had the time to chat with us, drink a coffee in a leisurely way. He also looked in on the elderly and brought fresh bread to those housebound, for contact was always part of the postman's job.

Postal service to the countryside only dates from 1829, but then it was an expensive service; it was the person who received a letter who paid for it — an unaffordable luxury for poorly paid servants and impoverished agricultural workers. Ruses were developed: if an envelope was marked in some way — a cross in one corner, for example — it meant it contained important information; an unmarked envelope was empty, a mere sign that all was well. The postage stamp came into use in 1849, and receiving mail became a more frequent event. Hounded by the ubiquitous packs of stray dogs, postmen slogged thirty kilometres a day, seven days a week, through knee-sucking mud in unpaved lanes to reach far-flung farms and villages. They often supped in farmhouses, imbibing much home-brewed cider, wine and cognac, for the mostly-illiterate country dwellers had come to depend on them; postmen could read letters, fill out forms, bring news of distant relatives. They represented contact with the rest of the world; they were open windows.

In the last two years, the French postal service has been modernized into a banking system. Mail delivery is no longer of the greatest importance, nor is personal contact encouraged. Postal employees have no time for visits, for conversations, for looking in on the elderly. They must justify each minute of their round, and thus, another cheery aspect of country life has vanished.

Pierre is scrutinizing me, his head held way back like it usually is when a smoking cigarette is dangling out of one corner of his mouth. "So what's going on between you and Didier?"

I feel my eyes open with astonishment. "What did you say? Going on? Between me and Didier?"

Pierre ignores the surprise, deciding it is merely theatrical. "You seemed to be getting along well enough with him on Friday night when you were both here in the bar."

"Why shouldn't I get on well with him?"

"Sitting over in the corner there with him and Philippe. Having a private conversation."

"Most conversations are private," I say. "Despite what people in this village think." There is, of course, more to the story than just chatting innocently to Didier and Philippe on Friday night, but I'm not going to reel out all the details just for Pierre's sake. Why willingly spread gossip — especially gossip about myself?

"But women like Didier," says Pierre.

"So what? That doesn't mean *all* women like Didier. What are you trying to do? Dream up a romance between the two of us? He's well over twenty years younger than I am. While you're at it, why not link my name up with all the other guys I talk to when I'm in here — Michel, "*le gros*" Gousset, everyone in the football club, the occasional travelling salesman. Or are you trying to tell me that I should stay at home like most of the other women in the village? Cement myself down in front of the television, watch the soaps and the game shows."

Pierre stares at me vaguely, but he isn't really listening. Why should he? He's heard me say this sort of thing many times over the years. That's what village life is all about. We repeat the same old songs over and over again. Everyone repeats and repeats. This way, we all feel nice and familiar with each other. As though we all know each other inside out and still have a lot to say.

"It's just that the two of you — you and Didier — have a lot in common, don't you?" says Pierre. "Politically speaking, that is. Both of you are dead set against the housing development. Both of you are always on about animal rights. What are you two? The rebel faction of the village?"

I decide not to take up the challenge. Once again, this is ground that Pierre and I have been over many times. I'm a vegetarian; he hates vegetarians, serves only meat in the restaurant. I'm opposed to separating baby calves from their mothers when they are born, raising them in tiny sheds without light; Pierre serves veal slathered with cream and wine sauce as a speciality. These arguments are ones that neither of us will ever win. I divert the conversation. "The theory over at the Douspis's is that Didier hasn't come to work for the last few days because he has a sweetheart somewhere. Is holed up with her and can't pry himself out of bed."

"Doubt that," says Pierre, shaking his head ever so slowly. "Doubt that a lot." Despite the cigarette, he manages to quirk his mouth into an all-knowing leer. "Rumour is, as far as romances go, our Didier generally only has the hots for married ladies. Only when a woman's married does Didier get into action. Can't see him holed up for three nights in some merry marital bed."

A warning buzzer starts beeping inside my head. "Oh, really? Married women, huh?" I say this blandly enough, while feigning great innocence and certain boredom. "I guess that lets me off the hook as far as romance with Didier goes. So who gave you that bit of news? And what exactly did you hear?"

But Pierre keeps on shaking his head and wearing the leer. His eyes glow mockingly; he has picked up on my curiosity, all right, and it has given him a sudden surge of power. "You hear things when you run a bar. That's the role of the barman; he's the keeper of secrets, like a psychiatrist. You're here to listen. And then there are the people like you who come along. The people who want to know everything. You are just a little bit too nosy, aren't you?"

"Sure. That's me all right," I say, quickly switching to humble pie and hoping he will tell me more. If you want — or need to get — information, you certainly have to play humble pie and it usually pays off in the end; people just adore talking about other folk. "But even if I am nosy, everything everyone tells me never goes further. You know that, don't you? Everyone else does. In one ear, out the other. That's one really good thing you can say about me."

Pierre's head stops shaking, but his tongue starts wriggling the cigarette in the corner of his mouth. "Oh, sure. And you expect me to betray everyone's trust like that? How long do you think I'd keep my customers if I did?"

"Yeah. I understand. I guess you're right. I just never heard about any married women having a big affair with Didier," I say, lying through my teeth. "Thing like that would cause a scandal and a half in a village like this."

His expression becomes inscrutable. "I didn't say that Didier was having an affair with a married woman. I simply said they interested him. Customers — husbands — come in and complain about things like that. No man wants to be made a fool of."

"For sure," I say, nodding with great sympathy. In any case, his last statement has given me the information I want. Almost. Still, a few more little details wouldn't be amiss. But Pierre obviously isn't in the mood. He simply rips the cigarette off his lip, flicks ash into a vile green ashtray on the bar, shoves the fag back into the mouth corner and evanesces into the kitchen.

7

DIDIER IS A PRETTY BOY WITH SANDY HAIR, THE LONG THIN NOSE OF A
Grecian statue, a fine mouth. Only his high arching eyebrows kill any
tendency to sweetness and lend him, instead, a diabolic air. It always
surprised me that Didier took on the job of village employee. It seemed
to me that there were other things a pretty boy would want to do in
life, talents he would be desirous of exercising, tasks far more interesting
than cutting grass, planting and watering flowers, running the street-
cleaning machine, being at the beck and call of the mayor, checking on
us all, making sure we keep the sidewalks in front of our houses clean
and sparkling. It's not as if he isn't ambitious; he is certainly ambitious
enough. Something about him lets you know it too: the swagger of his
hips, the smug smile, his self-confidence, his unflagging stare.

The job of *garde champêtre* did once have a certain status attached to
it, but that was way back then, when colourful characters took up the job.
Before the Revolution of 1789, lands and fields, aside from communal
pastures, were the exclusive property of the aristocracy; they alone could
hunt on them or exploit them, and their private police and gamekeepers
made certain these rights were maintained. But after the Revolution, the
villagers, who had long been the victims of robber bands, thieves and
various con artists, were finally accorded protection with the creation,
in 1791, of the post of *garde champêtre*. The applicant for the position
had to be a person of irreproachable morality and strong character, had
to have a good knowledge of the laws and had to be able to file reports
correctly. He had to be observant, be a good listener, be able to converse
with the public correctly, be in good physical condition. His job was to
protect villagers from the unscrupulous: fraudulent tobacco and playing
card peddlers, illegal sellers of salt (once a highly taxed luxury). He
controlled public transportation, supervised fishing rights and the right

to sell stamps. He inspected fields, chicken runs, fruit trees and public monuments; tended to the sorting and burning of rubbish; swept the streets, gutters, the town hall and its steps; made certain water troughs were always full and that the church clock ran on time. When the street market existed, it was the *garde champêtre* who rang the bell signalling opening and closing times. In 1945, he was given the task of seeing that all chicken huts and cages were removed from the sidewalks.

But a *garde champêtre* is a man of flesh and blood. Village records show there were many less than scrupulous in the job. A Monsieur Drouard was relieved of his position in 1836, when found neglectful in reporting crimes. In 1861, a Monsieur Fitou failed to respond correctly when questioned about things spirited away from one place and found in another, "probably for dishonest reasons," the report states. In 1919, a Monsieur Lejeune's continual state of inebriation antagonized many. As for Didier and irreproachable morality, well, there are things I know, things Mesdames Sauvebœuf, Douspis, Filoche and Beauducel would give their best pair of support stockings to hear.

Take last Friday evening, for example. I had been sitting in Pierre's bar, twirling a beer mat around in utter boredom. The usual barflies were vociferously shouting out prognostications for the Sunday football match, and Didier, at a corner table covered in smeary, empty glasses, was talking with Philippe, the truck driver. He isn't the most honourable person around, Philippe; he's been caught several times chugging away with televisions and computers from pillaged warehouses, a leisure pursuit that lands him behind bars now and again. Everyone reckons he'll be jobless each time he's out and breathing fresh air, but Philippe, a man of infinite resources, always manages to land on his feet. At the moment, he drives the stinking vehicle that picks up dead animals — cows, chickens, pigs, horses and sheep — from the farms and takes them to the industrial treatment plant. It's a smelly, unpleasant job to say the least, but a job's a job and Philippe has three children from three different relationships to support.

Didier and Philippe were talking in low voices, but still I caught a phrase or two over the high-pitched, semi-hysterical blah-blah-blah about the match.

"Pick up a minimum of fifty dead birds a day," Philippe was saying.

"And those are the ones they manage to get out. The others just lie on the floors and rot or get eaten by other chickens."

"Because the conditions aren't anywhere near the norm, that's why," said Didier. He seemed to be aggressively angry. "Each shed up there is meant to house sixty thousand birds, but they cram in a hundred thousand instead. The chickens have diddley-squat space to move around in when they're little, and when they get bigger, they have to fight to get near the food and water. But you know how things work. Payoff the right people and you get away with everything. Hush money, that's all that counts."

My curiosity got the better of me. I stood up and ambled over to their table, Werewolf following me in a sleepy-dog sort of way. "Talking about Malabry's intensive chicken farm, by any chance?" I asked. Both men stared up at me, Didier unwelcomingly, Philippe with the usual hot, interested gaze he gives to all women on earth. "I walk up that way sometimes and see those huge sheds on the hillside. You can smell the place for miles. To me, it stinks of hot feathers, promiscuity and misery. All you can hear is the hum of machines — not clucking, happy hens, that's for certain. The place has an evil feel to it."

"Stink?" Philippe smirked. "Want to know why it stinks? Because the birds up there are kept in sheds with near-continuous artificial light, right? Because they spend their entire lives eating, sleeping and crapping on concrete floors where litter never gets changed."

"Why not?"

"Because there are too many birds packed together to do the job right. So the floor just gets greasier and greasier. And covered in shit. Stinks like hell."

"You know what they get to eat, the birds in battery farms?" Didier asked me, perhaps encouraged by Philippe's revelations. "Growth promoters. Recycled blood, offal and the feathers of dead birds. Then they're pumped full of antibiotics. But it doesn't matter; with a diet like that, they'll still get sick. Viruses just love breeding in filthy, cramped quarters, and the immune systems of chickens are weakened anyway by overcrowding stress."

"Isn't there some kind of control?" I asked. "How can the Malabrys get away with that?" Both men looked at me as if I were rather stupid.

"Look, all intensive chicken farms are shit," said Didier, disgusted. "All. Without exception. Except at some farms — farms like Malabry's — the conditions are just a little worse. There's more overcrowding. More drug abuse. Farms like that are scattered all over the country. But because the Malabrys are part of our *commune,* I feel responsible. We all should. Shit like that shouldn't be happening here. It isn't even allowed, as everyone knows."

"So why is it happening? If it isn't allowed and everyone knows?"

Philippe snickered, looked over at Didier. Didier leaned back in his chair, crossed his arms, stared up at me, stony-faced. I had the feeling that my participation in the conversation was definitely at an end. If there were any other bits of news to be shared, they weren't going to come winging over in my direction.

8

AN HOUR OR TWO LATER, I WAS IN MY OFFICE, AN UPSTAIRS ROOM AT THE front right side of my house, when I heard a sound. I didn't recognize what it was. Not at first, I didn't. It was just a noise: faint, spattering. Werewolf, sound asleep on the floor, suddenly looked up, his pointy ears wriggling in all directions, as if trying to work out where the sound was coming from. He growled softly. I also continued listening, albeit without the nifty talent of wriggling my ears. What could it be? Mice in the corridor? Then suddenly, I knew: the sound of pebbles hitting a pane of glass.

I went to the window, opened it, peered out. The street was blacker than the bottom of an old well, not a star in sight. Because it was already past eleven o'clock, the single street lamp in the square had already been turned off, as usual. I could just make out a figure standing below. "Yes?" I called softly.

There was a moment's silence. Then I heard a snicker. Then more silence. Then: "You got anything to drink in that house?"

I recognized the voice: Didier's. It had a definite slur to it by now; he'd obviously gone on to have a few too many in the bar. I scrutinized the square quickly. Not a light in any window anywhere. Everyone neatly tucked into bed. No one around to see the two of us holding this Romeo and Juliet conversation in the night.

"Go home!" I muttered. "Just go home and sleep it off." Then I heard another faint sound, a rubbing. Like the noise of a window being inched open. Great. In a minute or two, every single PVC shutter on the village square would roll up in unison, and the grinning faces of Sauvebœuf, Filoche, Douspis and Beauducel would glow in the night with those "I told you so" expressions.

"Wait," I whispered. I closed my window, raced down the stairs, and opened the door. I shouldn't have done it, of course. Didier was swaying.

"What do you want?"

"Come on," he slurred. "Let me in. Jus' wanna talk."

Sure, I thought. Once he was inside and sitting pretty in one of my armchairs, how exactly was I supposed to get rid of him, get him back out onto the street and lurching homeward? I hesitated for a minute or two all the same. Perhaps he wanted to continue the conversation we had been having in the bar, although, to be honest, the silly half-grin on his face didn't give him the air of a man just itching to talk about chicken farming.

"Talk about what?"

"Jus' wanna talk. Jus' came for a visit. A frien'ly visit. A drink."

Werewolf was standing beside me in the doorway, staring at Didier with soft doggy eyes, not with hostility, of course. He knows Didier too well, sees him on the street, sees him going into the Douspis's house with eggs, had just seen him in Pierre's café. He wasn't going to consider Didier an enemy now.

"Nothing to drink in this house," I said, thinking as quickly as I could. There had to be a way of getting him out of my territory and back onto his. "Nothing to drink, for sure. You got anything at your place?"

He frowned slightly. Swayed some more. Then said, "Sure. Plenny to drink over there. Whiskey, you like whiskey?"

"Doesn't everyone?" I simpered in an awful, semi-flirtatious tone. I grabbed my house key from the hook on the wall. "Let's go. A glass of whiskey would do me just fine."

And so Didier, Werewolf (determined not to be excluded from the fun of a glass of whiskey) and I crossed the village square in the direction of the pink cement house Didier lives in. We didn't go in the front door. Instead, Didier headed into the narrow alleyway that runs along one side of the house, stopped at a back door (probably once the servant's entrance to the old bar). It's a narrow dark alley, even in the day, exiting somewhere behind the confusion of old houses.

He unlocked the door and we entered. It was the first time I had ever been inside, and I saw that the interior wasn't in the least attractive. The main room, probably once large and elegant, was now broken up into small compartments by plasterboard walls. The furniture was downright hideous: a sofa covered in swirling orange and brown nylon, two white plastic garden chairs flanking a gruesome wood-look table that, at that moment, was topped by an unappealing cluster of filthy, sticky-looking glasses. There were no pictures on the walls. There was nothing of interest. Overhead, bright lights glared down from a brown, fake teak, swirled, plastic, rustic-style chandelier. The floor was covered in ugly, modern, white tiles.

"Whiskey?" slurred Didier as he sagged down on the couch. He didn't really look anything like a promising host, a man capable of heaving himself back up onto his feet, locating a bottle and a couple of clean glasses, and pouring us both out a drink.

"So what did you want to talk about?" I asked as I perched on the very edge of one of the dreadful garden chairs. "About Malabry's farm?"

"Forget Malabry's farm. Forget that shit. Why d'you always want to know so much?" He wasn't sounding so very drunk anymore. I wondered if it had been an act, an excuse for throwing stones at my window. "Loosen up. Stop being serious. Have a good time once in a while."

Which sounded like a fine idea to me. Except sitting here, in this ugly room with Didier, wasn't fitting into my idea of a roaring good time. Not by a long shot. Didier is the one person I know just too much about. So I stood up again. "Sorry. Changed my mind. No whiskey after all. I'm going home to bed."

He stared at me with one of those blank, enigmatic looks. Not angry, not surprised, certainly not disappointed. I was resisting his charms, and that wasn't affecting him one way or the other.

"Goodnight, Didier," I said. "Sweet dreams." I walked to the door, Werewolf by my side, pulled it open.

"Bitch," he muttered after me. "Bitch." But it was a comment without much rancour in it.

"Yeah," I muttered back. "That's me."

And I went outside, crossed the square in the direction of my house, my eyes scanning all the windows — from Madame Sauvebœuf's to Christelle's, past mine to the Douspis's and Madame Filoche's — and wondered what all that had been about? Why me? Why had Didier thrown stones at my window? What had given him the idea that I might be interested in him? What had he hoped to get out of it? I'm poor as poor can be. Didier is a man who loves money. He doesn't care much how he gets it either. I know this because I happen to be the possessor of a rather tawdry village secret.

9

IN MY HOUSE, IN THIS EX-HOTEL, THERE IS A DARK WINDOWLESS bedroom. Perhaps this room was once used by the "nieces," those gentle and nubile creatures being "trained in household duties" by the dubious Madame Bonpied, a woman of unknown origin. Possessed of good business sense coupled with clever political awareness (she had been trotting along on the heels of various armies for many lively years), Madame Bonpied allowed herself to doubt the famous and later most-regretted words of War Minister General Lebœuf: "The Prussian army does not exist." Anticipating the Franco-Prussian War of 1870 and the progression of troops westward, Madame Bonpied, six "nieces" in tow, arrived in Épineux-le-Rainsouin with the many wooden crates of provocative finery required by her young relatives, and set up business.

Certainly, this commerce greatly interested the village men, those gentlemen callers well versed in the art of "education." But the alluring feminine newcomers were still not ill-regarded by wives. "Men are what they are," it was agreed. "Their needs must be attended to." What a relief to be released from a most tedious duty of marriage and its inevitable result: eternal childbearing. To confirm their essential goodness, Madame Bonpied and the suitably clad nieces regularly attended Sunday mass. Oh yes, the hotel had become a jolly place indeed.

But by the end of 1871, the military was withdrawing from the area, and Madame Bonpied was, once again, obliged to be on the lookout for economic opportunity. She found it in the busy and lucrative port of Nantes, a hundred and fifty kilometres distant, whence she removed herself, her nieces and the wooden packing cases of frilly appurtenances.

Armies haven't passed this way since the Second World War, over sixty years ago, and village life has become less dramatic. Scandal still exists, although nowadays it is rather mild scandal to be sure. And I am careful, very careful indeed, that even mild scandal does not touch my own life. For, calm as I seem, innocuous even — the single foreign woman *d'un certain âge* who collects stories of the past, notes them down just as they are on the point of vanishing — even I have secrets.

One secret concerns the local veterinarian, Jean-Paul, a married man: he is my lover. And tonight, Thursday night, Jean-Paul calls me on the telephone. He says, his voice warm, deep, always excited at these moments, "I'll be there in an hour. I need to see you. I miss you so much. I can't stand being without you." And so I wait for him in the strange back bedroom, the little room that has no window, that betrays no secret.

Naturally, Jean-Paul is anxious to keep our passion hidden from the public eye: he parks his car at a certain distance from the village square, takes the precaution of looking to see if he can discern anyone at a window, anyone watching the street. He makes certain all shutters are shut down tight. To my mind, he is just that teensy bit over-cautious; if anyone saw him, I could always say that Werewolf needed a shot, for I, too, am rather good at deception, although unlike Christelle, I don't confuse lies with the truth.

So when the sun has set, when the streets are empty and the square is in darkness, when the windows of Mesdames Douspis, Filoche, Beauducel and Sauvebœuf have been shuttered, when all those living in Épineux-le-Rainsouin are sitting fast and fascinated in front of the televised game shows, Jean-Paul passes through the right-of-way running through Christelle's courtyard, pushes open the wooden gate (never locked) leading to the courtyard behind my house, passes through the ever-unlocked back door, follows the narrow corridor past the chilly kitchen and storeroom (before refrigeration, kitchens were, of necessity, placed in the coldest sections of houses), comes towards the stairwell, climbs the steps. I hear his footfall, one step at a time, as he climbs, climbs, climbs to where I wait in the windowless bedroom, and even Werewolf doesn't bark, for he is long accustomed to these intimate visits.

Here in the dim light, one can see the big, old bed in a curtained alcove. The beautiful sheets, scented with rosemary, are reflected in the large golden mirror on the wall. This is the dream room, the fantasy room. Here I wait, ever ready, hair smoothed into place, elegant, appealing but not perfumed, for that would certainly attract the notice of Chantal, Jean-Paul's wife. And how happy we both are that an hour or two has been found for us alone.

"I love you," he says when he sees me, when he sees me sitting on the bed in this room that reminds one of someplace else: a *hôtel de passe*, perhaps.

"I love you, too," I say, although even I know that were this really love, it would be more. It would be throwing away all in order to live with the other; it would mean fidelity. But this facsimile of love, it will do for the time being. And I caress his head, his shoulders, his forehead and cheek, and even if the game is a false one, I still love to touch him and I will probably miss it when this story of ours is over. Because eventually, it will end. I know that, even if he doesn't. You can't maintain a relationship like this for a lifetime. It's just not rewarding enough. Not for the mistress. For the married man, perhaps. But definitely not for the mistress.

"I've missed you so much," he says.

"You missed me so much?" I ask, keeping my voice teasingly light. "If you missed me, then why didn't you come on Monday night like you usually do? Why wait until tonight? Thursday."

He looks uncomfortable. "I wanted to. But I couldn't. Things came up. Complications. At a farm near Saint-Hilaire-la-Nozay. And then I had to get home; I was filthy. I couldn't come and see you in a state like that." He kisses the tip of my nose. "You wouldn't love me anymore if I did. I'd be out on my ear."

He's lying, I think. My lover has begun telling me lies. Why? What is there to hide? Surely he hasn't found another mistress? Surely not? But why not? He is not a faithful man. He has never been faithful to anyone. Why would he be faithful to me?

So he undresses (in a slow striptease), and we make love. And then, as always, we drink wine. We talk. The same as usual. It's always the same, and not in the least unpleasant. Not in the least something that I want to throw away. Not just yet. Not for the nothingness that is bound to follow, the emptiness of a life without love.

He talks about the funny things that happened in the last few days: his meeting with an ignorant peasant who, certain that a jealous neighbour had cast a spell, called in a priest to exorcise his sick cow; the consultation with the absurd lady who wakes at four in the morning to braise liver for an obese and "ever so fussy" poodle. Talks of the farmer who claims that bags of snakes are being thrown into his cornfields from German fighter planes (this last is a well-known and widely believed local rumour).

"So I asked him why he thought the Germans would be bothered doing this," says Jean-Paul, the hint of laughter bubbling behind the words. "What would be the point of it? And he answered, 'To destroy us, to destroy France, of course. The war isn't over yet. Not by a long shot.' I can explain until I'm blue in the face that vipers thrown down from planes would die. That this is a mere fairy tale, a rumour, a myth. But every time I do, people look at me as if I'm a poor dull tool." Jean-Paul shakes his head with frustration. "And do you know what he said, this particular idiot? He puffed himself up with indignation and said that in one of his fields, just last week, he found a bag, a canvas bag. And on the bag were the words: 'Made in Germany.' And that the bag was evidently one that had contained vipers. They kill me, some of the people here. They just kill me."

"They kill me, too," I say. "Just last week, Monsieur Vadepied told me that if you want to win the lottery, you put a grass snake's tongue in your change purse." And I tell Jean-Paul about the events of my life. Small local events, indeed, but I try to narrate them with a certain humour and energy.

But tonight, things are a little different. Something has changed, although I'm not certain what. Am I resentful because of our missed rendezvous on Monday night? Perhaps I can't rid myself of the suspicion that he has lied to me. What if I only want to make myself look interesting, appealing? So I recount the tale — with a great show of delighted amusement — of Didier throwing stones at my window last Friday night, about how drunk he was, about how I lured him away from my house and back to his. And I see how the expression on Jean-Paul's face changes (as I knew it would). He is no longer looking soft and happy. The creases of laughter around his mouth and eyes flatten out. At first he listens, watches me with amazement. And then irritation. And soon jealousy. Even anger.

"That little shit," he spits out finally. "That ugly, little shit."

But I don't stop here. He will be even angrier if I continue to talk, I think, but the words just spill out and I tell how, in the café this morning, Pierre mentioned that Didier usually went after married women.

Jean-Paul's expression changes again. Irritation and anger become something quite different: panic. "Chantal?" he whispers. "Pierre was talking about Chantal? Has he finally opened his big, fat, ugly mouth, Didier?"

For Jean-Paul is not the only one who has been unfaithful in the marriage. His wife, Chantal, once maintained a very passionate liaison with Didier, our *garde champêtre*. It wasn't an affair that lasted long, and it certainly mustn't have been one of which she could be proud. Didier, years younger than she but ever so handsome, is still only the village employee, one who waters flowers, cuts grass, sweeps streets with his mechanical sweeping car. He is at the beck and call of the mayor, his pink cement house is graciously provided, rent free, by the municipal council. That love relationship Chantal and Didier shared, it was merely a passing passion, a very secret one. I am, supposedly, the only one in the village who knows about it; it was Jean-Paul who told me.

But now he is terrified that the secret is out. Finally. He can't stay in the position he's in, leaning back against the pillows. He leaps to his feet, looks wildly around the dimly lit room, begins to grab his clothes that are strewn about here and there (the result of the earlier striptease), pulls them on in a sort of hysteria. Suddenly, he's been transformed into a man being chased by foaming-at-the-mouth, rabid hyenas.

I stay right where I am, right here in the bed, leaning against the pillows. Casual. Sensual. Amused. Very amused. But I am, I realize, also a little irritated. No, I am very, very irritated. Where is it coming from, this panic of his?

"You know what?" I drawl slowly. And mockingly. "Chantal isn't the only married woman in this village. You think that she's so attractive that Didier slept only with her? You think she's a right femme fatale, do you? The one and only femme fatale here in Épineux-le-Rainsouin? Just because she's your wife?" I'm not being nice but I don't care very much about that at the moment. Might as well let the truth squeak out every once in a while. And nothing brings out the truth better than a little serious provocation. Or rejection.

He looks blankly at me, his eyes haggard. It doesn't take a lot of genius to see that married men, no matter what they say, keep their loyalties safe and sound in their own homes. Even if fidelity isn't a strong point there.

"I'm going," he says in a funny, choked little voice. "I have to go home."

As if I can't see, all by myself, that he's running away. "See you around," I say coldly. And for the very first time in our relationship, I don't leap out of bed, throw on my silky robe, follow him down the stairs for a last kiss, a few more caresses and words of love. For the very first time, I don't even like him very much.

Too bad. Too bad for him. He has made me just angry enough that I haven't even finished the story. That it was a customer of Pierre's who had once complained about Didier liking married women — and Jean-Paul has never been a customer. In fact, he never sets a foot in the place, claiming he has enough dreary conversations when he goes out to the farms; he doesn't need gossip and chats about the football match to round off his day. That it most likely wasn't Chantal Pierre had been referring to anyway.

"Run quickly," I call out as he vanishes out of the room. "Run fast. Mama has dinner on the hob. Run to Mama."

Craven behaviour is a declaration of war, as far as I'm concerned.

10

Because I am angry when Jean-Paul leaves, because I don't have the desire or even the energy to get up and make myself a late dinner, I fall asleep in the room without windows. In the room without windows, you don't hear what's going on in the street. Which is why I miss it all, miss all the commotion on the village square in the morning. And because Werewolf is lying on the rug, sleeping, he misses it all, too. Neither one of us knows that the village square is filled with police and firemen and that there is a hearse parked in front of Didier's house. That absolutely everyone in Épineux-le-Rainsouin (except Madame Douspis) is gathered out there as fascinated spectators.

I am not around when Didier's body is carried out of his pink cement house on the other side of the square. I'm not there when it is pushed into the ominous black vehicle. I'm not there when it is driven away. I miss the whole thing.

"You missed the whole thing," says Monsieur Vadepied when I am finally out on the square and thinking of drinking my coffee at Pierre's with the mistaken idea that this is just another normal, sunny, unusually warm, late spring morning. "He's very dead, Didier. The mayor went to ring the bell at his house because he didn't show up for work again. And didn't show up yesterday. Or the day before either. Or on Tuesday. And he was furious because you got a job, you got to be responsible. Really angry, the mayor. Get a salary, have to do the job. Young people today, don't know what work means. When I was young, we knew all right. Whole nights we didn't sleep because we had to work. That's what things were like when I was young. And then the mayor, he rang the bell. And then he noticed that he didn't hear the bell ringing inside the house. The bell wasn't working. As if, for example, the electricity didn't work. Thought it was strange. So then what happened was, he tried the door.

Wasn't even locked. So he went in. The mayor went in. He knocked on the door once or twice and then he went in."

"And then he came out," interrupts Madame Filoche, her little eyes glowing behind the thick magnifying lenses of her glasses. She's leaning forward in excitement. "And when he went in, I saw him. I was watching through my window. He went in. And then he came out. And he was white as a sheet, I saw. And then he went home. Looked like he was going to be sick."

"To call the fire department. That's why. To call the police. That's what they do," adds Monsieur Vadepied with the air of a man who has learnt all about police procedure from television.

"And then they came," interjects Madame Ferrier. "The door wasn't locked and they didn't even have to break in. You know. In order to get into the house. They didn't even have to force the door or anything. It was strange that no one noticed, his door being open all these days and no one noticing. The door wasn't locked all this time and Didier was in there. Dead. The whole time."

"The house was unlocked. Just like that, unlocked," says Monsieur Douspis. "Anyone could have gone in there — thieves, murderers, anyone — you never know these days. And then they went in. And they saw, just like the mayor, Didier was dead."

"In his bathtub. He was dead in his bathtub. Completely naked," adds Madame Filoche, her little eyes dancing with eager glee. "Totally without clothes."

"Which would be logical," I add calmly. Just for something to say. But no one even blinks an eye.

"And the reason that the doorbell wasn't working is because there wasn't any electricity in the house," says Monsieur Vadepied. "Because of the short circus. You know why? Because Didier, he was dead in his bathtub … with his hair dryer. He had his hair dryer in the water. And that caused the short circus. Hair dryer plugged in the plug right over the sink. Sink right beside the bathtub. The way they always are in the old houses."

"And then the doctor came," says Madame Filoche. "And then they saw Didier having the bath. Naked in his bathtub. And then the doctor pronounced that he was dead. Has to be several days that he's dead in his bathtub because he didn't come and bring the eggs to Madame Douspis's house."

"And he didn't even come to work on Tuesday," says Monsieur Douspis with a triumphant note. "The whole time he didn't come to work, he was in his bathtub."

"It puffs up," says Monsieur Vadepied in a secretive, confiding tone accompanied by a dark, mysterious glare. "It puffs up."

"What puffs up?"

The ladies present emit excited little squeaks, but neither Monsieur Vadepied nor Monsieur Douspis are going to spare anyone.

"The body does," says Monsieur Douspis with great satisfaction.

"That's right," says Monsieur Vadepied. "It blows up a lot. Takes in all the water in the bathtub. Sometimes you can't even get the body out of the bathtub because it's blown up so much. Filled up tight."

"Then you have to cut it up," says Monsieur Douspis. "Cut it into small pieces."

"What? The body or the bathtub?" I ask.

"Body," confirms Monsieur Vadepied with a wise nod.

"So they really cut it up?" I ask. Everyone, except Monsieur Vadepied, is looking a little shocked. Perhaps it is rather traumatizing to think of Didier chopped up into small bits.

"They brought the body somewhere else, in any case," says Madame Filoche sternly. "They didn't leave it there. Took it away to the morgue, most likely. That's what they do with bodies nowadays."

"Was called into a restaurant years ago," confides Monsieur Vadepied. "Water in water tank not coming through to the kitchen properly. Had a roof-top system, water should've come, but no water coming down now. Went up there and took a look and saw why, too. Rats, whole lot of dead rats up there in the water. Bloated up. Bloated up big as pigs almost. From the water."

"Disgusting," says Madame Filoche, and the other women Greek chorus in agreement.

"Well, almost as big," Monsieur Vadepied concedes. "Small pigs."

"He was certainly dead anyway, Didier. That's why he didn't come to work. It's for that," says Monsieur Douspis.

"He could have come to work anyway," I mutter *sotto voce*. Just to lighten up the show a little. And to cut short the colourful details about rats and bloating. At least Jean-Paul is going to be happy with this bit of news, I reflect. And perhaps his dearest Chantal.

11

"Is all of this true? Didier is really dead?" shouts Christelle. As usual, her television is blaring; you have to fight hard to have conversation — or what passes for conversation — in Christelle's house. Her eyes are wide open with honest shock. Like me, she, too, missed the fuss and drama in the street; she was in bed with the usual crushing hangover. So we sit in her downstairs room, smoke cigarettes, drink a bottle of wine brought by me because Christelle claims she has no money for booze (both of us know perfectly well there are quite a few bottles stashed away in her cupboards), and chew away at the news.

I am, in any case, in need of a drink. All afternoon, I waited for the phone to ring, for Jean-Paul to call. I was so certain he would. What subject could be more interesting than Didier's demise? I want to know what his reaction is. I want to talk with him. He should be rejoicing. He should be thrilled. He should be trying to charm me back with sweet words after last night's behaviour. But he hasn't called after all.

"Yes, of course. I wouldn't make this up, you know. He's really dead, Didier. Electrocuted. Murdered by his hair dryer."

"That's stupid," shouts Christelle, then grins in a secretive but nasty way. "Really stupid."

"I agree wholeheartedly. It was a remarkably stupid thing to do. You take a bath to get washed, right? Not to get dry. And Didier, he knew that doing something like that was stupid. He knew about electricity."

"Yeah. But he was stupid. I always said he was stupid. When you are stupid, you do stupid things." Already her words are slurring together. She must have started drinking long before I arrived.

"And the rumour is, he had this little tendency to run after married women," I add casually. Just to see what will come up. Just to see if Christelle knows any of the local tittle-tattle.

"Yeah," she bellows. "That's what I was told." Nodding, she pours some more wine into her glass. Christelle can kill three glasses in the time it takes me to sip half of one. She doesn't know what it means to go slowly, to taste, to enjoy.

"You heard what exactly?" I ask, suddenly very interested. "What did you hear about Didier and married women?"

"Just that. That was all I heard." She shrugs as if this is the most boring question anyone could ever come up with.

"What things?"

"Rumours."

"Yeah, right. Got that. But what rumours?" I have the distinct impression that she is already regretting what she said.

"That he likes to go after married women, that's all. I heard it at the hairdresser's. When I had my hair cut there a month or two ago. Didier was walking by and some woman — I don't know who she is, just one of those bags who's always in there — said that he liked to flirt with married women. That's all." She stares at the television screen as if there is something really wonderful happening up there. As though, by not meeting my eye, she thinks I won't notice she's lying through her teeth.

"You often use the hairdresser here in the village?" I ask. Just to see how far she's really going to go this time. To my certain knowledge, Christelle went to Madame Beaupied's salon only once, several years ago, to have her hair washed, cut and dried. Afterwards, when the job was done, she'd stood up, announced she didn't have the money to pay, and she'd come by with a check another time. This hopeful little attempt at getting something for free once more didn't work. Christelle had underestimated the tenacity of a village businesswoman; Madame Beaupied responded, calmly enough, that she was calling the police. Immediately. Within seconds, Christelle had handed over the cash.

This sordid little tale has been a much-rehashed topic of conversation at Madame Douspis's ever since, although Christelle's version is quite different. And of course, hardly believable. According to Christelle, Madame Beaupied had agreed to cut her hair and let her pay later. But when the job was finished, Madame Beaupied saw that she had done a bad job. So bad that she knew Christelle would never return with the money, and so demanded to be paid immediately. But that's Christelle for you: she's ever the victim, even in her lies. She never again went back to Madame Beaupied's salon. I know that. She knows that. Everyone in the village knows that. So why am I even asking this question? So I can, masochistically, have the pleasure of hearing another lie?

Christelle stares with great concentration at the television screen, at a gum commercial showing a gorgeous young woman with swinging hair offering a chew to an impossibly handsome young man who is looking deep into her eyes. "Have to go sometimes," she mumbles vaguely. "Didn't always have time when I was in Derval just to have my hair done. Was too busy doing the computer course. Getting ready to get the secretarial business on the road."

"And what did she look like, the woman who said that about Didier?" I'm not in the mood to let Christelle off the hook, especially since Pierre said the same thing. And I don't want to hear any bullshit about her fantasy computer courses.

"What did she look like? She looked like everyone else here. Everyone looks alike in this part of the world. Wore glasses. Was getting a permanent, just like all the local bags always do. You know what they look like, the women in the village. She looked like nothing. How am I supposed to describe someone like that?"

On the television screen, it's back to the game show again. The audience, open-mouthed, is turning and twisting in excited glee, shouting wildly. Someone has fluffed the answer to the jackpot question.

"Okay," I say, deciding to give her an out. I know she's lying. She knows I know. It's a stalemate. "But you know how the village women love to gossip. They just make things up half the time. You know they do. They pick up on teensy rumours, stretch them out, elaborate, add a few characters, a bit of sex, a tale they've heard somewhere else. The truth is nowhere to be found after a while. So think, think hard. Who mentioned that Didier went after married women? And when did they say that? Did they mention any married woman in particular?"

Christelle shifts her gaze away from the television screen and over to someplace on the ugly plasterboard wall, squints, pretends to be concentrating — in order to seem to help me, of course. But I sense she is definitely annoyed. She doesn't, of course, understand why I'm so interested in this information. She doesn't know anything about

Jean-Paul, and she's not the sort of person who asks questions either. The lives of other people just don't interest her enough to do that. But she sees she has to come up with an answer of some kind. She has to cover her lie somehow.

She lets out a long, slow stream of smoke. Shrugs. "Look, it's this way. I have friends, you know. A couple of married men come to visit. Of course, I don't have any personal relationship with them. I know all they're interested in is having a screw, married men. I know they come and visit me because they think that's what they'll get from me. But I don't screw married men: that's my rule and they find that out soon enough. But they come here anyway and they want to talk. So they tell me stories. And one guy, he tells me about Didier. I think he's talking about his own wife. I think he means that Didier is interested in his own wife. He was nuts, the guy. He was jealous. Like, what am I supposed to do with a man like that? I hate jealous men. And here's this jealous man sitting in my house and he's jealous about his wife and Didier, and at the same time here he is, thinking he's going to screw me. I mean, that's shit, right? Guys like that are shit. But that's where I heard it anyway. About Didier and married women." She stops. Looks at me defiantly. "And I also heard it at the hairdresser's, of course."

12

THE ROLE OF MISTRESS IS BOTH HONOURABLE AND DISHONOURABLE. IT
is with her that a man is on best behaviour; he perfumes himself for her;
it is she, the woman he loves, who occupies his thoughts. As for the mistress, she must be clever, discreet, and, most of all, she must keep secrets
for she knows quite a bit. A wife can't imagine how many details of daily,
domestic life have been exposed to her husband's mistress: all the repeti-
tive frustrations of marriage, the wearied sexual life (a mistress must do
better in her role of dream woman). In many ways, the relationship
between mistress and lover is very intimate and quite ideal.

However, if a mistress has been playing her role for a certain length
of time, the hope that she will, one day, live with her lover in a happily-
ever-after has long since died. She knows he will never leave his wife. The
mistress has also become part of his routine — a passionate, necessary
part — but nothing he would make sacrifices for. She is just another
element in his comfort zone. The comfort zone of a man too cowardly
to make a decision, a choice.

And because no relationship can endure without a future, the
mistress's dream changes. She imagines the day she will dump her lover,
this man who has refused her hope. She wants to find true love, a real
position, not this one that is hidden, ambiguous and blurry. She hopes
that one day soon she will say the words: "It's over between us. I have
met someone else. Someone I love, someone I will be faithful to, a man
who will be faithful to me." And she relishes the thought of her lover's
confusion, for his weakness, his spinelessness, has long since made her
lose respect for him, for their love story.

Jean-Paul's hair is streaked with grey. He is neither short nor tall,
neither fat nor thin. Solidly built, his movements are nonetheless young,
flexible and lively. Chantal is not his first wife; once, long ago, he was

married to Caroline and with her had two children. They were a normal couple, Caroline and Jean-Paul, a nice couple with nice kids, a nice house, two nice cars, a pretty garden, several fine horses. And Chantal? She was simply Jean-Paul's assistant, a summer replacement from Paris: fresh, young, blonde and slender. A good manipulator, too. It was easy for her to charm Jean-Paul, seduce him (she was twenty-five, time for her to get herself a husband). Like all people caught in a frenzy, Jean-Paul could only see that blonde freshness, the Parisian sophistication. *And* her passion, the passion of a Madame Bovary. What a triumph it must have been for him! He was only a local man, a country vet who treated cows, pigs, sheep, the occasional dog or cat. *Le grand amour* that touched poets with magic had passed him by; life had dealt him mere stability. And now, wonder of wonders, this young blonde woman loved him, wanted him.

What Jean-Paul didn't see was that Chantal was also ambitious, humourless, that life with her would be, in the long run, as tedious as the one he was already living with Caroline. Caught, snared, he divorced; far from being Madame Bovary, Caroline was only the woman he had known from school days: a grey mouse who suffered from indigestion and light depressions. Chantal and Jean-Paul bought and moved into a fine old former convent just south of the village. Chantal became a weekend mother to Caroline's unrewardingly turbulent children. Abandoned, Caroline took a small overdose, one she easily survived for it had been simply a gesture. And Jean-Paul, the main figure in this drama, acquired a guilty conscience, an indefinable feeling of regret.

"Give me time," Jean-Paul says to me now. "I love you. I want to live with you. You are the right woman for me, I know that. But I need time. I can't leave Chantal just like that. She needs me. She loves me. She raised my children and we've been together for so many years now. She depends on me. I have to break with her slowly. I don't want her to do what Caroline did. Give me time. I need time."

When he defends his marriage, he says his wife hasn't become fat and shapeless but kept her good looks, her dress sense, her shoulder-length blonde hair. She tends to family and social business with great efficiency. But he claims he no longer loves Chantal. She no longer charms him.

"Stick with me," says Jean-Paul. "I want to live with you. I want to wake up with you every morning. But I need time. Let me do this my way. Let me do this slowly. We have our whole lives ahead of us."

Chantal saunters through the streets, her shoulder-length dyed hair swinging free, her head held high; she is, after all, the respected wife of the veterinarian. Her chit-chat concerns their children (she and Jean-Paul had two more together), their successes, the new grandchild. She talks about the flowers in her big walled garden. She is friendly to me because I am a foreigner — one from a reasonable country, Canada, and not, she says, from some Third World place of shifty welfare candidates. She tells me of holidays she and Jean-Paul take in faraway places, for she likes to assume an exotic air. But she has never invited me to her house to participate in the many amusing dinner parties she gives. A foreigner is still a foreigner. A single woman is a threat; inviting me would mean an odd number seated around the dinner table. Had I a husband of some standing, well, things would be different then. And, perhaps if I were French … Naturally, she doesn't know I am her husband's mistress. She is also unaware that I know about her liaison with Didier.

She thinks of herself as a romantic, Chantal does. Ever a Madame Bovary — not just another village housewife. And as such, she was very much in love with Didier — that's what she claimed in the love letters she wrote him. Those letters, they were a great error on her part, but a woman in love, one who is experiencing an *amour impossible*, is reckless. She takes chances, for she is hungry for release from the mundane into the poetic. It drives her to desperation.

I know about those letters because Jean-Paul, my lover, told me the story when the affair was over. How did he feel?

"I don't care," he said. "What's important to me is what we share, you and I. Our love story. I don't want Chantal anymore. I want you." This was in the second, passionate year of our own relationship, the year when feeling and loyalty is strongest.

"Don't you and Chantal still sleep together?" I asked. "Make love?"

He hesitated. Only for two seconds. Three. "Occasionally," he answered slowly. But he was embarrassed, I could see. "I'm telling you because I want to be honest with you. I want, always, to tell you the truth. There can't be lies between us."

This was, as I mentioned, in the second year of our relationship.

The time of greatest intimacy. But that confession killed some of the enchantment for me. Destroyed some of my self-respect, although the relationship has limped on for two more less hopeful years, less trusting ones.

How did Jean-Paul find out about Chantal and Didier? Because Didier had tried to use Chantal's letters to blackmail her. He'd sent her a letter, too, one day. I can imagine how she felt when she opened the innocuous white envelope; perhaps she thought her lover had sent her flatteries, delightful words, a delicate sonnet recounting the suffering and heightened emotion that impossible love begets.

Then she saw he wanted money, only vulgar money — and not a little sum either but a monthly rent — or else he would reveal all to her husband. To the whole village. She must have panicked.

I can't say she has my total sympathy (this is certainly not required of a mistress), but I admire her courage in presenting that horrid epistle to her husband. Although many other women might have paid up quickly, arranged the family expenses to hide the loss, Chantal wasn't going to be blackmailed. It was her courage that saved her. She and Jean-Paul became allies and together — hand-in-hand, says Jean-Paul — they went to call on Didier in his pink cement house. United, they threatened to make Didier's attempt at blackmail known to the mayor. He would be out of work for life; there would be letters from lawyers, visits from the police; he would be ruined if he persisted.

"It means nothing to you that your wife screwed me?" Didier answered, one high-arched, devilish eyebrow raised in derision. He was so sure of his power; perhaps Chantal's crawling devotion had made him feel strong.

But Jean-Paul had sneered right back, had said that their marriage was one of absolute tolerance and great openness. That there were no secrets between himself and his wife — a lie, of course; their marriage was fraught with secrets. But this show of solidarity destroyed Didier's attempt to obtain a supplementary income. He was to immediately hand over the letters Chantal had written him. And there, in the pink cement house, without even once glancing at them, Jean-Paul tore them into a million pieces, pieces he and Chantal later scattered in the river that runs by their house.

No more white envelopes or threats of blackmail arrived in their mailbox. Life continued on. Chantal, perhaps shocked by the inherent dangers in assuming the role of a modern Madame Bovary, now stayed true to her husband. And Jean-Paul continues to pass through the right-of-way in Christelle's courtyard, to come through the wooden gate, to enter into my courtyard and the ever-open back door of my house. Continues to make love with me, to drink wine, to give me words of love, words of passion, to tell me secrets. And I continue to play the role of mistress, the one who is irresistible, ideal, cherished. Unless something of importance happens. Unless there is danger. Then the lover is out of sight. Unattainable.

13

ON THE TABLE ARE THE LITTLE CUPS OF COFFEE IN THEIR SAUCERS, THE
ubiquitous bowl of fruit. Here is the long blue plastic box with its see-
through lid; in various compartments are the pills Madame Douspis
takes every hour of every day. Here is a vase of fresh flowers; here a
display of varnished, dried flowers, their stems stiffened by wire and
pushed into a little greenish cushion of foam.

At eleven-thirty, Saturday morning, Madame Douspis leaves the
leaf-green chair at her post by the window overlooking the village square,
sits down at the melamine table, begins to cut onions in preparation for
lunch. Because she has left the square (perhaps dangerously) unguarded,
Madame Filoche takes up the good work. From her seat at the head of
the melamine table she can, by looking straight in front of her, see all.

"It's calm now out there," she informs us. "It's very normal already,
after all that happened. You'd think that people would be doing
something different with Didier dead and everything, but no. It's as if
nothing at all unusual has happened. There's Madame Bourny going to
the bakery as if this were a day like any other. And people are going to
come and go in the restaurant. No one has any respect at all anymore.
That's the tragedy."

"And what would you like everyone to be doing?" asks Madame
Douspis with annoyance. "He's gone, Didier. They've taken him away.
He's dead."

"It's a lack of respect all the same, I can tell you that," says Madame
Filoche. "It's a terrible lack of respect. Here's Didier dead, and everyone's
acting as if nothing at all has happened."

"But they did all they could yesterday anyway, the police," says
Madame Douspis. "They had an officer posted at Didier's door to make
sure nobody else went in there. And they took all of the papers in his

desk, phone bills and everything. And they collected the glasses in his sink and put them in little plastic bags and put little white tickets on them. And they put his clothes in a plastic bag. And they dusted everything over with powder, just to see if there were fingerprints. Just as if it were murder."

"When? When did all this take place," I ask, slightly exasperated.

"Right after they discovered the body."

"I didn't see anyone doing that."

"Because you never look out of your window, you never take an interest in what's going on in the square. We do. We're interested in things," says Madame Filoche.

"But you couldn't see what was going on inside the house," I insist.

"Of course we could," says Monsieur Douspis with a definite note of satisfaction. "I was with Vadepied, and we were both watching them through the window. We stood there the whole time looking in. We saw everything."

"Oh," I say, meekly. "I should have known. And the police just let you stand there and stare at them? Really?"

"Well, I guess they didn't see Vadepied and me," says Monsieur Douspis. He doesn't sound so sure of himself suddenly. I'm certain he hopes I'll stop prying. "They were very busy, just like on that program *Crime Stoppers*, so they didn't have time to look at the window. Besides, we were very subtle."

"So you see? The police have been snooping around. Collecting evidence," says Madame Douspis.

"Evidence of what?" I ask.

"Evidence that he's dead," retorts hatchet-faced Madame Beauducel in one of her rare moments of wild loquacity.

"I would think that anyone who lolls around in a bathtub for days on end has made that point quite clearly," I say.

"Anyway, if they want evidence of anything, the police, they should come and ask us. We know pretty well everything," says Madame Filoche sourly. She is evidently offended. The police are going to have a hard job of work to get back into her good graces.

"And now that Didier's dead, there's no one to keep order in the village. No one to do the sweeping in the streets. No one to water the flowers," says Monsieur Douspis mournfully. "Didier, he was an ace at doing all that. The reason the village looks so nice is because of Didier's flowers. Grew them all by himself out on his plot of land over near the new development. Grew all varieties. You won't find many *gardes champêtre* doing that sort of thing, these days. He'll be hard to replace, Didier will. No, not hard. Impossible."

Madame Beauducel nods with both approval and disapproval. "There's no one left to take care of things here in the village," she comments darkly. "No one at all. The mayor had better be thinking about that!"

"No good eggs to be had either," says Madame Douspis who is always enthusiastic about her meals.

"The people here in the village aren't going to like things being neglected. The flower committee isn't going to be happy either," adds Madame Filoche. And suddenly, all four — Mesdames Douspis, Beauducel and Filoche, and Monsieur Douspis — stare at each other, silent for a minute, then all snicker in unison.

They don't like the flower committee. They thwart every attempt the committee makes to encourage us to decorate our houses with tidy geraniums. If we grow geraniums, perhaps our village will have the great honour of receiving, from the tourist office in Derval, a little star on the name panels that stand on roads leading in and out. This star seems to be essential to the flower committee; they view it as the highest possible achievement of our age.

The flower committee, whose members are also the village festival committee, is a small, exclusive circle. They are the resolute church-goers of the village; they are local tradespeople — roofers, masons, plumbers, and electricians; they are on the municipal council, are the mayor's friends (his wife is part of the circle). New associates are not welcome. Because this is so, village events and geranium planting are boycotted by those *exclus*. The festival committee does its level best to drum up enthusiasm for the yearly fête; they have modernized the event, brought in a local rock group, organized a bric-a-brac sale and featured children's marching bands. But only proud parents of the marching band members and friends of the rock group attend this sad fête that has been unsuccessful for years and is a far cry from what it once was.

It was formerly an event of great importance; it drew people together; it was a free day; it was a joyous occasion. There were droll and admittedly silly games on the village square: participants raced from one spot to another balancing an egg on a spoon clutched between their teeth; they hopped about in burlap sacks. There was a rifle stand, although live victims — bound ducks and chickens — had not been used for almost a century. There were carousels with wooden horses; there was the whirling ride called *pousse-pousse*. And at night, the peasants from faraway farms would lay down their tools and cross the countryside, often walking fifteen kilometres, to attend a ball animated by accordions, fiddles and drums. Only in early dawn would they straggle homeward, sleepy-eyed, to change clothes and return to their fields.

"All the flowers in the cement planters on the square will die now that Didier is dead," says Monsieur Douspis with grim satisfaction.

"Everything will go to the dogs," Madame Filoche agrees. And all present stare out the window with dour despair, as though the village square is already covered in spiked, creeping weeds and overrun with rubbish and rats.

"Who will want to come and live in the new housing development if the village is a mess?" asks Madame Douspis. "Who will want to come and take a walk here? How will the mayor draw tourists? Because that's all that interests him, drawing people into the village. It's bad enough now that our pretty little water wheel has been taken down."

"Oh yes," I say, thoughtfully. "There was all that fuss about the water wheel. Monsieur Pouttier's wheel. I had forgotten all about that."

"Didier was very opposed to the water wheel, of course. Said it was bad for the river, for the environment," says Madame Douspis.

"And the mayor hated him for it," adds Madame Filoche.

"But he was right!" says Madame Douspis with ferocity. "Didier was always right about things like that. He knew. He always did. And he opened his mouth and said so, too. Whether the mayor liked it or not."

14

WEREWOLF, WAITING PATIENTLY OUTSIDE ON THE SIDEWALK, FOLLOWS me into my house. I'm still thinking about the water wheel. It had been a modest, puny little project, but in an unaccented countryside such as this one, in villages of little distinction, a water wheel — even a tiny, fake, useless, decorative water wheel — is quite an attraction.

Marcel Pouttier, the electrician, has a house perched just on one side of the little river that cuts the village in two. His father, also an electrician, had possessed the first radio in the village; Sunday mornings, just before mass, a select group of villagers would gather in his front room to hear the news. When television made its appearance, the front window of the Pouttier house was enlarged and a set placed in it. What an attraction that was! All — mothers, fathers, children — would gather outside this display window and wonder. The sound couldn't be heard, but those flickering images were enough to nurture great dreams of possessing such a miraculous invention. Families scrimped and saved until the proud day arrived when they, too, could carry a set homeward, become the envy of less fortunate, less successful, less economical neighbours.

A dedicated member of flower and festival committees, an important man on the municipal council, Monsieur Pouttier Junior has an earnest desire to beautify our village with many tumbling arrangements of orange and pink geraniums and to see that well-won star appear on the village name panel. To this end, he decided to use his talents as electrician and man fascinated by gadgets. He constructed a miniature water wheel — complete with little buckets to contain geraniums — that turned round and round in the shallow, admittedly sluggish, little river. Word quickly passed of the wheel's existence; soon people were flocking in from surrounding villages and standing on the bridge, admiring this object of beauty. This result of a humble hobby, the geranium wheel, had become a centre of attraction, a claim to fame and source of great pride in Épineux-le-Rainsouin.

Until Monsieur Picot, owner of the former but very real fourteenth-century water mill (renovated in the 1970s into a modern bungalow with rustic-look terraces, wood-look beams galore, slathered over with arty-looking, swirled yellow cement) standing upstream of the little geranium wheel, reclaimed the ancient right of mill owner to control the waterway for a hundred metres in each direction. Picot demanded the wheel be removed immediately. He is a crotchety troublemaker, Monsieur Picot; he and his vinegary wife have little to do with the rest of us, the other villagers. And now they were pleased to see that they had a good excuse for causing trouble and exerting their importance; they threatened to instigate a lawsuit against Pouttier, against Lemasson, our mayor, against the entire municipal council.

It caused a furore. Monsieur and Madame Picot, ever disliked, were now loathed. Only one voice supported the wheel's destruction: Didier's. The newly constructed cement dyke on which the wheel stood slowed down the river even more, he insisted. It was creating a mini-ecological disaster: green scum was forming below the *lavoir*, was threatening the lives of the few remaining minnows who, unlike the bigger fish and once abundant crayfish, have miraculously survived the influx of nitrates, artificial fertilizers, weed killer and waste motor oil. Didier had the misfortune to state this at a meeting of the municipal council at a time when hatred of Monsieur Picot had united pretty well everyone else. His public declaration had been followed by an awed dead silence, aghast stares and horrified, open-mouthed grimaces.

Until, with no further ado, our mayor, Aimable Lemasson, a nervous man of short fuse and long-remembered invectives, had begun shouting, "No one asked for your opinion, you idiot. Fools like you should keep your stupid ideas to yourselves. Who do you think you are, you broom pusher, you ignoramus, you low-life nobody, you uneducated, interfering jerk?" He then, it was later recounted, paused, red-faced but still flapping his arms whilst scrabbling around mentally for even more dire humiliation. There had to be a sacrificial goat, and since neither the hated Monsieur nor the sour Madame Picot were present, Didier was it.

"Mortified, dishonoured and a pasty yellow-white colour," says Madame Sauvebœuf who, as keeper of the church key, always attends meetings. "Didier just stood up and, without another word, walked out of the town hall."

The incident caused considerable talk; a few of us admitted that Didier was right. It was, indeed, easy enough to see the almost daily increase in plush, flocked wallpaper-like algae. But if Didier persisted in his fight, would he also keep his job? Most people, of course, favoured the mayor. A mayor is a person of great importance in a village, and our own Monsieur Lemasson sees it as his lifelong duty to beautify all with yellow cement, to construct cement planters for geraniums, to have initiated the building of a new housing development. And he was determined that the water wheel remain, that the village maintain its reputation as a place of unique interest. But Monsieur Picot and his lawyer were tenacious; the ancient law had to be respected. And both water wheel and low cement dyke were quietly removed. Tourists no longer came to stand on the bridge and wonder. The village slipped back into its habitual, dreamless snooze.

15

"WE THOUGHT WHEN WE MOVED HERE WE'D HAVE A NICE LIFE. FRIENDS, dinners, things to be interested in. But it's not like that at all. This is a terrible area, as far as social life goes. We can't meet anyone. Almost no one invites us anywhere. The people here are anti-social, that's what they are. I can't tell you how much we regret the decision to move to this part of France." The man who is speaking is almost elegant despite a tatty little goatee. Well-dressed, grey-haired, a soft pouch of a belly puffs out the fine silk shirt he wears. He and a considerably younger woman have just emerged from the dining room and are standing at the bar, talking to Pierre. They probably belong to the big, flashy Mercedes parked outside the restaurant.

There's no one around to hear the complaint except for me and Pierre (and Werewolf, of course, but he never does pay much attention to anything that doesn't smell animal). I'm sitting a few feet away, drinking a glass of wine, the only person left in the bar at closing time. The lights in their overly cute seashell-like holders throw crinkly shadows on the pink textured bar walls and light up a tasteless painting of a little girl in braids having her underwear pulled by a fluffy, playful cocker spaniel, and a wood-look sign that states: "Don't harry the bartender; that's his wife's job."

"Where we used to live, in Bourges, well, I can tell you, we had a nice life back there," says the woman plaintively. She is wearing an expensive-looking linen pantsuit. Her makeup is light, her dark hair is clipped into a low ponytail and her long fingernails have been painted a frosty orange. Based on appearance alone, it's no mystery why these two have trouble integrating; local *haute couture* dictates the wearing of shapeless striped, checked and flower-printed acetate or manure-spattered blue overalls set off by rubber boots.

"We get the impression there's nothing happening out here. There's nothing of any interest going on. People are so closed off, they have no culture, no refinement. They're just primitive," says grey silk shirt.

"Primitive is the word. There's almost no one we can talk to. There's almost no one we can be friends with. Of course, there must be other people around of our level, but how are we supposed to meet them when everyone is being so difficult? So rural."

They're not talking to me, of course. They haven't even acknowledged my existence. I'm just some bag sitting at the bar. But because I am a cheery, friendly person, because I usually manage to weave my way into any conversation, and because I am curious about this couple — who the hell are they anyway? — I chirp in, "Yes, it can be difficult when you arrive here. People tend to stick in family groups. The best thing to do is join an association of some kind. A club. There are plenty of those around."

Pierre flicks a glance my way, gives a brief nod of assent. But linen pant suit and silk shirt don't even make a half turn in my direction. Neither can even be bothered looking, seeing who's talking to them; I'm just a little squeaking cricket-like thing they can't hear or acknowledge. Perhaps they've decided I'm not quite of their social level, a grey-haired woman wearing tatty jeans and run-down sneakers, sucking up red wine at the bar. I'm just part of the local, rural scenery. Way beneath them.

Pierre lifts his glass of beer, listens patiently. The two of them are his last customers on this Saturday night. The restaurant oven has been turned off. Soon he'll lock the door, turn off the lights, and head upstairs to his apartments to join his wife, Anne-Marie, for an hour or two of television. He isn't risking any comment. But what this whingeing couple hasn't yet worked out is that Pierre is a local, too: born here, raising a family here. He's part of this world, and like most folk in their own territory, he's proud to be part of it. As a local, his values run to family loyalty, regional loyalty. To him, the lack of social life outside family is normal. It's the way things are. He's certainly not going to have much sympathy with a couple of snobby complainers from somewhere else.

The man slides his credit card back into his wallet and the two of them exit.

"Who are they?" I ask, crinkling my nose as if there's a smell of rancid perfume in the air.

"Meet Nicole and Bernard Malabry," Pierre says as he grabs my glass, gives me a free refill.

"Malabry? Intensive chicken farm?"

Pierre nods expressionlessly.

"She's a lot younger than he is."

"She used to be his secretary, back in the days when he was an accountant in Bourges and married to someone else. They came out here to start a new life."

"How do you know she was his secretary?"

"They told me."

"So if Bourges is such a wonderful place, what are they doing out here? You'd think that someone like Madame Nicole Malabry would have put her glass-slippered foot down right in the beginning. I mean, she looks like someone who married the boss for Mercedes and money. Not to be an intensive chicken farmer's wife."

"Maybe she loves him. You think of that one?"

"No," I say. "When you look at people like that, you don't think of love. There's nothing warm and tender about them. If there were, they wouldn't be torturing our feathered friends up at their factory farm on the hill."

"You know all about love, huh?"

"No. Of course, I don't know all about it. But I've been around. And if I'm guessing correctly, Nicole Malabry is the sort of *nouveau riche* city girl who will complain and complain until hubby finally agrees to sell up and go back to city lights, take her out of all this, and put her back in all of that."

"I take it you don't like them," Pierre says, his voice dripping sarcasm.

"You like them?"

"Nope. Can't say I do. But they're customers. Good customers. If I only let people I liked into my restaurant, I'd have to run a place without a roof, without running water, electricity, chairs, or tables."

"You don't actually serve the chickens they raise, do you? Tell me you don't. Please. Just so I can sleep soundly. Just so I can believe you have principles."

Pierre shakes his head dolefully, goes to the door of the café. "Good night," he says. "There's a good, violent, space adventure movie on TV in five minutes. Don't want to waste any more good intellectual time on idle chatter."

16

ONE OF THE LESS APPEALING THINGS THAT CHRISTELLE DOES IS HAMMER on my front door in the middle of the night — say, three or four in the morning. She does it on the nights when she has done the round of country discotheques and is now too drunk to know — or care — that most of us are in bed and want to stay there, uninterrupted. These are times when she wishes to bare her soul, and she couldn't care less if I am interested or not.

"I have to talk to you. Something wanna tell you," she always slurs when I swing open my upstairs, bedroom window. "S'important."

"Then it will wait until tomorrow. Go to sleep, Christelle."

"Open the door. Something 'a tell you."

And so tonight, like all the other nights, I wearily trudge downstairs and open up. She isn't going to leave me in peace anyway, and once woken up like this, I can't go back to sleep. There have been times when I have tried ignoring her and her hammering, times when I threatened to call the police and charge her with disturbance of the peace. But I've never managed to dissuade her. And the next day, when I forbid her to ever do this again, she looks at me with amazement — real or feigned, it's difficult to know — and says, "I did that? I woke you up in the middle of the night?"

Now she is swaying, almost falling over, when I let her in. "What do you want to say?"

"Something I wanna tell you."

"What? What do you want to tell me?"

She sits herself down in an armchair beside the fireplace. No hesitation, no worry about being a pain in the ass. "Nobody to talk to here in this village. Nobody likes me. Bunch of jerks. Don' talk to me. Bunch of jerks don' know anything. Old bags, creeps. Assholes."

"Christelle, I'm going back to bed. This is boring."

"All think I'm scum. I know who's scum. They're scum. Don't gimme th' time of day."

"Christelle, I've told you time and time again, you have to be friendly to people. You're the one who doesn't talk to anyone. People aren't going to make an effort to be nice to you if you don't do the same."

"Conspir'cy took my daughters away. Social workers, ev'one all against me. My mother conspired with them to have the kids taken away. Like I'mn't good enough."

"That's not what you told me," I say impatiently. "That is not at all why the kids were taken away. They were taken away because the last guy you were living with was a drug addict and both of you were so out of it, you never sent the kids to school. They never even got to leave the house. And the father of your eldest daughter reported you to social services."

"Bullshit. S'all bullshit. Not with that guy anymore. Want my kids back. Gonna come live with me again."

"And you have to prove you can take care of them. But if you go out all the time, get drunk, how are you going to cope with kids if they come back? You'll lose them again." Actually, I can say what I want. Nothing makes an impact on Christelle anyway. She's too drunk to care, to listen, to understand. "Okay, Christelle. Out. I'm going to bed. Now." I move towards the front door, swing it open.

She glares at me from the armchair. Glares for another two minutes. Then heaves herself to her feet — almost falling over in the process — stumbles towards me, towards the doorway, down the two steps, and veers right, to her house.

Furious, I march back upstairs. Just another good night's sleep shot to hell. Thanks, Christelle.

17

Sunday, as I cross the square with Werewolf, I see the mayor, Aimable Lemasson, standing in a late-morning, butter-yellow streak of sun near Didier's house. He is surrounded by a little knot of people: Monsieur Vadepied, Mesdames Filoche, Beauducel, Houdusse, Sauvebœuf. Only Monsieur Douspis is missing; he and his wife have gone to a relative's wedding in the Paris region.

"I'm afraid both the police and I think it looks as though Didier committed suicide," the mayor is saying morosely. "He was depressed. We had a little conflict over something." His suntanned builder's skin is saggy and pale, the corners of his mouth hang downward in a catfish-like grimace. He looks, truly, to be a man in sorrow. Certainly, he doesn't think that Didier has killed himself because of the water wheel, does he? To my way of thinking, Didier would have been more likely to seek revenge than self-destruction over an incident that involved, as it did, a mere toy.

"You mean it wasn't an accidental death after all?" asks Madame Filoche with her usual happy delight at really bad news happening in someone else's life.

"It might have been an accident," confirms the mayor dully. "But it looks as though the police are looking at suicide."

"Why would a nice young man like Didier commit suicide?" Madame Filoche's little bespectacled eyes glow. "He had everything to live for. Wine, women, song. Chickens, too."

"Cousin over in Montagny committed suicide once," says Monsieur Vadepied cryptically. "Had a wife and ten children. Had everything to live for, too. One son in prison, another squashed by an earth-moving machine at work. Unmarried daughter in the family way. Had triplets, she did, eventually. Would have liked that if he hadn't shot himself. Half his head, right off."

"But it could also be murder, couldn't it?" asks Madame Filoche hopefully. "Have the police mentioned anything about that?"

The mayor drops his tone of affliction, replaces it with impatient annoyance. "Now why would they think something stupid like that? Why would it be murder? No one broke into his house. No one took his wallet, his digital camera, or his television. His computer, his scanner, the ones given to him by the municipal council, were sitting right there on his desk. No one touched them and it's good material, too. There was no sign of violence, no sign of forcible entry. His chequebook was right on the kitchen table; there was a full bottle of whiskey on the counter so no one came to steal his booze either. He was electrocuted, that's all. Why murder somebody for nothing?" He puffs with irritation, flings an exasperated arm heavenward, stalks away from the group, heads back over the bridge and homeward.

Monsieur Vadepied shakes his head doubtfully. "Wife's uncle's brother-in-law over near Flers was beaten to death with a metal rod. Police said it wasn't murder then, too. Said it was suicide. How'd they figure that out?"

"Police don't do their job these days, that's how," says Madame Filoche with satisfaction. "Too many young slackers on the police force. Think their uniforms are there for decoration only. I'll tell you what I think. I think it's all the fault of the Internet. The Internet has ruined everything."

"Don't forget what happened to Madame Soutif," says Madame Sauvebœuf, her eternal smile well in place. "Both husband and son hanged themselves, one after the other, in their barn, just outside the village. Last year, owner of the café in Sainte-Cécile hanged himself, too. Right in the main room. Wife had to cut him down before she opened up for the day. 'Was perfectly normal yesterday,' she said later."

"Used to keep the rope people hanged themselves with, in the old days," says Monsieur Vadepied. "Father had one out in the barn. Neighbours all came, said they wanted a piece of it. Said it brought good luck."

"Didn't bring much luck to the hanged person," I mumble, but am, as usual, ignored. Cynicism isn't highly appreciated in Épineux-le-Rainsouin.

"And then, when I was a young married woman," continues Madame Sauvebœuf, "right here in this village, Madame Pichot went shopping for dresses for her daughters one day, then came home and hanged herself in the woodshed two hours later. Just imagine going shopping, spending money, and then killing yourself. Lot of people do that around here."

"Lot of people get up to a lot of things around here," says Madame Houdusse with a knowing look. "Not just killing themselves either, but worse even. Never know when you look at a baby if it really looks like its father or not. Never can tell, although people always say that it does, of course. Fools, that's what people are. Say anything. Things aren't the way they used to be in the old days, not by a long shot."

"The old days!" Madame Sauvebœuf sniffs. "I remember the old days well enough myself. Farmer used to come into town for mass here, sixty years ago it was. Strange man. We all thought he was strange. That's what we all said. Probably too lonely out in his big farmhouse. Even then it was hard enough to get a wife if you were a farmer living too far out of town. Women didn't want that any more. Times were changing. Didn't want to be farmer's wives, wanted to marry shopkeepers, live in town. Too much isolation and hard work on an outlying farm. And that farmer, that odd man, he wanted to find a wife. So he put an ad in the local paper, and almost immediately a marriage was arranged with a village girl. Well, he showed up for his marriage with his fine carriage and fine horses because farmers did that then, just to show they were doing well for themselves. But after the marriage, six months later, the girl gave birth to twins. Not one child, but twins. The farmer, he went into the café. He went in and he said that he couldn't understand it at all. He hadn't even touched the girl yet. But she'd had twins. You can imagine how people laughed, especially later when he said how proud he was of his twins."

"I remember those days," says Madame Houdusse. "Newly married women gave birth to their children out in the farms, then waited a year or two before bringing them into town. A baby, you can see how old it is. But a child of two or three, who knows exactly? How many months, no one can tell."

"Now it's foreigners, those Romanian women, coming here to France to marry the farmers," says Madame Sauvebœuf. "Farmer doesn't want to stay a bachelor all of his life, and French women don't want to be a farmer's wife. Lazy, they are now, the young people. Want a husband but don't want to have to do anything for him. Farmer has to look elsewhere for a bride. Romanians more than happy to come here, to a land where they can buy things."

"Better than the English," says Madame Filoche. "Can't trust the English. Coming over here, buying up all of our houses, jacking the prices up so we French can't afford them anymore. Taking over, that's what they're doing."

"The French are setting the prices," I say, although I'm pretty weary of the old argument. "Not the English. They'd be stupid to jack up the prices themselves. But they have to pay what the French ask."

"English always killing people, too," says Monsieur Vadepied darkly. "Kill people all the time. And now Didier's dead."

"I don't think the English had a hand in that." I attempt to smother a grin.

"Killed Joan of Arc, didn't they?"

"No," I say. "The French did."

"Burnt her to death, the English did."

18

"WE HAVE TO TALK," JEAN-PAUL WHISPERS INTO THE PHONE.

"Why are you whispering?" I ask with irritation. "Is anyone there? Can anyone hear what you're saying? Where are you? At home?"

"No," he whispers. "No, I'm here in my office alone."

"In your office? On Sunday afternoon? There's no one there on Sunday, so why whisper?" Why the theatrics, I wonder, but don't ask. "You've heard about Didier, of course."

"Of course, I've heard about them finding Didier's body! What is everyone saying in the village?"

"Well, everyone has a pet theory about his death, of course. Some think it was suicide, others claim it was an accident. Even the word murder has made an appearance. My bet is, they'll all go for murder eventually. It's ever so much more exciting. Just like the good stuff everyone watches on television."

"And the police?" He's still whispering. His sense of humour has disappeared, too. "What do the police think?"

"How do I know what the police think? You think they come calling? That they come to my place and chat about their latest cases? Or go over to Madame Douspis's for a cup of coffee and a parley?"

"Be at the cemetery in half an hour." Now he's almost snarling; he really has lost all his usual cynical wit.

"The cemetery?" I ask, rather startled but still not abandoned by sarcasm. "Is this a new twist in our relationship? Sex and death as a turn-on?"

"I'll explain when I see you. If anyone else is present, don't talk to me. Just wait until we're alone."

Oh, right. As if no one's going to think it's odd, my being in the cemetery at the same time he is or my being in the cemetery at all. As if no one in the village notices that sort of thing — two people looking uncomfortable, throwing each other shifty looks over the crucifixes and plastic flower arrangements, then pointedly ignoring each other. Both just hanging around doing nothing, no blossoms in hand, no scrub brush to kill off the messy moss on the modern marble tombstones. Still, if Jean-Paul needs all the high drama of an assignation with his mistress in the village cemetery, I'll play along. Not that I'm so excited about it. No, on the contrary, I'm feeling rather blasé at the moment. No sudden thrill at hearing Jean-Paul's voice, no shaking hands, no knocking knees. No desire to even smear on lipstick. It's all part of what I call the mistress blahs: you finally have accepted, despite a few delicious promises, there's no happy end to the story. You know that indifference, well dosed with irritation, is just around the bend. And it doesn't make you sad, not at all. The whole thing has only been a momentary passion, a bit of love's facsimile in the desert.

I take the cul-de-sac in front of Christelle's courtyard, pass the chunk of metal in the stone wall where a pump previously stood, and begin to climb. In antiquity, cemeteries were banished to distant fields, but by medieval times, they had moved into the centre of villages right alongside the church, and burials by the huge crucifixes on country crossroads or in back gardens were greatly discouraged by the clergy. Only the excommunicated were refused a place in holy ground, but it was not uncommon for secret interments to take place there in the dead of night.

They were not sad places, cemeteries. They were places of pilgrimage, of refuge; here one communicated with the deceased, included them in life's activities. Dances, even markets were held in them; houses were built within their walls; some dwelt among tombs. People met here after mass, exchanged gossip and news while the hired professional mourners, the *pleureuses*, tore their hair and wailed vociferously in most public grief.

By the eighteenth century, however, attitudes were changing; death was becoming an unmentionable spectre, one best hidden from view. The old cemeteries around the churches were dug up, covered over and the dead were banished to less visible plots of land. Our own cemetery is now on a hill behind the village — a dangerous situation in times of cholera, plague and typhoid. Rainwater rushes down from fields higher up, leaches into the earth in the graveyard, trickles down into village wells. "It was poisoned water they had to drink back then," says Monsieur Vadepied. Not that it was worse than what was collected in ditches, streams, ponds, and polluted by sewage, kitchen waste, manure: far healthier to drink cider or wine. In 1955, piped water finally arrived.

I pass the grave of Aymé Tisserand at the cemetery entrance. A friendly soul, he requested to be buried in his hat in order to salute friends when they came to join him. Jean-Paul is already standing at the top of the hill, up where modern gravestones — huge blocks, pretentious and gilded (the dead must keep up appearances) — stand in military order. Soon the few remaining sagging old stone crosses will disappear; when families cease to pay rent for plots, old bones are hauled out, flung into a mass grave.

Jean-Paul sees me, looks around nervously, probably terrified that someone — alive or dead — will take note of our meeting, pass on the good word. But it's only when I'm standing right in front of him that I notice how white and pinched his face is. Even his hair has faded, lost its shine, and his eyes flicker anxiously. He seems to have aged suddenly — or is this the way he always looks in daylight? My usual vision of him, restricted to the half-light of my windowless back bedroom, is that of a man bent on seduction. Which is quite definitely far from his mind now.

"Tell me what's going on. What are they saying?" Jean-Paul whispers.

"They who? Saying about what?" I ask, trying not to make it so obvious that I'm gaping at him with curiosity and not a little vicious amusement. "Saying about Didier?"

He nods impatiently. "Of course, about Didier."

"Why are you still whispering? The dead aren't big on eavesdropping."

He isn't in the mood for vacillation either. Or humour. "Come on!" he whispers.

"Just what I said on the phone. That he either killed himself or he was murdered. It's only everyone having a good gossip. That's all. I just happened to be out on the street when the mayor was talking about suicide. He said it couldn't be murder because it was obvious that no one broke into his house and there were no signs of violence. The police are going for accidental death or suicide. That's all." I wonder why Jean-Paul is such a nervous wreck. Unless he has a bad conscience about something, something that threatens to shake his profitable, comfortable world. "What have *you* heard? Don't people chat to the local vet about things like death?"

He doesn't answer. Just shifts his eyes over in the direction of some conifers in the far distance.

"You look awful," I say bluntly. "What's got you in such a state? What are you so worried about? You should be happy that Didier is dead."

"Happy!" he spits. Continues examining the row of pines on the hill. "Why should I be happy?"

"Because now Didier can't open his big mouth about his affair with Chantal. Because he's no longer around to tell the tale, that's why. And that's all you're worried about, right? That's what's been keeping you on tenterhooks for ages now, you and Chantal both. What's important to you two is keeping your reputations squeaky clean here in the community." I know I'm not being sweet and supportive, but, frankly, I'm just not in the mood. He's a disappointment, this lover of mine, this man in whom I have invested much emotion.

His eyes jerk over in my direction. Finally. "Well, I'll just tell you what I'm worried about if you can't figure it out by yourself." His teeth are clenched, his lips drawn so tight they've almost vanished. "Number one: what if Didier made copies of Chantal's letters? What if he didn't give them all back to us? What if he kept one or two? Chantal didn't check to see if they were all there. I didn't even look at them. I didn't want to. The whole situation disgusted me. I just grabbed the things, tore them into a million pieces. But what if they weren't all there? What if the police found them, then what?"

"Never thought of that," I say slowly. "So if the police found them, they'll come around and ask you questions. So what? You can't be the only person whose wife has had an affair."

"And what if the police also come to the conclusion that someone bumped Didier off? What then? Who would be a likely suspect? The wronged husband, of course. In other words, me."

"Oh. I get it. A crime of passion."

"Exactly."

I almost snort with derision. "I thought all the passion was gone between you and Chantal."

He stares at me blankly. No lover likes being caught out in his little white lies. And I don't feel like letting him off the hook. "Anyway, according to what you told me, Chantal and Didier's romance has been over with for some time now. That means if you bumped him off just the other day, you can't even plead to a crime of passion. You would really have to catch them in the act for that plea to hold nowadays. Nope, you'll be tried for straight, cool-headed murder."

"Is this what you call funny?"

"Okay, okay. So you are one scared man at the moment." I'm not appreciating his nasty, tense tone of voice. Not at all. You don't use a tone of voice like that on a mistress although I do have to admit it: Jean-Paul's not exactly in a cosy position. But if he's not being nice, I'm not going to be nice either. Eye for an eye. Still, that doesn't mean I should be horrible.

"You're the one who told me that everyone's gossiping about the guy. Saying he had the hots for married women. One married woman or several married women? If it's one married woman, singular, then they're probably referring to Chantal."

"So, did you do it?" I ask, wondering how angry he's going to get now. "Did you kill Didier? Try to make it look like an accident? And you're pissed off that the so-called accident might look suspicious after all?"

"Sure," he says scathingly. It's a wonder he can talk at all through such a tight mouth. "Sure, I killed that little shit. Instead of enjoying being a nice and happy cuckold, I decided to go one step further. Be a murderer."

"Could be. You wouldn't be the first either. Despite your usual, oh-so-cool attitude towards Chantal and the love affair she had."

But Jean-Paul isn't really paying attention, so my words don't even provoke him anymore. Instead, he's staring over at the pine trees again. "Here's what you have to do for me," he says slowly, quietly. "You have to snoop around, ask people questions, and keep your ears open. Listen, really listen. Contact me just as soon as you hear anything. Call me immediately."

"Hear what? What am I supposed to be listening for?"

"Just find out if Didier was having an affair with other married women. Listen to rumours. See if anyone mentions me or Chantal."

"And while we're at it, why me? What does this have to do with me? Nothing, as far as I can see. This is your story. Chantal's story. Not mine, buddy."

When Jean-Paul shifts his eyes back my way, I can read a certain amount of humour in them. Finally. Unless it's sympathy I'm seeing. "Why you? Because you spend your life talking to everyone, that's why. You can't sit still for one whole minute without asking questions. And in the end, that's what everyone expects from you. Yes, I know; you always ask questions because you are an amateur ethnologist. But you're also seen by people as sort of a crank, you know."

"Great," I say sarcastically. "And when a big-shot veterinarian needs someone to save his skin, he comes and consults a crank."

But Jean-Paul isn't into sarcasm at the moment either. Or criticism. "Do me the favour, just keep on asking around. Find out if anyone else had a reason to want Didier out of the way. He was such a shit. I can't be the only one. And believe me, I didn't kill him. Honestly, I didn't. But I have to know if anyone suspects me."

His fingers reach out, caress my cheek briefly. As if this nosiness of mine has made me somehow endearing. Or as if he thinks a little tenderness will secure my loyalty. At the same time, it's not as if he's asking me to do something strange. I am nosy. I'm going to go on asking questions anyway. And in a strange way, I feel flattered. Because he thinks I'll turn something up. "Why not?" I agree finally. "Might as well poke my nose in everywhere. Keep up my bad image."

"And don't be too obvious."

"Obvious?" I stare at him. This man, he's nice and flattering one minute, and the next, treats me as if I'm an idiot. I'm okay for local gossip but not for in-depth investigation? "What kind of obvious?"

"I mean, don't ask questions that are out of character. Just find out what people are gossiping about. And there's another thing." He looks embarrassed suddenly. "I won't be coming to see you for a while. Let's wait until all this blows over, okay? I don't want to take any risks."

"Sure," I say and shrug my shoulders as if I couldn't care less. I could, of course. I'm just acting. It's my pride that's hurt. Pride dislikes being kicked, being brushed off like dandruff. He's a coward, I decide for about the one-hundredth time. A coward. I always knew it.

"I love you," he says. "Just remember I love you. Even though I'm not around, okay? When this is over, we'll go away on a little trip together. Just you and me. Do something nice. Okay?"

Yeah, sure, I think. Sure.

19

I'M SUPPOSED TO START ASKING QUESTIONS ABOUT DIDIER? WHERE? To whom? And no one's going to think I'm being odd? Oh, right. Didier wasn't even a friend of mine. So why am I so curious all of a sudden? And what exactly does Jean-Paul think I'm going to do? Knock on all the doors in the village and ask each and every wife if she's had an affair that she'd really like to keep hushed up? And by the way, is her husband a jealous sort of guy, one likely to commit murder?

Married women. Which married women? Who were Didier's friends? The English couple, Tim and Fiona, they used to hang around with Didier, I remember. Quite a lot of the time, actually. But that was a while ago, before their separation and divorce. And why did they divorce? I know none of the details. Why should I? Our acquaintance had only been a very casual one; when we ran into each other in Pierre's bar, we chatted; once I went to their house for dinner with my friend Martine who lives in Saint-Hilaire-la-Nozay — she thought that as native English-speakers, we would have a lot in common.

And now I start wondering: could Didier have been sleeping with Fiona? Is that why she and Tim split up? Did Didier try to blackmail her? If chasing after married women in order to extort money had been his usual game, then why not? Perhaps it was Tim Pierre had been referring to the other morning, although I haven't seen Tim in the café for quite some time now. Hadn't seen him hanging around with Didier recently either. Strange.

Five years ago, Tim and Fiona bought a tiny house just outside the village, on the road to Saint-Hilaire-la-Nozay. Once, it had been a gardener's cottage on a long, poplar-lined lane leading to a seventeenth-century castle owned, in the late 1940s, by wealthy Parisians known for weekend sexual orgies, dabbling in black magic and experimenting with drugs. One summer during a wild party, there was a fire (no one in the village really knows how it started), and all that's left of the castle today is a pile of blackened carved granite lost under a savage tangle of briars, nettles, sticky willy and thistles.

The gardener's cottage, long since abandoned, was hardly in a better state when Fiona and Tim first saw it: the roof had caved in, the beams rotted. There were no windows, no doors. But the grey stone walls were straight and steady, and both Tim and Fiona fell in love with the place. Tim is handy. He loves building and restoration, and he was determined to turn that old cottage into a palace.

The villagers were flummoxed, of course; who would want to buy a roofless rubble of old stones? "Only the English," they sneered. "The English buy anything and everything. Offer them horse manure and they'll take it. Pay top price, too. They're in love with France. Everything here fascinates them. They write books about how we're such quaint characters, and they go into ecstasies about the food. Want to sell old wrecks? Sell them to the English. We don't want them." Villagers are clear about their preference for concrete and breeze block, for the new housing developments with streets named after trees: *la rue des Frênes* (Ash Tree Street), *la rue des Marronniers* (Chestnut Tree Street), *la rue des Ormes* (Elm Tree Street). But in developments, no trees are allowed to grow tall and block the view; regulations stipulate the height of a hedge, the colour of front doors, the variety of flower that can be planted in gardens.

It was, apparently, a good marriage that Tim and Fiona had. Their grown children, unwilling to resign themselves to the dullness of a small French village, had remained in London. Living temporarily in an old caravan, Tim got to work making windows and doors, copying old, traditional models, for many of the English tend to be purists. They do not renovate; they restore. With the help of visiting friends, with Didier, he put up new beams, covered them with grey slate tiles. A year or so later, the cottage had recovered much of its former charm.

Fiona, less interested in building, attended to the couple's social life. She was a friendly woman, and, although her French was limited, she did her best to communicate with all and sundry, to integrate, to become part of the village — as much as foreigners can hope to do in this rather xenophobic region. They invited everyone — neighbours, new acquaintances, drinkers in the bar — to their home. And because people are more than happy to freeload, they came in droves. The invitations were rarely returned, but that didn't matter to either Tim or Fiona. Their house was an open house; everyone was welcome to gather, to dine, and to impose. And drink: Fiona and Tim were great social drinkers.

Because he was a congenial person, a helpful one, Didier had quickly become their friend. He was often at their house. Very often. I know this because Madame Sauvebœuf told me so at the time. And Madame Sauvebœuf certainly knew. From either one of her doors, she can well see what takes place on the road leading out of the village in the northerly direction.

"Every night, he goes there, Didier. I can't help seeing him. When I just happen to be outside, in front of my house or just behind, I see him, six-thirty sharp, after he showers and changes clothes and the day's work is done. Every evening I see him, all right, heading down the Saint-Hilaire-la-Nozay road, out in that direction. And I guess where he's going because what else lies in that direction? Nothing much but the village of Saint-Hilaire a few kilometres distant, but there's not even a café in that place so why would Didier go that way every evening? Not that it's any of my business; not that I care. Everyone can live his or her own life; it's nothing to do with me. It's only that my husband just happens to go for a walk every evening — the doctor says it's good for his heart you know, we're not young anymore — and one evening he went out in that direction, went by that cottage out there, and what do you know? There was Didier, sitting out in front of the house with that English couple. Just as comfortable as comfortable can be. Just as if he lived there."

But Didier hadn't gone there to freeload. Tim and Fiona were no different than many of the other English in the area; they had difficulty with the language, and Didier, wishing to help, offered his assistance. Together, he and Tim bought sand and lime, plumbing supplies, roof slates, wood, old red floor tiles. In a very short while, Didier had made himself quite indispensable, so much so that Tim and Fiona had become quite dependent upon him. And they drank together, ate together, came to the café together to guzzle before staggering back home again, quite in their cups. Or so my friend Martine told me. She knew. She and Fiona were very close back then.

And then quite suddenly, Fiona left the country, went back to England and didn't return. Didier no longer wended his way down the road in the evenings after work. Tim's behaviour changed radically, too; he no longer frequented Pierre's bar. Martine told me that he and Fiona were divorcing, that it was a miserable divorce, an ugly one. She wanted money, a lot of it. The battle through lawyers had begun. I saw him once, sitting alone in the front yard of his isolated gardener's cottage, looking as cheery as a man whose morale had been sawn in half. I'd waved. He'd flipped his hand, a vague, unwelcoming gesture.

So I can't just go over to Tim's house. Barge in and begin asking questions. It would seem odd, especially just after Didier's death. No, I'll go to the bar this evening. Sit and listen. See if there is any information I can pick up — a vague hint, a clue, a tidbit dropped unaware. And if my little theory about Didier and Fiona proves right, I'll have some news for Jean-Paul. How grateful he'll be! For even if ours is not an ideal love story, it's at least something. Something, out here in the country.

20

AT EIGHT-THIRTY ON SUNDAY EVENING, I CROSS THE SQUARE, TAKE THE steel and cement bridge to the other side of the village. On the right, just downstream from where the little water wheel once stood, is the *lavoir*, the former washhouse. This was once a meeting place *par excellence*, for the time spent rubbing the clothes on the stone ledge also afforded hours of delicious gossip as well as a chance to assess neighbours' financial situations by the quality and quantity of linen sheets, embroidered towels, trousers and underclothes. For this reason, not all dirty linen was exposed to public view; the more shameful tatters were dealt with in barns and courtyards, well away from public censure.

First boiled in wood ash in a big pot at home, the wash was brought to the *lavoir* for scrubbing before being hung on hedgerows to bleach and dry in the summer sun. Wealthier households, post houses and hotels had servant girls for the task, and these would chat freely of visitors from far-off places, of romances, dark family secrets, besmirched honour. It was certainly a place of education, the *lavoir*.

Perched at the river's edge, the squat wooden building still possesses the stone lip on which clothes were rubbed clean and the pulleys that raised and lowered the floor in keeping with the water level in the river. But the *lavoir*, no longer in use, has become nothing more than a place for the flower committee to hang baskets of geraniums.

In Pierre's café, I order a beer, sit ... and am ignored, quite pointedly, by the men present: the short, stocky Piednoir brothers — Serge, Georges and Robert — agricultural workers, Monsieur Hautbois, roofer, "*le gros*" Gousset, deliverer of cattle to the slaughter house. Even Pierre, relatively forthcoming when we are alone, is paying no attention to me now. In the early evenings, I am considered an intruder, for this is the highly exclusive male moment of the day. This is the time when discussion is serious, deep, meant for sophisticated, masculine ears alone.

This afternoon's football scores are compared, past football triumphs are resuscitated, praise of football heroes sung. Then, football regretfully exhausted, the discussion goes on to the benefits of new tractors, vans and cars, the price of diesel fuel, the meanness of officials who impose speed limits on the roads, colourful details of gruesome traffic deaths with maximum carnage. Eventually, Didier's name crops up, although, heaven knows, that sad subject should be quite exhausted now that everyone has been chewing away at it for several days.

"Stupid thing to do, taking a hair dryer into the bath. You'd think he'd know better," says Serge Piednoir.

"Just like Claude François," says "*le gros*" Gousset, referring to the accidental bathtub death of that popular French singer in 1978. "Made a law after he died. Plugs have to be a certain distance from the bathtub these days. But that's only in new buildings. Lemasson renovated Didier's place in '76. Plug right beside the tub, just over the sink."

Serge Piednoir shakes his head in a morosely happy sort of way. "Still like that in plenty of houses, plugs beside tubs. Lot of other deaths going to be happening until they do something about all those. Men, women, children, innocent people just taking a bath."

"They should stick to rubber ducks when they do that. Not play with hair dryers," I say flippantly enough. My comment is ignored, of course. It just doesn't have the right note of gore.

"Mayor white as a sheet, I hear, when he came out of his house. Bet he doesn't feel too good now either. He's the one did the renovations anyhow. Said you could smell Didier all the way out to the main road. Body that stays in water like that turns all yellow. Seen it myself a few years ago when a dead man come up after a few weeks in the lake near Sarnes. Was fishing at the time. Looks like it's under wax, the face and all. Doesn't even look human anymore. And you never smelled anything like it. Nothing worse in the world. Put me off my fishing for the afternoon, I can tell you that."

"Pulled a man out of the water once when I was a volunteer fireman," says Georges Piednoir. "Been there a week or two. Rotten, bloated arm came off right in our hands."

"Strange things, bodies," says "*le gros*" Gousset with an all-knowing air. "See that story on television about the guy on a motorcycle driving on the highway near Paris? Driving behind a truck carrying steel bars. One got loose, not tied down well enough. Flew through the air, sliced off the cyclist's head neat, just like that. Neat. Body went on all by itself. Everybody seen a headless bike driver driving along the highway, two, three, four kilometres or more before it finally stopped, keeled over, just like that. Plouf."

Everyone grunts in appreciation but not surprise; we've all heard that old fable at least fifty times, right here in this very bar.

"See that story on television about man died in his own home? Dead a week when they found out. Nothing left of him 'cause his dog ate him. Even the bones gone. Television showed it all."

Georges Piednoir throws Werewolf (who's not listening) a fleeting but suspicious look. "Seen on television the other day about dogs eating children whole. Killing them and eating them. Can't trust dogs. Kill children all the time, dogs do. Owners aren't responsible these days, television says so."

I sip my beer, observe all. The Piednoir brothers are married with young children. "*Le gros*" Gousset, a man often on the road, is also married. As is Pierre, come to that. But there seems to be no resentment in the air, no hints about Didier being a chaser of skirts that are the property of other men. The well-known tales of blood and guts roll on, all containing elements most pleasing to modern *Homo sapiens*: pain, suffering, decomposition, putrefaction and televised tragedy. Were bar conversations always so, I wonder? Were they like this in the days when a few original old crocks were regulars: a strange little man who conversed in a series of clicks or a bug-eyed creature who maintained odd, disjointed conversations with no one in particular? How about when Tim and Fiona brought in their bonhomie? And Didier, his protest? But Didier and the old crocks are dead, and Fiona has started a new life in London.

"Anyone seen Tim around lately?" I ask idly. Everyone turns to me and glares, obviously offended at this feminine attempt to change a fascinating line of conversation into the banal. Pierre stares at me quite blankly for a minute or two, as if wondering what I'm up to. Then, blandly enough, says, "Haven't seen him much since his wife left."

"He was Didier's friend, wasn't he?"

Pierre shrugs impassively. The others look at each other, ignore the question. Either they have nothing to say or nothing they want to say to me about that.

"Going to be hard to get that house of Didier's cleaned up and smelling sweet for the next *garde champêtre*," says Robert Piednoir, tastelessly picking up the juicy conversational thread once more. "I know all about the way things stink after a few days, and the weather's been warm lately. Hasn't made things better. At least if it happened in the winter, Didier dying, then it's cold and the stink's not so bad. Was a cow died a few years ago in a barn out near Saint-Hilaire-la-Nozay. Farmer just let it lie for a few days. Was summer that time, too. Let it lie before calling in and having it hauled off to the treatment plant. Don't know what made him do that. Folks are strange. Plenty of folks strange plenty of the time; never know what makes them tick. I come into that barn — what, days later — and believe me, you smelled that cow. Ponged, it did. Smell got itself into the walls. Into the wooden floor, that's what it'd done. Just soaked right into the planks."

"Know that smell any day," adds Serge Piednoir. "Just smell a dead animal on the road. Roadkill tells you where it is, all right. Pongs, it does, roadkill. But nothing got a stink to it like a man dead in a bath for four days probably. Probably not."

"Is everyone absolutely sure about the four days?" I ask.

All turn and stare at me as if I've posed the stupidest question this year.

"I mean, does anyone know what day Didier actually died?"

"Of course. We all know," says "*le gros*" Gousset. "Mayor told us it was Monday night. Didn't show up for work on Tuesday, Didier didn't. So it had to be Monday night, didn't it."

"Monday for sure, huh?" I wonder if this is rumour or fact. Does one really need fact? Is fact considered just an intrusive little bit of detail? Still, I would think the police might want a little more precision.

"Poor sod," says Georges Piednoir. "Poor sod, Didier. He didn't know he'd pong like that."

There is another communal assenting grunt.

21

BEFORE SHE LEAVES TO DO HER EARLY MONDAY MORNING ROUND, I CALL
my friend Martine on the phone. She's a nurse but also an amateur
psychologist; you can't stop her analyzing everyone and everything, and
she's just the person to talk to in this case. This whole story has snagged
my attention, and not just because I want to do Jean-Paul a favour either. But it's given me a project, an activity; it's a nice little puzzle for
me to gnaw away at.

"You've heard that Didier, our village *garde champêtre*, is dead, of
course," I say when she answers the phone.

"I've heard."

"Well, the mayor claims he committed suicide or that it was an
accident. But everyone else is sure he was murdered."

"Who's everyone else?" She doesn't sound in the least bit interested.
Bored, irritated, exasperated, even. I know Martine never liked Didier
very much, and, as a practical sort of person, she isn't all that crazy about
spreading or listening to gossip either.

"The village biddies."

Martine sniggers. "Village gossip. People aren't satisfied with suicide
or accidental death. They watch too much television and want drama in
their own lives."

"But what if somebody did murder him?"

"You hoping to make an arrest?" Her voice oozes unadulterated
sarcasm.

"Of course not," I say quickly. I'm not about to roll out the story
about Jean-Paul. Not to Martine. Not to anyone.

"So what's your interest in all this?"

"No interest. Just nosiness. As you say, thanks to television, I'm just
looking for a little drama in my own life."

"You don't have a television."

"The biddies say that the gendarmes were swarming all over Didier's house after they discovered the body. That sounds to me like the beginning of a homicide investigation, right?"

"No. You're dramatizing. It sounds to me as though the police were there to see if there were any *grounds* for beginning a murder investigation. Big difference."

"Right. Do you think they did an autopsy?"

"Why should they have? It's obvious how he died," says Martine, still exasperated.

"Yeah, sure. He died in his bath, electrocuted by a hair dryer."

"So? Where's the mystery?"

"How about the exact time of death? Don't people do autopsies in this country?"

"Not often. Only when the cause of death is unknown."

"How about if something looks suspicious. I mean, who takes a plugged-in hair dryer into the bath with them?"

"Someone who wants to kill himself," Martine answers. "Of course, the police could always arrest the hair dryer and charge it with murder."

"Come on. You know what I'm getting at."

"Look, there are only two medical examiners in this entire *département*. This isn't North America. This isn't even Paris. Forensic medicine is a job nobody wants. The installations for doing autopsies are rudimentary, and that means medical examiners are limited in the laboratory tests they can carry out. Not only that, it's also an unpleasant job, it's notoriously underpaid, and you have to be available any time day or night."

"So you figure they didn't do one on Didier?"

"Almost certain they didn't. Not unless his family insisted that they do one. Even if the police did want an autopsy done because there was some doubt about the manner of death, they'd need the family's permission."

"Oh. So did he have a family, Didier?"

"How do I know? He was my best friend? As far as I'm concerned, he was just a perverse jerk."

"How? How was Didier perverse?"

"I don't have time for this," says Martine. "I have a job to do. Patients are waiting for me. And what I know about Didier would make a long story."

"One you'll be happy to tell me, I hope. In person."

22

JEAN-PAUL'S VETERINARY PRACTICE IS OVER ON THE OUTSKIRTS OF Derval. It's a breeze block and yellow cement horror with lots of plate glass, just the sort of sterile construction that reassures people with sick pets. I park my car in the empty space near the door, attach Werewolf to his leash, and march up the steps. Werewolf doesn't mind going to the vet; a vet touches him all over, and that's ecstasy as far as he's concerned. He doesn't even care when he gets a shot.

"You have an appointment?" the ever prim and sour receptionist behind the big plastic counter asks. It's a moot question. She knows very well I don't, but she thinks I ought to respect the big man's time. Her put-upon expression tells all.

"I'm sure he'll see me. If he's not busy."

She throws me one last, lingering look of disapproval, then heads for the door that leads into the surgery. A minute later, another door opens. Jean-Paul is standing there. He's looking nervous again. "Come in."

Werewolf's nails ticktack on the tile floor as we sweep by.

Jean-Paul closes the door, waits for a second or two, probably just to make sure the receptionist is back at her post and not standing with her ear glued to the cracks. "You have any news?" He's back to whispering.

"No news. Just a question."

"What kind of question?" He's as wary as a trapped rat suddenly.

"About Monday evening."

"What Monday evening?"

"Last Monday evening, the night you were supposed to come and see me but didn't. Monday evenings are our times together, remember?"

Jean-Paul blows out an exasperated puff of air. "Look, I was busy, right? I can't always come and see you when you think I should."

I am almost amused. Only almost. What the hell is he thinking?

That I'm here in the role of offended mistress? Demanding an excuse for a missed rendezvous? Well, if he does, he's dead wrong, but I don't feel like clearing the matter up for the moment. "I'm not asking you to explain why you couldn't come. I just want to know where you were."

He closes his eyes, rubs his forehead with a balled fist. Massaging the grey matter and hoping something good will come up? "What difference does it make?"

"A big difference." I wait.

He looks at me warily. Then drops the fist to his side, a gesture of resignation. "I was at home. With Chantal."

"Oh. Okay." How cosy. Lover boy and wifey. I push back the jealousy; mistresses don't have any right to that particular emotion. "I suppose Chantal will back you up?"

"Yes, yes. She'll back me up." He looks guilty as hell suddenly. And hangdog. "Look, I had to stay home. It was our anniversary."

"Cute."

"I didn't want to handle a domestic war, okay? I came to see you on Thursday. Wasn't that good enough?"

"Sure. It's fine."

"So?"

"So, I'm just snuffling around. Isn't that what you wanted me to do? Snuffle around? And this coincidence just might interest you: Didier definitely died on Monday night. That means, if someone killed him, it was then."

Jean-Paul stares at me wordlessly. He can't believe I really think he might be guilty.

"So I'm just checking out your alibi. Of course, even if you killed him, Chantal would back you up. Unless it was Chantal who killed him, of course. Or perhaps you both did. Both of you going to his house on Monday night for a friendly little visit."

"Are you crazy?"

"Nosy. Not crazy. Thanks for the info." Werewolf and I head for the door, swing it open.

"I didn't do it," I hear him call after me. "I told you I didn't do it."

The receptionist stares at me with undisguised curiosity as I pass her. But it's too late for her to rush to the closed door and slam her ear against it.

It's when I have the car already pulled out of the parking spot and am turning east that I see the big, shiny Mercedes slowing down, coming to a stop, parking in the space I've just vacated. I pull over to the side of the road and watch Nicole Malabry, chic as chic can be in orange silk, step out, smooth back her hair, straighten her dress, rub her raspberry rose lip-sticked lips together and head into Jean-Paul's building. "Not an ailing cat, not a sick dog, not even a dead chicken in sight," I say to Werewolf. "Just a friendly visit to the local vet. In high heels and silk stockings."

23

"NORMALLY WHAT HAPPENS AT A WEDDING IS THAT FIRST, YOU GO TO the ceremony at the church," says Monsieur Douspis, his face red with indignation. "Then outside the church, the couple greets the guests — especially those who have come from a long way. Then everyone goes for the meal in the village hall or a local restaurant. And if the groom belongs to the football club or the fire department, then his pals dance around or do a skit or sing a song. You know, a demonstration of some kind. It situates things. Then everyone sits down and the couple goes from table to table and greets everyone again. And you eat a big meal. Really big. And then there's another big meal in the evening. And a dance. And after the dance, when it's late at night, there are more things to eat: cold cuts, salads. And in the old days, there was a noon meal the next day. That's normally what happens. That's what people are supposed to do."

Of course, even Monsieur Douspis's idea of a proper wedding is a very watered-down version of the traditional affairs held in my old hotel years ago. In the hotel's best bedroom the bride received the hairdresser, and was dressed in the traditional black wedding gown and white veil. On her father's arm, she first proceeded to the town hall for the official wedding, then to the religious ceremony in the church. Formalities over with, bride and groom led the wedding guests to one of the cafés on the square for a toast before the feast. Back at the hotel, long tables, covered with flowers and leaves, formed a square around the main room; the newlyweds sat at the place of honour just in front of the fireplace, now covered with a cloth bearing the couple's initials in palm leaves.

The meal was copious; the few old menus still kicking around in my old hotel testify to that. One began with soup, went on to fish in homemade mayonnaise, then the chickens used for the soup, then tongue, string beans, a roast of veal, salads and desserts, fruit salad, a wedding cake, petites fours and coffee. The meal over, waiters and waitresses passed a hat to collect spare change from the guests, which was exchanged in the grocery shop next door, always open during such events, for the wedding gift: a small clock or a china bowl for washing. Then all would depart to drink in all the other village cafés, for a local marriage meant that all should profit. Later, back at the hotel again, each member of the wedding party would sing solos until it was time for a second meal, slightly more frugal: consommé, cold cuts, roasted chicken and beans, salad, fruits, pies, cakes and coffee.

Musicians would arrive, usually an accordionist and drummer, and dancing began: slow, traditional dances that allowed the peace necessary for banter, for weddings were occasions for folk to fall in love.

"This wedding we were at on the weekend certainly was modern," says Madame Douspis, who is selecting shallots for the midday meal. "It wasn't in a village hall or a restaurant. It was held in a château. Conspicuous consumption, that's what it was. Who needs a château? A village hall was good enough for us. And no one greeted us when we arrived. And there was no skit, no singing, nothing. We had come all the way from here; there were other people who came from even further, from Brittany, and there was nothing. We sat down; we had plates of chic nothing to eat."

"Times are changing," says Madame Filoche with malicious glee. "Young people today, they don't know anything. They don't know the proper way to do things."

"Bland food," Monsieur Douspis complains. "Modern and bland. The tiniest slice of pâté. Veal stew with shrimps."

"I don't know what shrimps are doing in veal stew," says Madame Douspis, violently assaulting one poor shallot with her sharp little knife. "And three kinds of rice, there were. So what, three kinds of rice. There wasn't enough to eat on the plates. We were hungry."

"And the wedding couple, they didn't come around to the tables either. Not enough to eat, and I don't know how much it cost them but that caterer, he wasn't up to much. Wasn't worth much, although they paid dear. Must have cost them a fortune. Nothing much, the château either. Just bare walls. It was supposed to impress us. There was dancing, but it started even before the meal was over. Not music you could dance to, just disco stuff so loud you couldn't talk. So we left. We went back to our hotel. And since there was nothing the next day, we went to visit our son in Paris."

"That's the way things are going now," says Madame Filoche. "For young people today, the traditional way of doing things is no good. A château, it's supposed to show everyone that they've let their origins drop."

"And the groom, he wants to show he is a big shot, that he's too much of a big shot to belong to a football club or a fire department. That's for bumpkins. This new generation, they just want to show they can make money."

"Parisians!" Madame Filoche sniffs and looks pleased that the Douspis's weekend to which she wasn't invited (they weren't relatives of hers) has turned out to be a disappointment. "Not that things are better out here. Murders, thefts, wars. Can't trust anyone these days, not even the police. Not even them, just a bunch of young bucks, young bucks who don't do anything at all. Look at what happened to poor Didier, and the police don't do anything at all. Not since they went through his house collecting evidence. Didn't see them again the whole time you were at that wedding, and now it's already Tuesday. Didier has been dead for over a week."

"What did the police do wrong?" I ask. "I mean, if Didier took a bath with a hair dryer, the police certainly couldn't prevent that, could they? Not unless they thought he was going to do something stupid and stationed themselves in his house, day in, day out."

There is a long silence. Monsieur and Madame Douspis and Madame Beauducel all stare at me with something that looks, strangely enough, like pity. Madame Filoche shakes her head, as if confronted by the ultimate stupidity. "Tsk tsk," she says. "Tsk tsk."

I stare back. "Well?"

"I never wash my own hair," says Madame Douspis, mysteriously. "Instead, I go to the hairdresser. Madame Beaupied does everything for me. And when I was young and I had thick hair, healthy hair, I only washed it from time to time because it was never dirty. Even now, Madame Beaupied tells me that I have hair of superior quality, and you don't often see that in women of my age. Even though I keep it cut as short as possible now."

"Mine is also excellent," insists Madame Filoche, whose copper dyed tresses are ever rolled into the elegant chignon. "One must always take care of oneself. My husband was from Paris and when I moved to Paris after my marriage, I knew that a woman always had to take care of herself, be careful about her appearance. My husband was a civil servant, and I had a certain position to keep up because I was a civil servant's wife. I always had to be elegant even though I was a simple housewife. No laziness permitted."

"Well, Monsieur Douspis was an engineer," says Madame Douspis proudly. "That's not nothing, you know. People also expected me to look good. It wasn't easy with four children, especially during the war, I can tell you that. But I always had neat hair, beautiful hair because my hair was of great quality."

"Well, I never go to the hairdresser," insists Madame Filoche. "I can take care of my own hair. And I don't need a hair dryer either. And certainly not in a bath. But some people are so vain, you can't teach them a thing. Hair dryers in baths," Madame Filoche snorts with derision. "You need to be a stupid to do a thing like that, but I'll bet people do it all the time."

"That's true enough," says Madame Douspis. "Person who did a thing like that would have to be stupid. But Didier, he wasn't stupid. He wasn't vain either. And more importantly, he had even less hair than I do now."

Then Mesdames Filoche, Douspis, Beauducel and Monsieur Douspis all stare at me again. Stare, as if waiting for something, for some brilliant flash of inspiration on my part.

"Well?" says Madame Douspis. "Well?" She looks as pleased as punch with herself — the cat that killed the vulture.

"Well what?"

"Think a little. And then tell me that you are going to be able to sleep safe and sound in your bed every night. You, a woman who lives alone. In that big old house of yours. Where no one can hear you if you scream for help. All alone, and a murderer on the loose."

"Look, there is really no reason to think Didier was murdered."

"Of course there is," she announces triumphantly. "We know

that now. Definitely."

"This is crazy," I say, deciding that malicious gossip really has gone too far. "How do you know that Didier was definitely murdered?"

"We worked it out, that's how. Just used our heads, we did. Put the facts together. I don't know why it had to be us, though, and all the others don't even know how to use the brains they were born with. Didier, he dies with a hair dryer in his bath?"

"Exactly," I say. I'm still not catching the drift. "And his death was either an accident or suicide. Even the mayor says it might have been suicide."

"Police say that because they're too lazy to do a decent job of work," says Madame Filoche. "Mayor says it because he doesn't want trouble. But why would Didier go out and buy a hair dryer? Now why would he do that, you tell me. Didier, he had short hair. Short as short can be. Why, in heaven's name, would he need a hair dryer?"

"Oh," I say as the penny drops. "Oh. I never thought of that."

"But we did!" trumpets Madame Douspis. "We did! We did think of that. No way on earth a man with hair as short as a mowed lawn would need a hair dryer." She shrugs, now attacks a piece of garlic. "You don't think of these things because you don't pay attention to what's going on. You don't watch everything the way we do. Didier was a single man. A single man always has a single man's life. It's not as if he can't do what he shouldn't." As she drops the white peel on the table, looks up at me with an expression I can only interpret as sly. "What we decided is, if Didier died with a hair dryer in his bath, it's because someone else threw it in there."

And all four of them, Mesdames Douspis, Filoche, Beauducel and Monsieur Douspis look at each other with beaming, satisfied exaltation.

"Okay, okay. But still, the police must have thought of that, too. And if they did, they'd investigate if it looked anything like murder."

"Wrong again," says Madame Douspis. "Because the mayor is responsible for law and order in a village. And if the mayor says to the gendarmes that something looks suspicious, they'll investigate. But if he doesn't, they won't. That's how things work here." She slices deep into the clove of garlic.

"Case over in Derval," says Madame Filoche. "Brother-in-law told me about it. Algerian woman hanged herself about a month ago. First person to find her was her sister. She cut her down, tried to give her the kiss of life. Husband came in, saw her doing it, called the police. Police came and arrested the woman, almost accused her of murder. Was touch and go for a while. All that because she was Algerian. But people like the mayor, the gendarmes listen to him, to what he has to say. Not to a bunch of old people like us."

And all in the room nod in total agreement.

24

"ALWAYS KILLING OFF THE BEST OF THEM," SHOUTS MONSIEUR VADEPIED.
I am sitting at the table in his front room, surrounded by his wife's im-
mense collection of stuffed animals, costumed dolls, souvenir cups and
saucers with their drawings of tourist destinations, dried flowers, and
six shrieking canaries in tiny cages hooked against garish orange, brown
and red swirl wallpaper. At the end of the table, the television is blasting out the sports news at full force, but no one is watching or listening to it. "Didier was one of the best. Like with his chickens. Couldn't
have it better, chickens couldn't. People like Didier around, no need to
kill off all the wild birds. Kill them off, they do, in foreign countries.
Migrating birds. Pet birds. Look at China. Killed all the sparrows and
crows. Sparrows and crows eat insects. Then what happens? Insects eat
all the rice, all the crops. Everyone dies of starvation. Saw it on TV last
night. Hunting down all the wild birds, cutting down trees they live in.
Then feed sick chickens to tigers and leopards in the zoo. So they get
bird flu."

Madame Vadepied looks at me with worried eyes. She's a woman one
never sees on the village square. Permanently glued to her television set
from dawn until midnight, she largely prefers the company of feathered
friends to that of mere humans. Now she waves her hand in the direction
of her pet canaries. "Not going to get my birds. Let no one in here."

"Keep them out," Monsieur Vadepied nods in agreement. "No one
comes in here unless they're invited. Me and my rifle'll make certain of
that."

"You have a rifle?"

Monsieur Vadepied stares at me with humour. "Everyone has
one. Keep mine loaded. No one comes in here. They'll find out soon
enough."

"Everyone has them? Loaded?"

"Loaded. Of course, loaded. You hear about what happened in Angers?" He hands me the cigarette he has rolled for me — harsh, crudely-cut, grey tobacco. "Man shot his girlfriend and three children on Friday night. Neighbours found them. Weren't even his three children. Were hers from another marriage. Just shot them, one by one. Then he killed himself so they couldn't take him. Nobody knows why."

"Killed all three children," Madame Vadepied leans across the table, her hands folded, begins shaking her head with great disapproval. "And in Chamrie. Chamrie, too. Chamrie, a man kills his two children and his wife with a hammer. Yesterday. Said she wanted a divorce. Didn't want a divorce so he killed them. All of them. With a hammer. One after the other."

"With a hammer," confirms Monsieur Vadepied, "Over in Chamrie. Then in Mers, man was told that his wife wanted to divorce him, and he hanged the two children then shot himself. On the weekend. Didn't want a divorce. You'd think they'd just piss off and let everyone get on with their lives instead of killing off the whole lot. What I say is, we put children on earth so that they can live, not so we can kill them. That's a fact. Wife's cousin, man she's living with, he's no better than that either. She's the third wife he's had. Come in here one day and her arm's black and blue. Says she ran into the door. Wasn't true. Know it wasn't true. Children told me. Said he threatened her."

"And she stays with him?"

"Not going to let her get away, he isn't. Says he loves her."

"And Didier ... Didier, too," says Madame Vadepied with a wise nod.

"Didier too what?" I ask.

"Didier, too. Not the first murder here either," says Monsieur Vadepied morosely. "Not the first murder in the village. No place is safe. Before you came here, it was. Of course, it was the nephew that time. Did in his uncle, the old man, on the main road a few years ago. Nephew thought he had money hidden in the mattress, came one night before Christmas, bludgeoned him to death. Said he needed money to buy his kids Christmas gifts. Same thing going to happen now as that last time. Same thing, with the police and all. Submarine cars going to be everywhere."

"The what, everywhere?"

"Submarine cars. Cameras in them. Police park submarine cars in the village. Tops open up, like a submarine. Cameras come out, film everything. That's how they find them, the criminals. Police film everyone with submarine cars and find out who's guilty."

"Never heard of those," I say with great doubt.

"Seen 'em myself. Douspis saw, too. One parked just outside his house, day they buried the old man. Photographed everyone went to the funeral. Photographed the nephew. That's how they caught him. Saw he was guilty."

"How? How did they see he was guilty?"

Monsieur Vadepied shrugs. "The police, they know things like that. That's why they're police."

25

THE POLICE RELEASE DIDIER'S BODY; THEY CAN'T KEEP THESE THINGS forever and anyway, everyone has worked out what the manner of death was. Now, Wednesday, we all stand around on the village square in front of the church, waiting for the funeral to begin. Pretty well everyone from Épineux-le-Rainsouin is present: Pierre and his wife Anne-Marie, Pouttier, Aimable Lemasson, the Thibaults, the Tribhous, Monsieur Douspis (Madame Douspis participates from the green fake leather chair in her window), Mesdames Filoche, Houdusse, Beauducel, Monsieur Vadepied, Jean-Paul (pained and uncomfortable-looking), Chantal (elegant yet prim in dark purple, looking as if she has spent every hour of the last month tanning in the sun), the entire municipal council, those new folk from the housing development, everyone from the surrounding farms. There's a sizeable contingent from the next village, Fontenay-le-Léger, headed by Marie-Jeanne, who runs the café there, and her meek husband, Loïc. Even our lady painter, "Her Majesty," is here — an odd character, not entirely pleasant, who lives alone in a huge, gloomy farmhouse she refers to as her "manor." Her black dyed hair is covered by a crocheted beret complete with cluster of bobbing linen daisies. To my great regret, she bustles up to me. "This is awful, awful. Just terrible. Awful." She has a breathless gasp of a voice. "Terrible, terrible, terrible."

"What's terrible?" I ask, rather surprised at this waterfall of emotion. She has, like the rest of us, had quite a bit of time to get used to Didier's death. But it's almost as though she heard of it just yesterday.

"Didier dead like this. Just terrible, terrible. Oh I don't know what we'll do without him, he was so helpful to me, such a nice man, knew so much about flowers, helped my little gardener, although he wouldn't really help, he wasn't all that helpful, you know what I mean, but he helped. Whenever I had a problem, I could call him and he would come up and help. He knew my problem with the church bells and how sensitive I am but couldn't do a thing about it, of course not with a mayor like Lemasson who doesn't listen to me ever. Terrible problem, the clock bells. I wish they would stop them from ringing. All the time, ringing, every hour, half-hour."

"I like the bells," I say, forcing my words in. "I like them. They regulate my day in a medieval sort of way. And all the other villagers, they like them as well. It would be a shame to stop them."

But she doesn't care about the way we feel. "I'm just more sensitive to the sound of them. I'm a very sensitive person. An artist is always a more sensitive person. But that's something the rest of you can't understand. Not ever."

Christelle isn't present, of course. She wouldn't be caught dead standing around with everyone else here. And anyway, it's only morning; she's probably still in bed with a hangover. Martine is nowhere to be seen either; she wouldn't grace Didier's funeral with her presence. Didier's former chum, Tim, is also absent. And nowhere to be seen are Nicole and Bernard Malabry. Perhaps they didn't know Didier all that well; in any case, his views on chicken farming wouldn't have made him an all-time favourite with them.

The police are even hanging around for some reason, watching everyone from their vehicle, which is parked just between Madame Douspis's front window and my front door. Very carefully I scrutinize the car, especially the top. I'm looking, of course, for the submarine camera. There isn't one. Why would there be? The gendarmes can see perfectly well from their car windows what is going on, who is here. The submarine vehicle is, disappointingly enough, merely another village myth.

"In the old days, a funeral was quite an affair," says Madame Sauvebœuf with great regret. "The funeral dinner used to be held in your place, in the Hôtel de la Boule d'Or." She is wearing her usual excited little smile. "After the mass and burial, people would all go in there and have a big meal. Sometimes there were so many people that they had to take all the beds out of the rooms upstairs and set up tables just so that everyone could be fit in. It was usually pot-au-feu that was served. They'd make a huge caldron of it in the courtyard out in back. And everyone said it was delicious. People would come in beforehand and ask what was being served, and when they heard it was pot-au-feu, they'd come just for the meal even if they weren't much interested in the funeral. One year, the cat fell into the cauldron. Got cooked with the pot-au-feu and nobody noticed until they got to the bottom of the cauldron and saw all the fur sitting there. Of course, no one told the guests they had just eaten cat. And everyone said afterwards it was the best pot-au-feu they'd ever had. But I found out about it anyway. I was just a little girl at the time and working in the grocery next door, and I knew."

Funerals were certainly more picturesque than that, before the nineteenth century rolled to an end. Back then, it was up to the *pleureuses*, the professional mourners, to go from house to house and announce a death. These women would also wash and dress the body, then hold watch, murmuring prayers, telling old stories that tended towards the macabre on such occasions. All who came to pay their respects to the deceased would first sprinkle the body with the holy water kept in a bowl at the foot of the bed, then wash their hands in another bowl, a tactic meant to foil the evil eye. Just before the coffin left the church, one *pleureuse* would go to the road leading to the cemetery and burn the straw that had filled the dead person's mattress — another act that kept ever-lurking evil spirits at bay. When the coffin was finally lowered into the ground, the *pleureuses* began their job of howling, screaming and moaning, a vocal performance to be repeated at frequent intervals in the graveyard for the following three months. These excessive lamentations were eventually considered to be in bad taste, and the clergy made an effort to curb them. By the 1880s, *pleureuses* were unemployed.

Today, it is in an uncomfortable silence that we all troop into the church. The coffin follows, feet first as tradition dictates (one enters life head first, leaves it the other way round). The priest gives a little eulogy, but there is no mass for that costs considerable money now, and I seriously doubt that Didier was religious. Then we traipse up to the front of the church, take the sceptre, dip it into holy water, sprinkle it on the coffin (to keep the devil at bay), then trail out to the street again and up to the cemetery. As we pass the grave of Aymé Tisserand (who is, no doubt, doffing his hat), I notice no one is crying. No one, aside from Her Majesty, is showing much emotion at all. The mayor makes a glorious speech about what a wonderful *garde champêtre* Didier was, about how he was a devoted employee. Everyone nods in agreement. The mayor's secretary hands out flowers. We throw them down onto the coffin. The ceremony is over. It is a very normal funeral, all things considered. Rather an anticlimax.

"Sad, so sad, isn't it," says Her Majesty before she turns into her gate. "Poor Didier didn't have any family here. He had no one at all to love him. No brothers, no sisters. So sad."

26

WHEN I STEP OUT OF MY FRONT DOOR ON THURSDAY, I SEE THAT MADAME Douspis's window is wide open and she's in the leaf-green chair, chatting to the ever suntanned Chantal who is standing on the sidewalk. I saunter over, determined to join in on the conversation. Chantal is dressed in an elegant flower print, her dyed blonde hair sweeps her shoulders and a pretty little woven basket for groceries is perched beside her on the ground. It's the sweet, country-girl look she's aiming at, although it is just too cute, too perfect, too expensive-looking to be real.

"I always feed the birds," Madame Douspis is saying. "Can't get out with these legs of mine except to go to the restaurant on Sundays. Just have to spend the days in the house, what with all the pills I have to take every single hour of the day. Have to amuse myself somehow, and feeding the birds is the only pleasure I have. And now they're saying on the television that we shouldn't feed the wild birds because they could all have the flu and could kill us. What kind of world are we living in, I ask you?"

"Yes, it's tragic. Just tragic," says Chantal. She turns to me as I come up beside her. "Isn't it tragic?" She's wearing a sympathetic, faintly sad expression, although the emotion isn't quite mirrored in those big, blue eyes of hers. Those are always strangely flat, bland. As if she is slightly, but permanently, high on something.

"Just keep on feeding them," I say to Madame Douspis. "We need the wild birds. Years ago, when they ran a campaign in China to kill them all off, the country was overwhelmed by insects. From one disaster to another."

"Oh, yes. Things are just awful in other countries," says Chantal. She bends down to pick up her basket.

"I brought Werewolf to see your husband the other day," I say quickly. Before she can get away.

She smiles blandly. "Oh, yes?"

"And he told me that you'd just celebrated your wedding anniversary. That's nice. So many couples breaking up these days, it's nice to see people still together." I'm such a phoney, I could kick myself. I didn't even know I was capable of coming out with such nauseating, honey-sweet garbage. But Chantal doesn't think this is out of character, apparently. She doesn't know me well enough. Doesn't care to know me.

But it's her reaction I find interesting. She simply stares at me. Blandly, yes. But with a shadow of vague, stunned confusion, too. As if my statement about the anniversary is news to her. There is a five-second pause. "Oh, Jean-Paul," she says faintly. "He's quite the romantic."

"Is he? He doesn't give the impression of being one. But then again, he's only my veterinarian — or rather, my dog's veterinarian. I go to see a general practitioner for my own rabies shots." I force out a chuckle as if I'm really amused by my own wit. Madame Douspis howls a response, although Chantal simply continues to look confused. Cheap humour isn't really her forte, obviously. "Did you do something special to celebrate?" I ask Chantal. I know. It's none of my business. I have no right to question her like this. If that great lover of mine, dearest Jean-Paul, gets wind of it, he'll come around to my house with a hypodermic needle full of anthrax. But scrabble around in my mind all I like, it's the only thing I can come up with at short notice. I really want to know if Jean-Paul's alibi holds true.

But Chantal has recovered her poise. Perhaps she senses I'm up to something. Up to no good. She is a loyal wife, even if she isn't a true one, and if her husband tells her to jump through the hoop, she'll do it. He'd do it for her, too, probably. "We had a very nice dinner party. With that lovely new couple. The Malabrys."

"The Malabrys?" I force myself not to look astonished. "Oh, yes. I heard them talking in Pierre's restaurant one evening. They said they were having a hard time of it out here. That everyone was so unsociable. So I guess they were pleased as punch to be invited by you, huh?"

"Yes, Jean-Paul told me the same thing a few months ago. That they were ever so lonely. It's hard for city people to adapt to life out here. So we began by inviting them over to our house. Jean-Paul thinks

Nicole is just adorable. Her husband is a teensy bit more reticent, but I suppose it's just a question of getting to know him better. Some people are like that, aren't they?" She raises one hand in a little wave. "Well, have to be off. Jean-Paul will be home for lunch soon. Have to feed my hungry lion." And she heads off across the square, leaving my thirst for incriminating information about my lover unquenched.

27

Lovers come and lovers go. Why suffer? They have different shapes and sizes, different voices; each relationship has its quirks. With age and experience, it becomes more difficult to separate the memories, remember with whom life was best.

Before coming to Épineux-le-Rainsouin, before Jean-Paul, there was Thomas and our life together in a farmhouse called La Basse Chauvière. He was a long string of a man, Thomas, an optimist, a droll person, romantically enthusiastic about me, about his very absent brood of ungrateful children from his previous marriage, about the old traditions of country folk. His zeal also extended to La Basse Chauvière, a tired-out building surrounded by weedy, untended fields, isolated from the closest village, Launay, by a long rutted lane.

La Basse Chauvière was once a traditional farm, built in the old way: long, rectangular, low. It must have had certain charm. There was a vast fireplace where the ubiquitous *soupe perpétuelle* — a mixture of lard or goose fat, cabbage, potatoes, onions, leeks — had boiled away in an iron caldron hanging from a *crémaillère*, a long hooked chain, or sitting on a *trépied*, a three-legged stand. Bread, made of chestnut flour and placed in *ruchots*, little woven baskets of briars, had baked in the curved brick oven. It was coarse, healthy bread, delectable when fresh and ruthlessly hard when old, but farm families were poor in the old days and bread, even stale and concrete-hard, had to be consumed; it was cut with an axe and soaked in water before being placed on the table.

The deep nook in one corner had housed a huge, canopied bed to be shared by all family members. At a long wooden table, the farmer, his workers and children ate (women dined standing, ever ready to serve). There must have been a high wooden cabinet for dishes, a large wooden saltbox which doubled as a seat by the fire, a huge, long-cased pendulum clock called a *comtoise*. There was also, no doubt, a wooden trunk for the carefully embroidered linen, a wife's dowry, which arrived in the household in a curious fashion. Several days before the wedding, the engaged couple and their friends, dressed like monks and nuns and carrying a cross and small coffin containing silver, money, bottles, linen and dishes, marched in procession to the house where the future couple would live. In a nearby field, a hole was dug and the coffin buried; tradition dictated it could only be recovered after the birth of the couple's first child.

Because Thomas so loved those old ways, he whetted my curiosity with them. Soon I, too, wanted to see his farmhouse set in the faint moderate swell of hills, the green tangle of mixed hedges, the soggy earthen lanes. We had first met in Ottawa — he was in Canada, a visiting ethnologist — and the images of rural France he drew were a heady contrast to the urban streets I had known all my life. I agreed, quite without hesitation, to return to France with him. I no longer needed to work; I had inherited enough money to lead a modest life, and there was no doubt in my mind that we would have a lovely time together. He was a fine man, Thomas was. A gentle, lovable, considerate one. And a man with a passion for knowing, investigating; there's nothing quite so appealing as that.

But the farmhouse, La Basse Chauvière, so lovingly described, was a disappointment when I finally saw it. It had been greatly modified over the years. Modern tiles covered the floor of beaten earth; the old furniture had vanished. An adjoining room, once a stable where, on the coldest winter nights, a farmer's family and workers bedded down with the animals, had been converted into a small, ugly kitchen. The old walls of sand and chalk were covered by plasterboard, the vast attic was sliced into cubicle-like bedrooms for Thomas's long-gone children.

I disliked the place immediately. Thomas insisted it had once been a place of joy, long ago, in the early days of his marriage. There had been friends, so many friends, back then. Life had been dreamy, innocent, filled with plans. There had been parties every weekend; there had been great music, discussions of overwhelming importance. But times changed: the children had left home and rarely kept in touch; friends had gone on to other things; the ideal marriage had ended in divorce.

Thomas had left to work in Paris, then Ottawa; briars had taken over the garden, the front porch had sagged, the roof tiles slipped. He would make the place whole again, he said. Once again, it would become a place of joy. I was the new woman in his life, the great love. Together, we would recover the former beauty.

Yet I was not happy in La Basse Chauvière. Those weedy fields littered with abandoned cars he had once planned to restore, the dark damp kitchen, discouraged me. It was a house of broken dreams; it was a ghostly place. New friends were difficult to make. The over-hearty phone calls to his children brought no return of affection. And in the end, even Thomas was discouraged. The anticipated repairs were put off until the future.

And then one night, all came to an end. There was a head-on collision with a driver who had fallen asleep at the wheel. With Thomas dead, La Basse Chauvière became an inheritance, one that was fought over between the children and their various lawyers.

The house still stands empty in the fields, and the May sun glancing off stone walls lends it no joy, merely emphasizes desolation. The briars and nettles have grown even higher. Young saplings Thomas once planted, overwhelmed by sturdier intruders, have given up the ghost. And the long tendrils of sticky willy cover all with their gauze-like veil, provide a hiding place for *couleuvre*, the huge but passive golden-green grass snakes that love abandoned places.

Once a month, on sunny days, ones like this pleasant Friday morning, I drive the fifty kilometres to La Basse Chauvière, park my car near the ruined barn, take a little gravel pathway to the rotting porch that has sunk a little more. The house windows have been smashed in, the door hangs from one hinge; interlopers, finding nothing worth stealing, have wreaked revenge. I open the rusty mailbox hanging from one nail, search for the letters that still arrive from time to time: invitations to exhibitions which Thomas will not attend, cards from distant friends who have been out of contact for years. All these I claim, for the dead cannot have their mail forwarded. These letters are my inheritance.

One day, the lawsuits will end. The house and land will be bought. Diggers will clear the field; builders will come in, hoist new beams, set modern windows in the place of the old, and put in a modern kitchen, central heating. The tangle of the yard will become a broad stretch of grass; the barn will be a two-car garage. Ghosts of the past as well as dozing snakes will be definitively vanquished.

What if Thomas hadn't died? Would I still be living here with him? It's hard to say. It seems as if a lifetime has passed. I was another woman at that time. Thomas is a distant memory. Yet I have stayed on in this country, refusing to return to the place where I was born. I am still determined, as I was when with Thomas, to fit in, to remain part of this world. His interest in vanished traditions became mine after his death. He is no longer here to read the stone walls of buildings, to find out their evolution. He is not here to follow the grassy paths the postmen took on their country rounds, not here to ask about music and dances, festivals and old ghost stories. But I am. I have taken on his job. It is a way of continuing our relationship. A way of defying Thomas's absurd death.

This previous life of mine with Thomas in this farmhouse, La Basse Chauvière, almost no one in Épineux-le-Rainsouin knows about; here, fifty kilometres represents a definite distance. Only Jean-Paul knows. He knows because lovers of the present always want details about those in the past. And Martine knows, of course. Because with close friends, one talks about the old days, the old stories, the old loves.

28

THE VILLAGE IS ALMOST MOTIONLESS THIS SUNDAY MORNING, A PLACE of suspended animation. Masses are said in the church only once a month, for attendance has dropped and one priest serves several villages. But not so long ago, the old café in my house knew its best business on Sundays; while village women prayed in churches where aristocrats and members of important families had the best pews in the front rows, the men would sit at long wooden café tables, smoke, drink wine and cider, chat. In one corner, behind a small partition, Monsieur Cheminais, Sunday barber, would cut hair and shave the men. After mass, everyone gathered in the square. Beside each church are little steps leading to a low platform; from here, the *garde champêtre* would read out local announcements.

These Sundays, people only cross the square to buy their bread at the bakery, then go home and stay there in front of their televisions. Monsieur Vadepied is, as usual, very present, although he, too, is scurrying homeward, no wrench, no hammer, no screwdriver in hand. He grins sheepishly. "*The Love Game* is on television in five minutes."

"What's *The Love Game*?"

"Program for young people, but we like to watch it. Three women, and they sit behind a screen. A man asks them questions. Then he chooses one to be his girlfriend. Winner gets a trip for two all expenses paid. Lots of expensive gifts. It's nice. Never miss it."

Werewolf and I leave the village on foot, cut left onto a sunken green lane between high hedges and rows of oak and chestnut. Here, the sun barely penetrates the dense foliage, and in the rainy season, the soft ground is transformed into sticky, boot-sucking mud. These lanes, once criss-crossing the country and connecting farms and villages, were formerly used by all manner of walkers: traders, tinsmiths, vagabonds, pilgrims, students, brigands and peddlers of everything from almanacs and rosaries to needles, thread and matches. Roof thatchers had passed here, woodcutters too, and that long-vanished figure, the *chemineau.* He was neither poacher nor filcher, neither beggar nor travelling handyman, yet he was all of these. An odd jobber, he would lend a hand to the ironmonger, help the farmer bring in the harvest, the lumberman cut wood and saw trees lengthwise. He passed from village to village, farm to farm, slept in barns or ditches and gathered his meals where he could — at a farmer's door or, when necessary, in his yard — stealthily sneaking away with a flapping chicken under his vest. He was a man of poor fortune, one of muddy clothes and long beard. Arriving in the dark of night, he would press his face against kitchen windows, inspire fear, inspire pity, rouse old superstitions. Country dwellers sighed with relief when he, once more, took to the road.

Although it has probably been over a half a century since a cart passed this way, their ruts are still visible in the lane. Horses, sunk to their withers in the winter morass, would be pried out by long poles pushed under their bellies. But now such routes are largely abandoned, though walkers' associations clear them. Werewolf and I stroll as far as the village of Saint-Hilaire-la-Nozay, meeting no *chemineau,* no brigand, no repairman of pots and pans, no seller of salt, no remittance man. Meeting no other walker at all, hearing no sounds other than those made by birds and distant tractors.

Martine lives in a little witch's hut of a place, one surrounded by roses, apple and chestnut trees, at the far end of Saint-Hilaire-la-Nozay. Once, her garden looked out onto a stretch of pasture, hedges and a copse of deciduous wood, but that was before a PVC warehouse surrounded by an asphalted parking lot ate up the view. Since then, she spends all her free time gardening, growing trees, a mixed hedge and clambering vines in an attempt to block out ugliness. When I arrive, she is planting flowers, shaking young plants out of their green plastic pots, pushing them into little holes in the earth. She never has been a woman who can sit still.

"So tell me why you said on the phone that Didier was perverse," I say.

"Who cares about Didier?" Martine gores out another hole with her little spade. "Who cares about that little shit?" Not that Martine could be expected to say anything nice about Didier. Didier was a male; Martine considers almost all males solely responsible for everything wrong on earth, from bad cooking to plagues.

"How?" I ask patiently. "How was he a little shit?"

"You liked the guy?" She looks at me briefly. Raises her eyebrows in fake surprise.

"I didn't know him all that well. It's just that everyone is talking about his death."

"So why's that so interesting to you if you didn't know him so well? Why call me on the phone to ask about autopsies? Why do you want me to analyze his character for you now?"

Inwardly, I sigh. This isn't going as easily as I thought it might. Martine isn't fond of telling tales about people and I probably never was meant to be an amateur detective. "Curiosity. That's all. Didier is the number one topic of conversation these days. And even if I didn't know him so well, a few days before he died, he threw stones at my window. At night. He wanted to come in for a drink, he said. Which I didn't let him do. But still, I wonder why he came to my house. I mean, I'm not exactly in his age or style group."

"And what age and style group would that be, exactly?" Martine sneers as she gouges out earth with great energy and a very decisive, hefty right hand. "A screw is a screw to someone like Didier. Old, young, or dead."

If I go on being discreet, I'm not going to get anywhere. "Was he screwing Fiona?"

Martine stops gouging for a minute. Spade poised in the air, she stares at me. "You think Fiona would be interested in that particular public dick? You think that's the best she could do if she needed a lover?"

"What do I know about Fiona? I talked to her in the bar a few times. I went to her house once. With you. Remember? Maybe she thought Didier was charming."

"And the reason you're asking all this? You haven't satisfied my curiosity." The spade is still poised in the air.

Damn! I should have planned this better, should have come with the right answers and excuses tucked neatly in my pocket. "Because everyone in Épineux-le-Rainsouin claims Didier had a passion for screwing married women. For messing up marriages. And I'm curious about that kind of person. I just want to know how they tick."

Martine puts down the spade, picks up a green pot, shakes out a timid yellow flower. "Married women? Interesting. Very interesting." She doesn't say anything for a minute or two — as if she's debating whether to release information or not. She pushes the flower into the ground, covers its roots. Then relents — probably because the desire to say something awful about Didier is just too overwhelming. "Okay, okay. Since you want to know so much, I'll tell you all about Didier and why I disliked him so much. And about what he did to Fiona and Tim. Because when it came to manipulation, Didier could have won medals. Oh yes, he made himself indispensable to Tim in the beginning. Helped him restore the house, translated for him, got him good materials. And as for Tim, he was just so damn proud that Didier was his best friend. Proud that he had a French friend who accepted him. More than that, even. He was half in love with the guy. But Didier, even in the beginning I didn't trust him. I saw what was going on. He wasn't capable of being subtle, and he just imposed his presence on Tim and Fiona. He was always there, always there at mealtime, every evening, all day every weekend. Of course, Tim and Fiona drank too much. They were always drinking. Even in the morning, Fiona and Tim drank beer, not coffee but beer. I never did see Fiona with a cup of coffee in her hand. 'Every day's a holiday,' she always said. 'On holiday, we do what we want. We have a blast.' And with Didier around all the time, Tim and Fiona didn't have much of a private life either. He never let them be. He just didn't. He had to be the main person, the centre."

"But Fiona liked him though?" I ask. "She didn't mind?"

Martine's grin is malevolent. She leans back on her heels. "Fiona didn't like him, not all that much. She merely tolerated him. She had to. Tim, her own husband, was so fascinated by the guy. I mean, Didier had become his whole life. He talked about Didier non-stop, repeated everything he said, looked at everything he did with admiration. Copied his every gesture like Didier was God on earth. And then one night, she, Didier and Tim went out drinking. Just like they always did, except

Fiona could hold her alcohol and Tim couldn't. When they came back to the house, Tim had had so much booze, he could hardly get through the door, and after falling on the floor about a dozen times, he finally managed to collapse on the sofa and pass out."

"Who told you all this?"

"Fiona, of course. Fiona came here, to my house soon after. In the middle of the night. Drove over here."

"With a bellyful of booze?"

"She had no choice. Just as soon as Tim was passed out on the couch, Didier jumped on Fiona, grabbed her. I mean, how's that for shitty behaviour? Her husband is there, passed out on the sofa, and this parasite she doesn't even like thinks she is going to have a nice little screw with him."

"And?"

"And she fought him off, ran to the bathroom and locked herself in. Screamed at him to go home, stayed in the bathroom, waiting for him to leave. About half an hour later, she didn't hear anything so she opened the door. And what does she see? She sees Didier is still there. Sitting in a chair near the bathroom and masturbating. So Fiona grabs her keys, races out the door, jumps into her car and comes here. Takes refuge in my house for the night."

"You believe this?" I ask, fascinated. The story is certainly interesting. But a little hard to believe.

"Why shouldn't I? You just finished telling me he liked screwing other men's wives."

"Well, Didier was a seducer, for one. And that sort of behaviour wouldn't seduce anyone. He'd know that. He relied on charm, not force."

"Well, you've got that wrong," says Martine, pinching down the corners of her mouth as she talks. "Of course, I believe it. Fiona came here, right? She couldn't go home, could she? She had to have help. Why leave your house in the middle of the night if you don't have to? And believe me, she was disgusted. And angry. I can certainly verify that. And furious at Tim, of course."

"Because he was passed out on the sofa?"

Martine shrugs. "Because he was the one who always defended

Didier. He was the one who couldn't live without him. And as far as Didier goes, believe me, men are all the same. They only think of their little thing. Think of stuffing it in somewhere."

"And then what happened?"

"The next morning, Fiona went home. Didier was gone by now, and she woke Tim up and told him what happened. He didn't want to believe her. She told him repeatedly. She was hysterical, Tim told me that after. She screamed and screamed, said he was a weakling, that he was pathetic. That Didier had seen what a wet he was and thought he could do what he wanted."

"You've talked to Tim about this?"

Martine nods. "He admits he couldn't imagine his friend Didier doing something like that. Why should he? Didier was his friend. His very best friend. Why try something like that on Fiona?"

"Why would he?"

"Well, here's the funny bit. From that time on, Didier didn't come back to their house. And that's what made Tim start thinking that perhaps Fiona had been telling the truth. It was proof, in a way. If Didier had been innocent, wouldn't he have shown up the way he usually did? Fiona went back to London about a week later. She said she needed a break. She and Tim had been fighting for months anyway; there was something fundamentally wrong with the relationship. Perhaps it had nothing to do with Didier. The marriage was probably over a long time before. People evolve, change, and Tim and Fiona had been evolving in different directions. After all, they'd been together for years. Perhaps the fact that Tim was dead drunk and didn't defend her, perhaps that was the last straw. While she was in London, Fiona decided she wanted a divorce. That she'd had it. She couldn't even be bothered going back to the cottage and getting her clothes."

"How is Tim taking it?"

"He's in a terrible state. He's ashamed of himself. Especially now. Because after that, Didier snubbed him whenever he saw him. Tim felt like the weakling Fiona said he was. And now Fiona won't even talk to him anymore. Everything has to go through her lawyer."

"So he was poisonous, Didier."

"Obsessed. Sexually obsessed. Like all men, when they get the chance," says Martine calmly, certain. "And Tim spends his days alone out there, drinking. That's no healthy way to solve a problem. He's digging his own grave, if you ask me. And you know what? I bet he's not in the least sorry to hear that Didier is dead. I bet he even feels like celebrating."

29

Tim is outside in front of his cottage on Monday morning, hedge trimmer in hand, sawing away at scraggy tufts of shrubbery. Even from fifty metres away, he looks just terrible. His face is red, unhealthy; he is thin and shrivelled, like someone who has gone through a washing machine boil cycle once too often. Gone is the self-confident man sure of his ideas, certain of his ability to learn French, to integrate into village life. Life without Fiona has obviously deflated him.

"Hi," I call out when I am still on the road, some fifty metres away.

He half turns, stares at me for a minute or two, as if he hasn't the faintest idea who I am. "Hi," he says finally, raises one hand, flaps a greeting. He doesn't look as though he's thrilled to have company, and he'd be mighty resentful if he knew I've come as a spy.

"Thought I'd look in and see how you're doing," I say cheerfully. "Haven't seen you around in ages."

He drops the hedge trimmer with a certain resignation, motions me over to a white plastic table and matching chairs. Although it's only eleven in the morning, I can see — and smell — he's already been at the booze. He fishes a pack of cigarettes out of his shirt pocket, shakes one out, lights it; I can't help noticing how his hands shake. "If you want to know how I'm doing, I'll tell you. I'm in a bad state." His voice is full of self-pity. "What do you expect? My wife has gone mad." He twists his lips into a bitter grimace. "I'd better amend that. My ex-wife has gone mad. Ex. I'm going to have to get used to saying that. Ex-wife. Ex-wife. Ex-wife."

I pull out the handiest platitude I can think of: "Divorce is always hard."

"Yeah, yeah," he says bitterly and takes a deep drag of the cigarette, blows out the smoke in a long stream. "Divorce is hard but soon everything will be just fine and dandy. I'll find someone new and fall in love all over again. Yeah, right. Just a matter of time. That's what everyone says when your world — not theirs — falls apart, right?"

"What do you think about Didier's death?" I ask, changing the subject, perhaps a little too abruptly. Just to make sure that the question appears to be casual and innocuous, I bend down, pull up a blade of grass and begin chewing on it, cow-like.

"Didier?" His look is one of disgust. "Who the hell cares about Didier?"

"He was a friend of yours, wasn't he? And it is strange, him dying in his bath like that. With a hair dryer." I chew on the hapless blade of grass some more.

"Good riddance to bad rubbish," he says. "I don't give a shit. You want something to drink?"

"Drink? What kind of drink?"

"Wine."

"No, thanks. Wine at eleven in the morning would kill me," I say. Then I change my mind. If I intend to come on all chummy with the guy, there's nothing like sharing poison as an icebreaker. "Okay. Why not? Just a small glass, though."

He stands up, disappears into the house, reappears with an open bottle of red and two inelegant mustard glasses. Evidently the pretty things I saw when I came here for dinner with Martine, the long stemmed glasses of yesteryear and Fiona, are no longer in use. These days, it's mustard glasses, a cracked flowerpot for an ashtray. But the hedges will stay trimmed. I wonder what the interior of the cottage looks like? A jumble of old clothes, a mess, more cracked flowerpots full of cigarette stubs? But I am not invited in. We sit out here in the golden sun, in the front yard.

The wine gurgles into the mustard glasses. He hands me one.

"Cheers," I say, chucking away the soggy blade of grass and taking a sip. It is truly dreadful stuff. Rotgut. No oily run to it as it goes down the throat, no dusty aftertaste. Just low-value plonk, harsh on the tongue, vicious to the gut.

He nods, distractedly. "Thirty years we were together, me and Fiona. Thirty years. We met in college. Fell in love right away, got married two months later. As far as I was concerned, I thought we'd stay together our whole lives. Then suddenly, we come out here and she goes mad. I'm responsible for everything. She gets the house we owned in London; she wants half of this one. She claims I told my best friend to rape her, just to have a bigger case in front of the judge. Lies, all of it lies. How could she do something like this? I did everything to keep us together, begged her, but it was no use. There was no getting through to her. Thirty years, and she just gets up and walks out the door. I love her. I want to go on living with her."

It is useless to explain to him that these days, it's usually the women who make the decision to end a marriage. These days, there's no going back. A woman suddenly has a vision of what love should be, and what it isn't; after that, there's no way a discarded husband can talk his way back into a comfortable nest complete with hot meals and clean rolled socks. Women call the shots. The old style loyalty of the past is dead; today, loyalty is to one's self.

"You can't let yourself suffer like this," I say, already hating myself for the sympathetic commonplaces I will roll out. "It will pass, the misery. It always passes eventually. Life begins anew, as they say. In the meantime, you should get out. Stop drinking. Take control of your life." Here I am: Miss Sunburst. Giving a pep talk. Not that he's interested in either me or my lecturing, Tim. He couldn't care less. But just to keep this conversation of sorts going, I go on a bit about male support groups, about meeting other men in the same position he's in and talking things out. About being free now, about not thinking about Fiona and the life that is over.

But he's not really listening anyway. I'm talking to the dancing sunlight, to the half-trimmed hedge, to the scraggly green grass. He is not looking at me; he's hearing no words. People in his state, they want to think they had *le grand amour*, the only true love on earth. The rest of us, we've only experienced mere phooey. So after a few minutes of pep talk, I decide to let it drop. Come back to the real reason I'm here.

"Did you hear that everyone is saying Didier was murdered? That it probably wasn't an accident?"

"No." He concentrates on pouring out another mustard glass of wine.

"Well, they are," I add lamely. "Look, you must feel some way about the whole thing. You and Didier always came to Pierre's to drink. He was always at your house. But you didn't even show up for his funeral."

"So?"

"So nothing. I'm just curious. You see, I have the feeling that Didier wasn't what he made himself out to be. He wasn't really a nice, jolly, concerned guy. He was sort of a phoney, wasn't he? That's what you found out."

But Tim is fishing out the pack of cigarettes again, lighting up another one. He seems to have decided that my question doesn't deserve an answer. "Thirty years," he says, a man obsessed. "And the other women out there, I'm not interested in them. They can go to hell. I want Fiona."

So we sit in the sun and sip rotgut. Then I stand up, say I'm leaving because, in the end, I'm bored. It's boring to sit and preach. It's even more boring when no one's listening. It's boring listening to someone whine. It's boring to watch someone self-destruct.

Tim, I think as I stroll back into the village, yes, he's definitely a man who won't miss Didier. Of course, that's assuming the story Fiona told Martine was true. How likely would that be? And why would Fiona lie? Because she, too, had succumbed to Didier's charms? Had Didier also tried to blackmail her?

Fiona will not be coming here again. No way of asking her questions ... but how convenient Didier's death is.

30

"Can't sleep at night anymore," says Madame Houdusse on Tuesday morning. "Not with a murderer on the loose." She and Madame Sauvebœuf are in front of Madame Sauvebœuf's house, two squat, square figures with bandy legs and dyed blonde heads. Just beyond the doorway, I can see the modernized interior: a white tile floor, a mass-produced table and chairs that look like they've never been used, a matching sideboard, striped wallpaper on plasterboard walls. It's a scene out of a furniture store: lifeless, soulless, characterless, dustless, perfect.

"Police don't do their job properly," says Madame Sauvebœuf. "Not a police car in sight since the funeral. And I can tell you, my husband has been watching, day in, day out, taking note of all the cars passing through the village, and he hasn't seen one belonging to the police anywhere. Not a one. Leaving us unprotected, they are. And who's most at risk? We are, of course: the elderly folk."

"No submarine cars seen around?" I ask.

"None," answer Madame Sauvebœuf and Madame Houdusse in well-coordinated chorus.

"You've actually seen submarine cars before? I mean, they really do exist? With a lid that opens on the roof? With a camera that circles around?"

"You can't see them just like that," says Madame Houdusse indignantly. "What would be the point of them if you did? You can't see it with the naked eye, the camera, but it's there all right."

"I see. But tell me, why is everyone in the village saying Didier was murdered? I mean, it could have been suicide."

"Why would Didier kill himself? He had everything to live for. He was good-looking, had a good job. Women friends. You don't go killing yourself just like that if you have all of those things."

"Of course, it was a murder," says Madame Houdusse. "Of course, it was. Why else would the police have gone into Didier's house when the body was discovered and put black powder everywhere to take fingerprints, just like on *Crime Stoppers?*"

"And you were watching them all the time they were doing this?"

"Of course we were. We were watching through the window with Monsieur Vadepied and Monsieur Douspis, and we all saw it all," trumpets Madame Sauvebœuf with great triumph. "And you tell me, if it wasn't a murder, then why was there an officer posted at the door to make sure we didn't go in? And why did they take all of the papers in his desk, phone bills and everything? And why did they collect the glasses in his sink and put them in little plastic bags with little white tickets on them? And why put his clothes in a plastic bag? If it wasn't murder."

"Because that's the way the police decide if a crime has been committed or not. To see if there is anything suspicious. But it doesn't mean that it was, you know," I insist, with great firmness. "And are you really sure they were putting things in plastic sacks with tickets on them? That they put powder everywhere? You actually saw them do that?"

"Can't see everything, of course, when you look through a window. Not with curtains on it and all. But we all knew what they were doing."

"How? How did you know? You might have all decided that's what they were doing, right? But not really have seen them."

"If that's what you want to think, go ahead. Problem is, you don't have a television set. You should buy yourself one, start watching a few programs. That way, you'd know what goes on. No point in asking all those questions about the old days. Times have changed. You have to keep up with the times." Madame Houdusse sniffs indignantly. "But you know what I think? I think the police should come to us all the same. They should ask us what we think. What we know."

"What do you know?"

"That it was one of his women who did it."

I stare at Madame Sauvebœuf, at Madame Houdusse, amazed. "A woman? Why a woman?"

"We're only saying it must have been a woman. But it could have been a man, too, if you like. But a man, if he wants to get another man into a bathtub, he has to fight him, get him undressed, and if there had been a fight in the house, that would have been easy enough to hear by all the neighbourhood. And the police would have seen all the smashed-up furniture, too. So it couldn't have been a man unless, of course, Didier was drugged first, which these days isn't at all far-fetched, all the drugs circulating around — ecstasy, cocaine, marijuana, all the rest of it. And it being sold right under our noses all the time; no place for decent people in the world anymore. And if he wasn't drugged, I can't imagine Didier taking a bath with a murderer in the house. That would be a silly thing to do. But with a woman there, that's different."

"Except he didn't know he was going to be murdered, of course. Or he wouldn't have been alone with whichever man or woman it was," says Madame Sauvebœuf with a sort of triumph.

"Perhaps he was already taking a bath when the murderer came in," I suggest.

"And the murderer just happened to have a hair dryer with him?" counters Madame Houdusse. "And he knew Didier would be bathing at exactly that time?"

"He could have used a hair dryer that was already there."

"But Didier never needed a hair dryer," says Madame Houdusse. "Everyone knows that. I wonder if the police have thought of that though. I wonder."

"Maybe it belonged to one of his girlfriends," I say. "Maybe one of them left it there."

Madame Douspis nods. "Maybe. Which makes his murderer a woman. Because a man would have to know that the hair dryer was going to be there. And if a man did it, it would be a man who had already been in Didier's house at one time or another. And he wouldn't have noticed a thing like a hair dryer because men notice nothing at all. But of course, it could have been a man, too, because, knowing Didier, there were a few jealous husbands in the village. Wouldn't have surprised me if Didier had been murdered by one of them. But not in a bath with a hair dryer. He would have shot him or strangled him, or stabbed him with a knife, or hacked him up with an axe, or sliced his throat open, or bludgeoned him to death. That's how men do these things."

A little light goes on in one corner of my brain. Slowly, I say to myself. Go slowly here, or the two of them will seal up tighter than Brittany oysters. "Bloodthirsty creatures, men. And I suppose this is the information you would give to the police if they came around and asked you questions, right?"

"That's for us to know," says Madame Houdusse sharply. "If only the police did their job properly, asked the right questions, there wouldn't be so many murders."

"Well, not all that many," I say. "Not all that many here in the village."

"But in other villages, there are. In the cities. All those women and children getting killed."

"Domestic murders. You can't expect the police to know when a husband or boyfriend is going to decide to run amok and kill everyone."

"They have enough information, the police. They know who's dangerous and who isn't. They know," says Madame Sauvebœuf darkly. "In the old days, people believed you could protect yourself. Against the evil eye, you could put salt in your pocket. Or you could put salt on the poles around your field or garden. Or you could put rusty nails around a well. Or you could plant ash trees at the four cardinal points around your house."

"Old superstitions," mutters Madame Houdusse.

"Sometimes, things like that work," says Madame Sauvebœuf. "We used to keep a log that was half burnt on the night before Christmas in our chimney. It would protect you from lightning all year round. And it made the dead die more slowly."

"But you have seen things, right?" I ask, impatient to get back to the bit about the jealous husbands.

"We've seen people going to and coming from Didier's house," says Madame Sauvebœuf. "Visitors."

"From the village?"

Madame Houdusse nods, although she lives over the bridge and near the café. It would be impossible for her to see Didier's house from her place.

"Oh, yes. Certainly from the village," says Madame Sauvebœuf. "Certainly. Seen things that we shouldn't have. Seen women going places that they shouldn't. Women going to visit Didier. In the bright light of day. Now I always said to myself, what would they be needing Didier for? He's not a repairman. He doesn't go from house to house doing things. It's not like Monsieur Pouttier, the electrician. I can see his house perfectly, and I know who comes to ask him to do work. But that doesn't mean anything because people need his services. But why do women have to go to Didier's house? That's what makes me suspicious. That's what seems strange to me."

"Which women?"

"The hairdresser, Madame Beaupied." she says. "But not because she was doing something she shouldn't. She once told me that Didier didn't like going to a salon to have his hair cut. That he thought it was a womanly thing to do. So she cut his hair in his house. If you ask me, that's strange, but then again, who asks me? And then there was Madame Berthereau, the cabinetmaker's wife. Before she left him. And then there was that English woman who was always in the bar — can't remember her name — lived out in that cottage outside the village."

"Fiona? Her name is Fiona. You saw Fiona going to Didier's house? Alone?" I ask with a certain thrill of discovery. "Without her husband?"

Madame Houdusse puffs indignantly; Madame Sauvebœuf sniffs. But their lips stay smugly sealed.

"Of course, that was some time ago," I prod. "I mean, Fiona left for England months ago."

"Well then, she must have come back again, mustn't she?" says Madame Houdusse. I can tell she'd like to keep this information secret but just can't manage.

"She came back? When was this?"

"Same week Didier died. Thought no one could see her, she did. Night and all. But we saw her all right, didn't we?"

"The same week Didier died?" I ask, astonished by the revelation. "The same week, or the same day?"

The two women stare at each other for a minute. As if they are uncertain. "Could have been the same day," says Madame Houdusse. "Could have been the day before, too. Or Saturday, even. But we saw her all right."

"Yes, we did," Madame Sauvebœuf confirms. "Both of us. And other women went to see him, too. Madame Besnard, the farmer's wife. You know who she is, don't you? Dyed blonde. Short. Fat. Always driving around in a Peugeot. Doesn't say hello to anyone. Thinks she's better than all of us but she's no better than she ought to be, I'll tell you."

There is a minute's silence.

"That's all?" I prompt.

"We don't spend our lives sticking our noses into other people's business," says Madame Houdusse huffily.

"But we know things," adds Madame Sauvebœuf. "Things like that been going on for years. In the old days, Madame Beauducel used to mess around with that night watchman. Back in the old days. When she was a young woman. She had the nicest husband. But she couldn't stay faithful to him. Her lover would go to that little house beside the *lavoir*, it was empty in those days, light a candle when he was there, and she'd see the signal and cross over behind the church and go see him. And what a lovely husband she had, too. But she couldn't stop herself. She was like that."

"There was the alcohol, too," says Madame Houdusse darkly. "She always liked alcohol a bit too much. Bad, when women start on alcohol. Madame Malabry, too. Thinks she's better than us all in her Mercedes, city girl that she is, from Bourges, never a hello or a nod. Thinks she's better than everyone, she does, rich farmer's wife that she is."

"Madame Malabry drinks?"

"Wouldn't know if she did. Up there on the hill, no one knows what's going on."

"What does she have to do with this?" I'm really losing the thread, if thread there be.

"Over at Didier's house all the time. More than all the others, if you ask me. Saw her three, four times with my own eyes."

"Oh," I say. It's a perfectly witless response to an astounding revelation. For heaven's sake, why would Didier sleep with Nicole Malabry, the enemy, the very person who treated chickens like mindless, soulless commodities? And what would her husband, Bernard Malabry, do about it? Murder someone perhaps?

The two women launch into a new conversation, one about a

woman in Derval who drank herself to death in 1956. Having nothing to contribute and finding ourselves ignored, Werewolf and I cross back over the square and go into the house. "Funny they didn't mention Chantal," I say to Werewolf as I detach his leash. "Must have been more discreet than the others."

Werewolf heads for his water and food bowls in the kitchen. He couldn't care less about who sleeps with whom. "Still, even you have to admit it," I say to his disappearing, stubby tail. "Didier was a busy man."

31

MARTINE UNCORKS THE BOTTLE OF ROSÉ, POURS OUT TWO GLASSES OF wine. It is late Tuesday afternoon, and we are in her little glassed-in terrace, a construction dating from the fifties. It doesn't suit the house at all. It's not even a pleasant place: it's tiny, the furniture in it is made out of white plastic, there's no air. I don't know why she wants us to sit here. There are better places out in the garden.

She lifts her glass. "*Santé.*"

I raise my glass, too. "*Santé.*" I sip. Put the glass back down. "You forgot to mention something the other day."

She looks at me. Her face is closed. "I did?"

"Yeah. You forgot to mention that Fiona was here, in France, around the time Didier died."

"So?"

"So, you knew."

"Of course, I knew. She stayed here. With me."

"Right. You don't think that's odd? You don't think there's any link?"

"Any link to what?"

"What was she doing here?"

"You like the wine?"

"I like the wine. Why was Fiona here?"

"You think she killed Didier?" Martine isn't being friendly. On the contrary, I have the feeling she's going to tell me to go home. Fast.

"I'd say it's a possibility."

"Because the little creep masturbated in front of her? Come on, Fiona's a big girl, not a delicate violet. She's seen it all before. You don't chuck a hair dryer into a bath and kill someone because of that. And you know what?" Martine leans forward in her chair. Her face is only inches from mine. "You know why I didn't tell you she was here? Because you're too nosy, that's why. You ask too many questions. And you are just the type of person who jumps to conclusions."

I decide to ignore her accusations. "So why was Fiona here?"

"To consult a French lawyer, that's why. To see about getting a French divorce. To see if there was any advantage in it. All right? She wants the house. She wants Tim out. She wants to get the best deal. Satisfied?"

I pick up my glass. Take another sip. It isn't all that nice, really, the wine. A little too sweet and bland for my taste. "I guess I have to be." Martine's right. You don't kill people because they are a little insistent about wanting to get laid. If that's the only thing I have to go on, it's pretty weak.

"She's a friend of mine, Fiona is. A good friend. Tim's a friend, too. I'm not one of these people who lets divorce come between friends."

"Fine," I say. "And just out of curiosity, if friends of yours kill someone, would you protect them?"

Martine leans back in the ugly white plastic chair. Grins. "Probably."

32

I wait until the village has gone to sleep. Over at Pierre's, the café lights are out, the shutters rolled down. I sit at my window in the darkened room, making certain there's no one about in the streets. At eleven o'clock, the one street lamp illuminating the square goes out, as ever. Cars pass occasionally, on through the night, on to somewhere else. "I'll be right back," I say to Werewolf as I pull a black sweater over my head and head for the door. He is disappointed, of course. He sinks to the floor with that abandoned, unloved dog expression he has managed to perfect. The only thing better than a juicy bone is a walk, as far as Werewolf is concerned. Still, this is a one-person operation; I don't want to be recognized, be seen snooping around by anyone. Do something perfectly innocent in Épineux-le-Rainsouin — forget to water your geraniums, for example — and the whole village will accuse you of being an anarchist. I decide not to take my keys either; I'm only staying in the neighbourhood, after all. Going for a stroll. More or less.

The door barely makes a sound when I pull it closed behind me. I cross the square quickly, feeling as though I'm sticking out like a sore thumb with feet, despite the lack of light, despite my dark clothes. My eyes skim the dark, severe-looking houses surrounding the square; could someone be watching me from one of those many aligned windows? Someone standing behind a crocheted curtain, someone peeking through the crack of a shutter, someone in a dark room? It's impossible to tell.

I head towards Didier's house, towards the little alleyway that leads to the back door, the former servant's entrance. Didier and I took that entrance the night I went to his house. That night, we approached it from the square, as I'm doing now; but the alleyway, I've never actually seen where it leads. I've never been to the end of it, although some of

Didier's women must have approached his house that way. If not, there's no explanation for why Chantal was never seen by any of the village "ladies" — or by anyone else. Chantal certainly knew Didier intimately; she was someone he wouldn't have minded having in his house while bathing. So I just want to make sure it's not a dead end; I want to see where it goes.

It's very narrow, this alley. The walls are so close, I can reach out, touch both sides with my hands. It must have been part of a now-vanished medieval network of lanes, renovated out of existence sometime in the nineteenth century. It's dark in here, too, a sooty black. It must once have made a most excellent hidey-hole for those bent on nightly pillage and robbery; to discourage evil, inhabitants were eventually ordered to hang candles in their windows, to go about carrying lanterns, swords and daggers. I have nothing sharp and nasty at my disposal, of course, and the last thing I need in my hand is a lantern to let everyone in the village know I'm out here and intent on snuffling around.

For the very first time, I notice that the back of Didier's house is attached to another building, one with rough-stoned walls and shuttered windows, a tiny house, one that no one lives in to my knowledge. I feel my way along, one foot in front of the other. There is no pavement here, just old cobbles — the way all roads were before tarmac became *de rigueur* in 1965. In front of me is the looming darkness of another wall, and it almost seems as if the alleyway doesn't have another entry after all. But just before the wall is an arched opening on the left, not a large one, but wide enough for a person to pass through easily enough. The alley continues, takes a right turn, continues for five metres, turns right again. And comes to an end at the forked village lane: one direction leads to the graveyard and the Malabry farm; the other passes the hairdresser's, then heads south, past Jean-Paul and Chantal's dwelling (a vast, swanky-looking former convent), goes by outlying farms, heads on to the next village, Fontenay-le-Léger.

"Right. So where has this got you?" I ask myself. "Nowhere concrete," I answer. I head back into the alley again, back towards the arch. And suddenly, have the strange, prickly feeling I'm not alone. Not that I hear footsteps. Or smell anything unusual. It's sixth sense that's cut in. And sixth sense is telling me to get the hell out of this situation fast. Still, I stop. Listen hard. Is that a small stone scrabbling across a cobblestone near the narrow opening? Or is it my madly beating heart? I can feel a clammy sweat breaking out on my forehead and I attempt to reason with my fear — or is it imagination that has snared my senses? Who knows I'm out here? Come on. Surely no one has been standing out in the night just waiting for me to appear. Or watching my house for some reason. Surely not. Why would they? But logic is a flabby bulwark against raw panic.

Stupid idea, leaving Werewolf at home. Stupid idea, coming out here in the night. Very stupid idea, indeed, if Didier really was killed. Stupid, stupid, stupid. But all I have to do is reach the square, reach it before whoever — or whatever — behind me gets too close. If there really *is* someone or something there ... At least once I'm on the square, I can scream bloody murder and all the PVC shutters will rattle up instantly, all the PVC windows will swing wide open, all the nosy but suddenly loveable faces of every village gossip will be poking out. No, I'm not going to run. I'm not even going to show that I'm terrified. That would be provocation. I stroll steadily through the alley (as steadily as I can over the uneven ground), reach the square, head across it, pass the church. Reach my unlocked door — what foresight that was — slam it closed behind me, turn the lock.

Werewolf is wagging his tail, happy to see me again, unaware that I might have just narrowly escaped transformation into dog meat. I go to the window, look out at the square. Nobody. Nothing. Just the dark, the silence, then the sound of a car coming into the village on the Saint-Hilaire-la-Nozay road, heading out again, going on to somewhere else.

33

"THIERRY'S GOING TO LEAVE HIS GIRLFRIEND," CHRISTELLE ANNOUNCES on Wednesday afternoon. She's busy rolling cigarettes on a little machine because they're cheaper than the ones bought in packs. I pay, nonetheless, the usual tariff: thirty *centimes*. I don't want her to think I'm taking advantage, only coming here for cheap smokes. "He's going to leave her for me. He says it will just take a little time. I have to be patient. It's a money problem; they have investments. But he's going to take care of that. Make sure she doesn't get what's his."

I look at her. She looks smug, confident. This Thierry is a mysterious, shadowy person I've never met, although she insists he comes to visit her, mostly on afternoons when he should be out on the road selling electrical wire. I find it hard to believe any man would fall for Christelle and her lies. She's too transparent. But you never know. She has plenty of these guys, gentlemen callers who pay her visits. A whole mass. Doesn't Thierry realize he's just one of many? Doesn't he care?

"And what makes you think he means it? I mean, all men who are married or even just living with someone say that they're going to leave their wives or girlfriends eventually. They all say that." It's hard to understand how Christelle, usually street-smart, sly and wary when it comes to men, has fallen for sweet words.

"He will," she says, as smug as smug can be. "He will. He doesn't love his girlfriend. They've been together for years. He wants out. It's just the investments that keep him there with her. But he's going to find a house for us. I'm out of here just as soon as he does. Out of this village of jerks."

"And into happily ever after."

"It's all up to me. And my business," she says, setting aside the cigarette roller and shoving the cigarettes into a little metal box. She looks at me with triumph. Everybody in this village seems to be feeling some kind of strange triumph. Except for me and Tim. And Didier, of course.

"Your business?" I ask, wondering which business she's referring to today.

"The private secretary business." She lights a cigarette, takes a long drag. Looks at me with what she thinks resembles absolute candour. "The business I'm going to be running on the Internet. I told Thierry that I'll be making enough cash soon to tide him over until he gets his affairs straightened out. I'll be in the position to make us a good life together. Eventually."

"Eventually," I say, just to make myself agreeable. With Christelle, something big is always going to happen. Always. At some later date. Thierry will be finding that out soon enough; business is for the few hours Christelle has left over after sleeping until noon, smoking a few hundred ciggies in bed, coming downstairs for television game shows washed down with glasses of plonk. And even if he's the sort of guy who doesn't mind that sort of initiative, she'll still manage to screw the relationship up somehow. She always screws things up.

"In the beginning, Thierry's going to invest in my business. Just so it gets going. Just until I get a client list. He has faith in me. He knows I'm a businesswoman, and he's going to be putting money into my bank account any day now. Then after that, when I get the show on the road and there's money coming in, he'll let me slow down. He'll be taking care of me. It's time I got married again anyway. Time I had another kid. I'm tired of all this scrimping and saving."

"How's the business going anyway? I suppose you have the Internet connection now."

"Yeah. My office is all set up in the bedroom upstairs. Printer, computer, scanner. All top quality. Did I tell you social services gave me enough for a laptop? Just in case I have to go out on jobs. Got to be prepared, you know."

"How many clients do you have already?" I really do set myself up for hearing bullshit. I must take a certain pleasure in it.

"That's how I've been spending my time. Making contact with future clients. And let me tell you, it's not easy. The guys you chat to on the

Internet, the potential clients, they think that all a woman is interested in is finding a mate, not setting up a company. They don't take you seriously if you're a woman with business sense. They just want to chat and then meet up with you someplace. Start a romance."

I stare at her. I can't believe what she just said. "Wait a minute. You mean you're looking for potential clients for a secretarial service in chat groups? Are you serious?"

"Plenty of people out there need a secretary," she says with a tangible amount of hostile defiance. "You find them where you can. And Thierry, he thinks it's a good idea, too. He's a great supporter of mine, Thierry. He's the man I want. He has class. I have class. I need a man with class. He isn't as smart as I am, of course. But he has class. I'm used to class, just like my mother is. She was a fashion model, you know."

"So you told me."

"You've seen her picture. I showed it to you."

"You have indeed." The old photo shows a dumpy woman wearing spike heels and a huge floppy hat over long, straw hair cut and styled by a very dull butter knife. Her eyes are racoon-ringed with black makeup, her lips smeared with wobbly, blood red. Christelle thinks everybody but herself is an idiot.

"Father was a photographer. He took one look at her and said he would make her into his model. That was before he got his yacht, left the country and went to live in the Caribbean."

"So you told me."

"Made a fortune out there."

"As a photographer?"

"Owned lots of land in the south of France, too. Prime building land. When my lawyer gets my uncle out of the picture, when I finally get my hands on my inheritance, I'm going to build a big house down there. Thierry says he doesn't mind moving to the south." She stops to punch out her cigarette and light another one. "Know what Thierry said to me the other night? Said it was time I stopped taking birth control pills. Time we started in on having a baby. Woman he lives with, she's too old for that. That's why he wants one with me. Wants to start in right away. So I've stopped."

She turns away, begins looking up at the television screen, thereby missing my horrified expression. "Oh, no," I say with dismay. "Don't you think you should wait a little? See if Thierry really does come to live with you? Does leave the woman he is living with?"

"He will."

"Look, Christelle, don't force things by getting pregnant." After all, I'm talking to a woman who has already lost two children to social services because of neglect.

She turns to me angrily. "I know what I'm doing. I know what I want. Besides, my eldest daughter has been writing to me. She and her sister are going to come back and live with me soon. In a month or two. Now that the social workers see that I have a stable life with a steady income."

"Thierry knows this?" I ask, pretending to go along with a lie I've already heard several times over the last few years. "He knows that your two kids are going to live with you?

"Thierry loves children. He's really happy about my daughters coming to live with us. That's why he wants a baby with me. As soon as possible."

"You'll lose your welfare payments if you live with him."

She glares at me as if I'm an idiot. "So who cares? I don't need welfare anymore. I don't need social workers, I don't need anyone. I have my business. Besides, with my two daughters living with me plus a new baby or two, I'm entitled to a nice pile of money from the state. In child benefits."

Good work, Christelle. She always knows the right station for catching the gravy train.

Before the First World War, for poor, landless peasant families, the more children you had, the "wealthier" you were. Children did mean more mouths to feed, but because they laboured the fields of others, they represented additional earning power. Produced in droves, sent out to work as young as ten, these young wage-earners handed over all their earnings to their fathers. During the First World War, young men left the farms as soldiers, and for the first time, caught sight of the big, wide world. When the war ended, they determined to stay in the livelier towns and cities, to take up the new job opportunities there. They were no longer willing to pass their lives slogging away in fields belonging to other people or to scratch out a living on handkerchief-sized family farms. And because children would no longer stay home, because they no longer increased the family income, the birth rate among country poor dropped. Birth control methods started to be practised; young men began marrying older women to limit family size, and such unattractive expressions as "It is in an old pot that one makes the best soup" came into being.

Today, despite high unemployment, disastrous urban spread and almost unmanageable pollution, each successive government of France blindly encourages large families. To this end, parents receive payments for each child born. And like in the old days, for people like Christelle, children still mean wealth.

34

WEDNESDAY EVENING, BERNARD AND NICOLE MALABRY COME OUT OF
the restaurant section of Pierre's, stand at the bar, pay for their dinner
with a nice, shiny platinum American Express card. Interesting. It's not
just any run-of-the-mill chicken farmer who has one of those out here
in the sticks.

Monsieur smiles at Pierre. "A very nice meal, as usual." Tonight he
has a white, silk scarf casually wrapped around his neck, perhaps to draw
attention away from his soft paunch. "The duck breast with raspberry
vinegar was delicious."

Madame, dressed in violet silk with matching shoes, throws me a
three-second, utterly vague look, as if she's never seen me before. I'm
that forgettable, obviously. There's no faint smile of hello.

Pierre slides the card into the machine. Bernard Malabry taps
out the code. The machine whirrs, burps. Pierre hands back the card.
The couple wish him good night, head for the door. Already I've been
forgotten. Once again.

"Doing well for themselves, the Malabrys," I say sarcastically when
the purr of the Mercedes indicates they are seated inside and out of
earshot. "New industrial farmers."

"You against farmers making money?"

"Farmers making money? Hell, no. But that's not farming, what
they do. An intensive chicken farm has nothing to do with farming
— or rural life either. Not as far as I can see. People like the Malabrys are
industrialists; they have long sheds where fowl are packed together like
lice in a sack. They are the modern inheritors of agriculture and have
nothing in common with the old idea of what a farmer was. Those two
are the very people Didier was talking about that night he was here with
Philippe. Both Didier and Philippe were saying that the Malabrys' farm

is a disaster. That the chickens live in abominable conditions up there."

"So I've heard," says Pierre, ever noncommittal.

"Philippe has to take the truck up there every day, pick up dead animals, victims of the lousy conditions."

"A job's a job."

"And that sort of thing is allowed? No controls anywhere? No one's interested?"

"Happens all over the country. That's what intensive farming is all about. Of course, you're going to tell me that things shouldn't be like that, aren't you? But get it straight: this is the modern world. That's modern farming. Have to get used to it."

"Modern world doesn't have to have only flaws," I say, charging away on my usual high horse. "It doesn't have to be synonymous with suffering and misery. We can do better than that, can't we?"

"Lots of people to feed in the world. Farming is big business. Things have changed. You sound like Didier used to. Those chickens of his: he was always on about them, making a big fuss about the animals. He let them live on forever. You can't do that when you're a professional in a competitive market. Anyway, no matter how things were done, you'd be against it. You don't even eat meat. You're just an unfuzzy, oversized rabbit."

I refuse both the change of subject and the provocation. "Didier and Philippe said that the chickens live on antibiotics, growth promoters, recycled blood, dead animals and offal. You run a restaurant, right? You feel good about serving up animals raised on that kind of crap? Just hide the horror under a little wine sauce, huh? Shove a few chemically peeled potatoes around the side, decorate with a ruby-red, artificially coloured tomato that never knew what earth was, and you're on your way."

Pierre rolls his eyes heavenward. "Thought that I wasn't going to have to listen to this kind of bullshit after Didier died. But here we go. I should have known."

"Okay, try this one on for size. The night I talked to Didier here in the bar, he mentioned payoffs. In other words, he hinted that the Malabrys pay people off so they can run that horror show up there on the hill. What do you think of that?"

"I think that you are going to get yourself into a lot of trouble if you stir things up," says Pierre. "Might even put yourself in danger, if that's true. But as far as I'm concerned, I think you have to take what Didier said with a grain of salt. He had a thing about the Malabrys. Hated their guts. Wasn't really part of his job as *garde champêtre* to criticize local entrepreneurs, was it?"

"Well, in a way it was, you know. I looked up the job description because that's the sort of thing that interests me. Once it was an important part of a *garde champêtre's* work to inspect chicken runs. And obviously Didier took that duty seriously." I'm feeling more and more excited. Like finally, I'm on to something. I'm not certain what exactly, but it feels right. It explains why someone would have wanted Didier dead. "Do you know what time Philippe goes up to the Malabry's to pick up dead birds? Is it the same time every day?"

"Sometime around noon." Pierre says this with certain reluctance. And suspicion. "But if I were you, I'd be careful. Sounds like you're going to get yourself into trouble. You may not like Nicole and Bernard Malabry — and I can't say they are my own favourite people either — but the village is happy they came here. They run a successful business. They pay professional taxes, and that means the village has money for improvements, for flower decorations, for the village fête, for roads. Villages here aren't rich without businesses, you know. We have no factories here in Épineux, no industry. So we're all nice and pleased about the revenue that intensive chicken, cattle and pig farms bring in." He reaches for my empty glass, puts it in the sink with a gesture of finality. No second round for me tonight. "So take my warning and don't go around stirring up muck."

"Slurry," I say as I get off the barstool and begin moving in the direction of the door. "Slurry is the modern product. Muck's old hat. All those cows and pigs permanently locked up in the barns on intensive farms produce stinky slurry. You can smell the stuff when it's poured over the fields, then carried by the rain down into ditches and rivers. It increases the growth of blue-green algae in the water, did you know that?"

"No. And don't care much either." Pierre holds the door open. If I don't leave of my own volition, he'll probably push me into the street.

"And the algae uses up all the oxygen so that the invertebrates and fish die and their decomposing bodies use up even more oxygen," I say, determined to get through to him. Because people should start thinking about this kind of stuff. Local people, because it's their world that's being messed up. "You ever look at the river that runs through this village? Ever decide to go and sit down on a nice mossy bank, smell the air and meditate?"

Pierre slams the door behind Werewolf and me. Pulls down the shade to block out the very sight of us.

Werewolf and I go over the bridge, pass the *lavoir*, Didier's old house, the opening of the alley, the church, cross the square under the one bright street lamp. No one following me tonight. No one is in the least bit interested in my movements. Was there really someone there last night? I suppose that's something I'll never find out.

35

AT ELEVEN ON THURSDAY MORNING, THE BIG MERCEDES PASSES ME JUST before I turn into the road leading past the cemetery. The driver is, of course, Nicole Malabry, forever chic. She ignores me as usual, is intent on manipulating the bend. Where's she off to now? Going for another friendly chat with our local vet, Jean-Paul? What was the word Chantal used? Adorable. Jean-Paul finds Nicole Malabry adorable. Now, what I wouldn't give to have a little chat with the lady: a chat about lovers, about her new life far from the city she grew up in. But I can't just knock on her side door, ask if she has a few industrial eggs to sell me, can I?

I climb the hill between high banks covered in a tangle of pink, purple and yellow wild flowers and shaded by high, straggling elderberry, pass a few simple stone farmhouses. It is a bucolic scene up here, an infinitely lovely one. And one where loveliness comes to a dead end right where Malabry's intensive chicken farm begins.

There's not a soul around. Not an animal to be seen. There are certainly no clucking chickens; their noise has been replaced by the hum of ventilators beside the long, low, evil-looking buildings with high food silos. No, this is no longer what I can call a farm. This is a prison where chickens spend their lives fighting for access to food and water in barns where perpetual daylight reigns. This is a factory — a food factory — where animals are treated with industrial brutality.

Up here, there are no trees, no hedges. The wind teases twelve nodding tulips that have been planted along the yellow cement walls of the main house in a stab at rural atmosphere. Can anyone see me as I stand here waiting for Philippe's truck? It's impossible to tell. But this is not a place where I care to spend too much time. It has a deathly, evil feel to it. So I go back down the road again towards the village, stop just where the hill begins to flatten out. I have no idea how long I'll have to wait, so I just sit myself down on the grassy bank, think of the way farms once were: lively places surrounded by trees, vegetable patches, where the odour of healthy manure and baking bread reigned.

Workers woke at dawn, went to the farmer's gate, waited for him to appear. All breakfasted together around the farmer's table, on farm bread and that *soupe perpétuelle* bubbling away in the big caldron. When the church bells pealed seven o'clock, the men left for the fields, to plough, to plant, or to harvest — a work done in rhythm, scythes swishing back and forth.

Farm animals were treated with a measure of respect back then, especially workhorses, those large-boned, thick-legged creatures depended upon for fieldwork and transportation. Farmers conversed with them, nurtured them, often refused to sell them in their old age. Only on the poorest farms was ploughing done with cows, although some were even too poor for that; around here they still tell the story of one man who was known to hitch his wretched wife to the plough.

Cows were the favourites of farm women; they provided milk, butter and cheese that could be sold in markets. But pigs, the creatures closest to humans in intelligence, were nameless, despised beasts, referred to with disgust, seen only as a soulless source of food and revenue. When slaughtered, all parts would be used (even the ears, intestines and lungs), incorporated into pâtés, formed into sausages that were hung in the chimney and smoked. Farm dogs, too, led sad lives, their territory restricted by a short chain near the farm door, although cats had it better; dwelling in warm kitchens, they kept rats and mice at bay.

And everywhere chickens roved, scratching, pecking. Eggs of a good oval shape were considered the best for producing young chicks. Chickens not sacrificed for weddings and other feasts would live out long years in farmyards.

A clashing of gears and a dull roar alerts me, finally, to a truck coming up the hill. It rounds the bend, a huge, smelly vehicle with an ominous-looking crane on its back. It is, indeed, Philippe, easily identifiable by his hairdo — long head shaved to a crown of bushy spikes, a tepee-like structure sporting a thatched roof. His gold pirate's earring flashes as he turns his head briefly in my direction. He waves. I flap my hand to make him stop. He brakes, lets the motor idle, rolls down his window, his eyes suddenly hot and provocative, as ever they are when spying a female of the species.

"How've you been?" he shouts over the roar of the engine.

"Fine. Just fine. Could we talk for a minute?"

"Sure. Jump in." He reaches over, swings open the passenger door. I walk around, heave myself into the cab.

"What's doing?" he asks with his usual lopsided, flirtatious leer, as if he thinks I've been sitting here in the sodden grass for the express purpose of seducing him.

"Could we talk about what you and Didier were telling me that night in Pierre's bar? You remember, the stuff you were saying about Malabry's farm."

"You being nosy?"

"As ever." I nod.

"Not healthy, getting too nosy."

"Probably not," I acknowledge. "So you're on your way to pick up the dead now?"

He widens the leer until it becomes a grin. "One of my daily pleasures. Or you can say I'm picking up what's left of the dead. What's left after the live birds have been pecking at them, the ones who aren't strong enough to get to the food troughs."

"You like this job?" I ask, my teeth chattering to the truck's vibration.

"Yeah. It's great." He shrugs, stops grinning. "Look, what's a man supposed to do? Got myself involved in some shit a few years ago, right? Not every employer going to come running to my door with a classy job offer these days, right?"

"You feel as strongly about the wrongs of this farm as Didier did?"

He stares at me for a minute or two. "Don't think so."

"Meaning?"

"Meaning, this is just a job to me, right? I see what's going on, I know the whole thing's shit. But I keep my mouth shut, right? Normally, I keep my mouth shut. Not in my interest to bite the hand that feeds me, right? But Didier, he asks questions. Lots of questions. So to him, I talk. But Didier, he can't keep his mouth shut. Funny guy, Didier. Half the time he's soft-hearted, half the time he's hard as nails. Can't figure people like that out. No blueprint for them."

"And?"

"And Didier, people don't like him asking questions. Don't like him stirring up shit. Starting trouble. Dangerous thing to do."

"You've heard that people are saying his death wasn't an accident? That it was murder?"

Philippe pauses for a heartbeat or two. Looks away from me and out the cab window. As if this is a painful subject for him. And maybe it is, too. I haven't missed the fact that he keeps using the present tense when he talks about Didier, as if the guy is still alive and just temporarily kicking up a fuss in another dimension. "Yeah, I've heard. That's what I'm getting at. That's what I'm warning you about."

"And what do you think? That he was murdered because he was stirring things up?"

"What do I think, what do I think?" He continues looking out the window as if for the very first time, he's trying to work out exactly what his thoughts on this particular subject are. "I think farmers, big farmers like Malabry, like Thibault, the pig farmer a few miles down the valley, like other modern intensive farmers in the country, people don't want to upset them, right? They're not like farmers who grow corn or sunflowers and who live on government subsidies. Intensive farmers pay professional taxes in the villages they live in, and as long as all of them are doing well, the whole village does well, right?"

"Right," I parrot. "And therefore no one gives a shit if Malabry's chickens are crammed together in horrible conditions, that the space they have to run in is as large as a piece of paper. That they die like flies."

"Right. Because I'll tell you something. What people do care about is having a meal on the table. They want to go to the supermarket and buy a chicken and cook it. They don't even want to think about what its life was like a week earlier, right? And I'll tell you something else. I pick up the dead animals at the farms, right? Wait until September. That's when babies start arriving at the turkey units. You think chickens have it bad. Turkeys have it worse. Got to be ready for the holidays, turkeys. Got to be big and fat. You can't even walk into a turkey shed without a mask, so much stink of antibiotics and chemicals in the air. But like I say, the customer doesn't care. Customer's only interested in something big and roasted on the serving plate."

"No one cares," I agree. "It's true. No one except Didier."

"Right. And Didier's dead. And some people are mighty happy that he is. So, got enough information? Can I get on with my job now? Feed my kids?"

"Two more questions?"

He looks at me dolefully, the look of a man forced to think about certain things against his will. But still, he doesn't refuse. "Shoot."

"One: did Didier have a thing going with Nicole Malabry?"

Philippe's hot grin returns, spreads like thick ink over his features. "Now, that would be interesting."

"Wouldn't it just. Sleeping with the enemy. Probably adds a right hot spark to good old-fashioned sex. Well?"

But Philippe only shakes his head. "Didier never tells me about his sex life. Never. He keeps his gob shut."

"Too bad. Okay, last question: Didier and you were talking about payoffs, that night in the bar when I joined you at your table. Payoffs to whom? What kind of payoffs?"

"Didier was talking about payoffs. Not me. I don't know everything he knows, right? You getting out now? Interrogation over?"

"Yeah, yeah." I open the truck door. "Thanks." I jump out of the cab, then suddenly realize that I know pretty well nothing about Didier. Maybe Philippe does. "Tell me, was Didier born here in the village, in Épineux-le-Rainsouin? Was he raised here? Does he have any family anywhere?"

Philippe jerks his mouth down at the corners, thinks for a minute or two. "No family that I know of. But no, he's not from this village. He's from Fontenay-le-Léger. I think so, anyway." He slams the truck into gear, as I close the door.

Fontenay-le-Léger? How interesting. For in Fontenay, there is the café, the one run by Marie-Jeanne, another inveterate gossip.

36

Once six cafés teemed with life in Fontenay-le-Léger, but that was back in the days when the local population was counted in hundreds, when the road was a busy one, when a train line zigzagged through the countryside, when the little branch line station still functioned. But the train line was disbanded after the war, the new *autoroute* avoided Fontenay altogether, and people sold up, left for employment in the towns and cities. Eight kilometres down the road from Épineux-le-Rainsouin, Fontenay is now nothing more than a hamlet: fifteen small houses crouch around a minuscule church and sleepy café.

Some years ago, there was an attempt by Marie-Jeanne, the café owner, to instil new life into the place by resuscitating an old tradition: the *veillée*. Farmers and villagers alike once passed the long winter evenings at *veillées*, gatherings at which everyone would shell nuts, carve wood, weave the baskets in which bread was baked, and cook apple and milk jam (both local specialities). The reason for their existence, originally, was to save fuel; it was thriftier to have a crackling wood fire and burning oil lamps in one house rather than in several. But their popularity continued, for here young people could meet, friendships between farming families and villagers could be consolidated, imaginations fired. The highlight of a *veillée* was storytelling: funny tales, depending on the wit of the narrator, or terrifying accounts of dangers lurking in the dark — bandits, wolves, *houbilles* (restless night spirits who stole sheep and crops), *hopitres* (evil ghosts who changed form and descended chimneys), *fades* (who bore coffins in the dead of night), and those other unfortunates captured by evil sorcerers and forced to roam the countryside as vampires.

The *veillée* began disappearing in the 1950s, a victim of prosperity. Farms were enlarged, people were able to acquire new equipment and no longer needed to share implements or duties with others. Jealousy of the neighbour's new car, tractor, or increased acreage edged out friendship; television dulled the tongues of storytellers.

Marie-Jeanne's attempt fell flat. By the year 2000, the old stories had been forgotten. Modern men and women no longer believed in spirits lurking in the dark; wolves had been exterminated; superstitions, when held to the light of violent films, were found wanting in suspense. The few participants at Marie-Jeanne's *veillées* could only relate the sad offerings of televised drama. The café, a shabby, scruffy country place, now feeds its rare clients their preferred fare: beer, cheap wine and gossip.

A vast, oval-shaped woman, fond of gaudy clothes, heavy makeup and cheap clinking jewellery, Marie-Jeanne does not greet my arrival in her café with any great enthusiasm this Thursday afternoon. She considers all women rivals for the affections of her man, Loïc, a timid, browbeaten shadow who spends most of his largely silent life taking refuge in his damp garden, hoeing potatoes, squashing thrips between his smutty fingernails, torturing weeds and executing terrified caged rabbits.

But I ignore the frosty welcome, take a seat at the bar as if I'm quite at home and will be staying for a long time indeed. Just now, a short, unpleasant, burgundy-faced man is enthusiastically recounting a highly repugnant tale of woe. "Doctor said I was filled up with water. Didn't have enough potassium in my blood so I just filled up. Couldn't bend, couldn't move my neck. Could hardly move my legs. Couldn't move my arms, fingers as big as sausages. I was bloated out to here." His arms describe a full circle. "No potassium in my system, that's what it was. Water just filled up the places it should have been, filled up my body like a pot. Just to here, it filled it up." His fingers slice just under his chin. "Gave me a prescription for potassium, doctor did. Took it. And just like that, all the water ran right out. Like a bathtub."

"I was bloated up, too, after my accident," says Marie-Jeanne who has divided her life into two time periods: before a minor car accident (when life was apparently a breeze) and after (life is no longer a breeze). "After my accident, couldn't wear any of my old clothes. And then my memory hasn't been the same since. Can't remember anything like I did before the accident. Can't even care about things anymore the way I used to since the accident. Don't care about anyone else either. Can't be bothered, since the accident."

"Water up to your neck and all of it inside doesn't help your memory any either," continues the burgundy man, determined not to be outdone. "Memory going fast anyway, what with age and all, but water filling up inside takes away what's left. Suffer? You don't know what the word means, I'll tell you that. Don't know if I'll be the same again, these things take their toll, they do. Round as a ball, I was. And full."

I wave my fingers to draw attention to myself, order a beer, and reflect on the fact that sometimes life seems to be an endless, joyless proposition. Useless to attempt to conjure up other, visually more agreeable images in my head. The red man has started the whole litany once again — for my benefit this time. Just in case I missed the best bits.

After ten minutes or so, I signal he has lost my attention by staring down at my beer mat and whirling it round and round on the counter. Marie-Jeanne has also taken up another activity: rinsing glasses in the sink behind the bar. No new audience appearing, with a greatly reluctant shuffle, the man leaves the café.

"How've you been doing?" I ask in a tone cheery enough to keep dread misery and wailing woe at bay.

"How can I be doing?" she answers bitterly. "Since my accident, things aren't like they used to be. And Loïc, he's been drinking as usual. And watching porno on television. I know I'm not the kind of woman he wants. He wants one of those he sees on the porno sites, that's what he wants. It's disgusting. Men are disgusting. They all make me sick."

"Did you hear that everyone's saying Didier was murdered?" I cut in, veering abruptly to the point rather than risk of being sucked into this dangerous conversational swamp. "Didier, the *garde champêtre* at Épineux. You were at his funeral. I saw you there. I heard he originally came from here, from Fontenay-le-Léger."

"I heard he drank all the time," hedges Marie-Jeanne who always looks for — and usually finds — the worst in everyone.

"As far as I know, he didn't. Not all that much, anyway."

"Well then, it must have been the previous *garde champêtre*. That's what I heard."

"Possibly," I temper. "It seems quite a few of the old *gardes champêtre* used to be overly fond of drink. But times have changed, you know. Didier was a very responsible man. He was born here in this village?"

"No," says Marie-Jeanne.

"He wasn't?"

"Wasn't." She picks up a doubtful-looking, greyish towel, begins drying the glasses. "Was born on one of the outlying farms. Out there where his mother lived."

"Is she still around?"

"No. Died years ago. An alcoholic. One of the worst. She spent more time lying in ditches than she did in her own bed. A lousy mother, of course. Miracle, Didier doing so well for himself with someone like that as his mother. Now that he's dead, everyone here's saying it's all her fault."

"What's her fault? I mean, with her being dead for years and all."

"She treated him badly. Never loved him the way she should have. He was always begging for his mama's love and never got but a drop of it. Just a lot of bad treatment and punches. She was always sneering at him, telling him he was no good. Never did get married, and that's no surprise either. Bitch, she was. Drunk. Sleeping around with everything in pants. What man wants that for a wife? Didier always did what he could to take care of her though, try and please her, but it was impossible. No one in the world could do that."

"What was Didier like when he was a kid? Do you remember anything about him?"

"He was very good looking," mumbles Marie-Jeanne cautiously, as if she's hiding something.

"And?"

"He liked women," she says cagily. "Liked them a little too much, if you see what I mean."

"You mean he screwed his brains out?"

She turns pink, but I doubt it's because of my language. Shrugs wordlessly.

"Screwed his brains out, and did it with no conscience? A sex addict? Is that how it was?"

Marie-Jeanne looks at me, her made-up eyes sharp and wary behind her blue plastic eyeglass frames, as if she's uncertain how much information she should be handing out. Or perhaps, how much will compromise her. "Loïc passes his time watching porno films."

"Tell me more about Didier. What have you heard? Did he ever have a steady woman friend? Did he ever have a long-term relationship?"

"Never cared about anyone but himself. Had no conscience. Did whatever it took to conquer women, but he cared about no one."

Perhaps he didn't even care very much about himself either, I think. He set himself up in dangerous situations — as a seducer of other men's wives, as a protester who just might have offended all the wrong people. Situations in which, if he were caught, the consequences could be dire. Were, in the end, dire. "Did Didier ever come back here after he took the job in Épineux? Did he ever come into the bar here?"

"Of course."

"By himself? Never with a woman? Never with anyone else?"

"No," says Marie-Jeanne, shaking her head of half-dyed orange-and-mouse hair. She's getting into full swing now, unable to resist the delicious lure of gossip and slander. "Used to come here and drink with that nurse, Martine, and the English couple, Tim and Fiona. Good friends with Didier for a while. Only for a while. And then they weren't friends anymore."

"Didier told you that?"

"Tim did. He still comes here from time to time. They're divorced now, he and Fiona. Did you know that? I'll tell you why, too. Because Fiona's a bitch, a jealous bitch. She hated Tim being friends with Didier. They had everyone in the area over at their house all the time, but as far as Didier was concerned, she hated him. Probably because he and Tim got along so well. She was just jealous. Not that Didier cares now, of course. But before he died, I also heard Didier had been having a tough time with your mayor. Some problem. Starting with the water wheel, he said. Mayor, municipal council underestimating him. Then came in here one night, said that there was a scandal going to be brewing in Épineux. Something to do with the mayor's enterprise. About getting all the construction jobs in the village, but how it isn't legal when you are mayor and the company belongs to you."

"You mean Lemasson Enterprises?"

Marie-Jeanne shrugs. "Probably. Who knows for sure? That's all he said. He wasn't a big mouth, Didier. But he was angry. And pleased with himself, too. Said he knew something and was going to use the information. Or at least that's what Loïc and I understood. Didier didn't say anything definite, but he looked like he was looking for trouble of some sort with Lemasson. But there's dirty linen in every village, isn't there? I was on the municipal council once in this village. Years ago. You should have seen what those meetings were like. First, it's only official business. Then everyone sits around and talks about who's sleeping with whom. Whose wife is being forked — that's the expression they use — by which other man. Or which husband is forking someone else's wife. They laugh and joke about how everyone is a cuckold. They think they're so smart. But what they don't know is that the same thing is happening in their very own homes. Their own wives are doing exactly the same thing. I know because just as soon as someone left the room, everyone would laugh about it. That's what village life is like. Everyone screwing around, but all of it's supposed to be a big, big secret. No one knows what the word honest means. Anyway, heard you have other problems in Épineux. Hear the church was robbed. That two chalices disappeared."

"True."

"Foreigners," she says hatefully. "That's who's doing that kind of thing. They have no respect. We go to their countries. We respect their lifestyle, their traditions. We don't rob them blind. But they come here and do they do the same for us? No. They come here and rob us. Should send them all back to where they came from. All of them."

37

IT'S AS IF NOTHING HAS HAPPENED IN THE LAST FOUR DAYS. AS I PULL UP to Tim's house in my car on Friday, I see he's still in the front garden, still sitting in one of the white plastic chairs at the white plastic table, still boozing. He still looks like shit, too, like someone who lives on cigarettes and red wine, and come to think of it, that's probably the case. The hedge surrounding the house has obviously ceased to receive any further attention: the trimmer is still on the ground where he dropped it on Monday; above it, the bushes are scraggly, as if a herd of goats came in to have a nibble, got bored with the taste and left.

Tim watches me without warmth, without welcome, as I get out of the car, slam the door shut and saunter over the grass in his direction. "How are you doing?" Even to me, my voice sounds obnoxiously bubbly.

In answer, he raises his glass of red, his hand shaking like a bowl of half-set, flesh-coloured jelly. I can smell, a mile off, that he doesn't want me to be here. That he reckons I'm up to no good. That I'm cruising around for information that he's not, under any circumstance, going to hand out.

I sit myself down on the grass at his feet (a chair not being offered). "Getting on with your life?" I ask.

"What am I supposed to get on with? My life's shit," he answers, evidently deciding to fall back on the usual tired-out-but-familiar song of "poor me."

"And why's that? Husbands leave wives, wives leave husbands every day of the year. And people survive." Here I am, sounding like Dear Abby again.

He looks away towards the hedge while his trembling jelly fingers snag the inevitable pack of cigarettes from his shirt pocket. He shakes one out, lights it. Doesn't ask me if I want a smoke, of course, and the atmosphere isn't really homey enough for me to actually come out and beg him for one.

I wonder why he's being so truculent — unless, of course, he, or he and Fiona, or Fiona alone, chucked the hair dryer in Didier's bath, and he reckons I've worked that out by now. Whatever the reason, he just sits there without saying a word, without looking at me. So there's nothing left for me to do than blunder on ahead as usual. "I've been gathering a lot of information about Didier. Were a lot of husbands who didn't like him, you know. Had a reputation for screwing their wives. The way I figure it, perhaps one of them murdered him."

Tim keeps looking over at the hedge for another minute or two as if there's something wildly exciting swinging around over there: monkeys, Tarzan, the lot. Then rips his glance away, glares at me. Finally ... although he's not actually going to go so far as to look friendly. "So?"

"So it could be you who did it," I say, casually enough. What I'm wondering, of course, is if Tim will deny that Fiona had had any kind of relationship with Didier. If he'll fall back on the story Fiona told Martine: that Didier tried to get it on with her and she refused him — a tale I still find hard to believe. It won't surprise me if he does, however. As a jealous husband, Tim might be more than happy to go along with something that would confirm Didier had been the devil incarnate. But evidently, he just can't be bothered keeping that particular myth alive.

Instead, he snorts. It could be with laughter, of course, but to my old ears, it's a noise that sounds a hell of a lot more like derision. "Yeah. Right." He takes a big, long drag from his cigarette. Sends the smoke straight out in a steady stream through his nose. "Like, I'm stupid, right? Like, I'm going to kill him when it's too late. For revenge or something. Is that what you're getting at? Well, if it is, you've got it wrong. I should have killed him before Fiona left me. When I finally worked out she was crazy about the guy. Not after. Got that? I should have proven to her that I'm a caveman, a he-man. A club-in-hand hero, jealous and possessive. Just to impress her. Win her heart again."

"Okay, okay," I say in an attempt to placate the guy. I mean, he has more or less admitted that Fiona did sleep with Didier. "You didn't kill him. You didn't. So who do you think did?"

The sneering air of derision collapses, and once more, he's looking at me with those rabbit-red, martyr eyes. "You want my opinion?"

"That's why I'm asking," I chirp. There's very little that irritates the hell out of me more than self-pity.

"Piss off. Forget the whole thing. Get yourself a life."

Pot calling the kettle black, I think. But don't say, naturally. Tim is looking away again and taking another long drag. He's definitely not going to answer my question. "Look, why don't you help me out?"

"With what?" he says to the jagged, goat-chewed hedge.

"By telling me some things."

"What things?"

"The things Didier talked to you about back in the good old days, back when the two of you were best buddies. Tell me about the clash he had with the mayor over the water wheel. About his preoccupation with Malabry's chicken farm. Stuff like that. You did talk about those things, didn't you? I mean, he must have confided in you."

Tim doesn't react for a minute or two, as if he's having one big, long debate with himself. Then he nods, just one brief movement. "So?"

"Go on." I wait, watch Tim smoke. And try to figure out why he's being so reticent, now that I've made it clear I know about Fiona and Didier. It could simply be because he's sad about Didier's death and at the same time he hates Didier's guts and he's angry. Or he's blissfully happy Didier's dead but can't actually come out and say so without looking suspicious. Or he's decided that his own life is in so many tiny broken pieces, it isn't worth expending any more emotion on anything or anyone else. Or perhaps he just can't stand me asking so many obnoxious questions.

"Go on about what?" He suddenly leans forward in his chair. Stares down at me. He's getting angry, I can see that well enough. "I'll tell you what. Why don't *you* come clean, for once? Tell me what your interest is in all of this? What the hell does it have to do with you anyway? Why the fuck are you harassing me with your stupid, fucking, rude questions?"

He's right, of course. I've been unforgivably rude. There's no reason on earth why he should tell me anything. "Okay," I say. I mean, it's not as if I have a whole lot to lose by telling the truth. It's just that I'm not comfortable with my life, with what I've been willing to settle for, and

I've never really admitted that until now. "Just as long as you keep this to yourself."

He nods, sucks on his cigarettes, blows out smoke, waits.

"I've never told anyone before, actually. And I'm not giving any names, okay?"

"Okay."

"There's this guy in the village. He's married. He's my lover, right?"

"Right." Tim stares at me. "Go on. This is getting good."

"And Didier slept with his wife."

Tim actually smiles. A nasty smile. One devoid of humour. "Surprise, surprise."

I nod. "Yeah. Just up Didier's street, I know. And then afterward, he tried to blackmail her. So because of all that, my lover is a worried guy. He thinks he's going to be accused of killing Didier. So he asked me to ask around."

Tim isn't looking at me any more. His face is pastier and a whole lot more tense than it was seconds ago, but I can't even begin to guess what he's feeling. Anger perhaps? Rage? Does he know how often Fiona went to Didier's house alone? "It wasn't the water wheel," he croaks finally, in a voice that sounds as though it's coming up from Hades. "It was the money. Everything was always money and power. Always. Sell your soul for money and power. The two big gods. That bastard."

"What money?" I ask, feeling fairly lost. "Blackmail money?"

"Not blackmail. The raise. Everyone working for the village got a raise. Four percent. Only Didier didn't. Pissed him off. Got nothing because he was honest about the water wheel, about pollution in the river. He gave his opinion in public, and the mayor didn't like that. He was pissed off about the intensive farming, too, Didier was. Said it was a scandal. Couldn't keep his mouth shut about that either."

"Everyone got a raise because there were payoffs?"

"That's what Didier claimed. I don't know any more than that. I don't even know if it was true. He just talked about payoffs from farmers to the municipal council."

"And what was he going to do about it?"

"He said that he was going to sound the alarm. Said he found out that the mayor was billing for materials they weren't using in the new housing development. That it was against the original agreement. Said that they were using cinder blocks because they were cheaper than bricks, but still billing for bricks. Said that the wood used in the roofs was cheap stuff, not what the tender said they would use. Said that an enquiry would bring the house down. Then everything that Lemasson Enterprises had done in years would be inspected. Find one thing wrong, then everything gets poked at. Shit like that."

"He wanted revenge?"

"Yeah. He wanted revenge. That's all he cared about. He thought he had power in that shitty little job of his. Because he saw everything, knew everything, thought he was indispensable. That no one would ever fire him because he knew so much. That he pulled all the strings." Tim takes a hefty slug of wine. Just to keep his whistle wet after such long declarations. "He was crazy, Didier."

"I see," I say, the light slowly dawning. "Didier had principles. But only if he wasn't being paid off not to have them, right? You think if he had gotten four percent like everyone else, he would have gone on keeping his mouth shut."

Tim looks at me with hatred. "He was a shit. I told you he was a shit. You know what a shit he was. Ask your lover boy about it, too."

"Got the message. Did Lemasson and all the others know Didier was about to blow the whistle about the inferior materials?"

"They confide in me?"

"Okay. Stupid question. That's all you know? That's all Didier told you?"

"That's all."

"And you don't care if his murderer gets caught? Because he ruined your marriage and now that he's dead, that's justice enough? Even if it's the mayor who killed him? Even if it's someone else on the municipal council, the plumber or roofer, who thinks he has the right to bump people off when they interfere? Because he just might have to take a cut in income and he doesn't like that idea? I mean, what is this? Mafia world? And you don't give a damn."

"You've got it."

"Anything else you can tell me?"

"Nope."

"Anything you want to talk to me about?"

"Why put the pressure on me? Why ask me about all this crap? You've got a better victim."

"What's that supposed to mean?"

"That means, go lean on that bitch friend of yours."

"What bitch friend?" I am totally mystified.

"Your friend, the nurse."

"Martine, you mean?"

"Martine?" he sneers in a falsetto, mocking me. "Lousy, fucking bitch. Fiona thought that every word came out of her mouth was gold. But your Martine, she hated Didier. She hates every creature with a pair of balls between their legs. She was the one who told Fiona to leave me. She's the one responsible. Not Didier. Didier helped me. We put up the roof on this house together. We did the slates together. He showed me how to make a stone wall. We planted trees. He translated for me. I mean, what the fuck! He helped me and Fiona. This whole dump became a fucking palace all because of Didier. He busted ass for us, and he didn't ask for a penny in return. You want a killer? Then don't look at me. Go get that bitch, Martine, instead. She's capable of it."

"Maybe," I say slowly, but I'm thinking hard. "Maybe she would be. But there's one tiny little problem. Motive. Martine had no motive for killing Didier."

"She hated his guts, I tell you. She couldn't see what sort of person Didier was underneath. She couldn't see he had a kind of beauty. And a heart of gold. Under all the crap, crap like having to screw every woman who crossed his path. And you know why he did crap like that? You know why? Because he thought he was weak if he didn't. That he wasn't a real man. That no one would think he was. Martine, she wouldn't understand someone like Didier. She just saw him as a shit with balls."

Strange. Now he's really defending the guy. Hate to love in a matter of seconds. Very strange, indeed. After all, Didier did screw his wife. And this doesn't seem to bother Tim one whit. No word of castigation in sight about that. "It's not enough just to despise someone," I say. "If people went around killing everyone they despised, we wouldn't have an overpopulation problem in the world."

Tim doesn't say another word. We just sit in silence for an eternity or two. Then I stand up. No point in hanging around where I'm as welcome as a covey of ticks. "If you think of anything, will you come and tell me?" I know full well he won't.

"Piss off."

"After all, it sounds like you cared about the guy." Almost more than that, even. How had Martine put it? She'd said that Tim had been half in love with Didier.

"Piss right off."

"Right." I lean over, pick up my car keys from the grass. "Nice talking to you." I start to walk over to the road, then come to a sudden stop, hit by a brilliant flash. For the first time, one loose end seems to have tied itself up neatly. I turn around. "Tim?"

He stares at me.

"Want to know what just crossed my mind?" Although I'm pretty sure he couldn't care less. "I think you're possibly more upset about Didier being dead than about Fiona leaving you. That's what I think. Tell me that I'm wrong."

"Fuck you."

"You loved him, didn't you?"

"Piss off!" He's screaming now.

"You loved him. You would have done anything for him. You didn't even give a shit about Fiona. Maybe you thought he loved you, too. Possibly you even slept together. And then you somehow found out he was sleeping with Fiona. And you realized he would never be true to you. That he would screw anyone because there was no real love in him. No loyalty either. He was sneering at you, at everyone. That's what happened, wasn't it?"

Tim stands. He looks ice cold sober. And angry. The drunkenness has quite fallen away, just as if it had been a bit of theatre, a way of getting out of answering too many questions coherently. For a brief and highly unpleasant moment, I think he's going to come over to where I'm standing and punch me. Or kill me. I feel my body tense and I force myself to turn, command my legs to toddle off, as quickly as possible, the last few metres to my car. And wonder why, once again, I haven't been smart enough to bring Werewolf along with me. He's not big, really, but at least he's my feisty defender.

But Tim doesn't advance towards me. Instead, he turns away. And with the lurch of a man desperately trying to control his fury, heads for the open doorway of the house. Goes in. Slams the door behind him.

I turn the key in the ignition, start the car and roar away with definite relief. And think about Tim and Didier. Now if Tim had been in his house, Didier might very well not have minded taking a bath. Because he was comfortable with him. Because it was something he might have been used to doing. Or even to taunt him. Because Didier must have known how much Tim wanted him.

38

"So you see? The situation was totally different from what we thought it was. Both Tim and Fiona loved Didier." I'm talking to Martine's back. It is Saturday morning, and she's planting tiny lettuces in her vegetable patch. The summer sun has temporarily vanished, swaddled in a cloud of dusky grey, and I hunch against the puffing little wind that ripples over the fields, rustles the leaves of a gigantic, ancient chestnut tree twenty metres away. "That's the real reason the marriage broke up. They were rivals in love."

"Actually, it just confirms what I said before. Didier was perverse." Martine yanks out an enthusiastic but doomed dandelion. "And people who are perverse have no feelings, no compassion for others. They use relationships to manipulate people."

"Still, Didier must have given people the impression he liked them. He charmed all and sundry. Except you, evidently."

"Sure, he gave the impression that he got along with everyone." Martine half turns to look up at me. "Perverse people look like they're living well in society. But their main interest in life is having power over others."

"Obviously Fiona made up the story about Didier masturbating in front of her. But why?"

"Maybe that was her way of getting revenge."

"Because, in the end, she realized Didier had no feelings, no compassion?"

"Possibly. You know, while you're in a relationship with someone perverse, you don't understand what's going on. You try to identify with the perverse person because you think that he or she resembles you, has the same makeup as you do. But they don't function in the same way. You can't project onto them and you can't understand them. It screws you up."

"So is it possible Tim killed Didier because he realized Didier had never returned his love? And he also wanted revenge?"

Martine frowns, shoves herself into a standing position and brushes earth from her baggy pants. "I doubt it. It all depends on what his relationship with Didier really was, what his relationship with his own family was when he was a kid. If what Tim felt for Didier was even stronger than love — if Didier represented his big brother, for example, and then this 'brother' rejected him — I suppose that might be stronger than love."

"If Didier was Tim's first experience in loving another man, and he felt betrayed and used by him, then mocked and rejected when Didier dropped him, that could also have dire consequences, couldn't it?"

"Tim did love Fiona, you know," Martine equivocates. "He loved two people."

"Okay, so let's get back to Fiona. She hated Didier for destroying her marriage — because he did do that. He took her husband away, he ruined her life. And what if she had really been deeply in love with Didier? What if she thought they would go off together, hand in hand, into a rainbow future? And then she discovered that Tim, her own husband, was in the same position she was. That he loved Didier. That he was his lover. Looking at this carefully, Fiona had even more reason to kill Didier than Tim did. And, in case anyone eventually accused her of murder, she invented the story about Didier trying to rape her as a way of justifying her action."

Martine says nothing. She's folding together all the little plastic pots that the tiny lettuces came in.

"So what do you think?" I prod.

"What do I think about what?" She stops jiggling the plant pots.

"About what I just said. Who murdered Didier — Tim or Fiona?"

Martine raises one hand in an upward gesture of exasperation. "Neither one of them."

"I thought you'd say that, so I have another theory ready. We agree that Didier was perverse, right? Now, what if the person who killed him was even more perverse than he was? What if Didier didn't realize someone close to him was dangerous? Still is dangerous."

Martine rolls her eyes heavenward. "Oh please! Just because someone is perverse, that doesn't make them a murderer. Perverse people want to manipulate others, not kill them off. Besides, they instinctively recognize other perverse personalities and avoid them. They need people who *aren't* perverse as their victims."

"So, we're back to square one again. Someone fell in love with Didier, someone who later felt so angry, humiliated and hurt by him that they committed murder." A sharp, unpleasant gust of wind slices across the garden, has the baby lettuces shivering. "Of course, it could be another thing altogether. It could be that Didier really pissed someone off, someone on the municipal council. Someone who had to kill him off to be safe."

Martine bends down, scoops up her trowel. "And that's something you're never going to find out about either."

"Probably not. You want me to tell you what Tim said? What he said about you?"

Martine nods.

"He said you killed Didier."

"What for?" She isn't even angry. Or fazed. Just mildly surprised. "Why would I do a thing like that? What would I get out of it?"

"That's what I told him."

"And what did he say?"

"Nothing of importance that I can remember. But what if you killed Didier because you are in love with Fiona and wanted to do something nice for her? What if you're the one with an ultra perverse personality?"

Martine shakes her head in mock pity. "Look, why don't you do the whole world a nice big favour? Leave the investigation to the police. If they had suspected anything in the first place, they'd have gotten on with the job. Just stop trying to stir things up."

39

"So tell me, Pierre, any police been seen driving around the village yet? Stopping at people's houses, following up on local gossip, asking about Didier? Encouraging everyone to dredge up all the deep, dark secrets?"

He throws his head back to avoid smoke from the cigarette stuck to his bottom lip. "Have they been to see you?"

"Why should they have? All I can blather on about is what went on in around 1873. Didier wasn't even sperm back in those days. By the way, haven't you ever heard anyone mention that cigarettes kill you in the long run?"

"That's what you came here to chat to me about? Cigarettes? At closing time on Saturday evening? When I could be sitting on my sofa with the wife, watching the sports news, not wasting what's left of my life being lectured to?"

"No, that's just to get you into a good mood. It's a starter. What I really want is for you to tell me how the municipal council works."

"All of it?" he mocks. "In two hours, three? Or is this an all-nighter?"

"Look, just explain how building contracts are awarded. I mean, it hasn't escaped my notice that Lemasson Enterprises gets all the contracts here in the village. That's not exactly legal, is it? I was told that a mayor doesn't have the right to profit from public building in his own village. So how does it work?"

Pierre looks at me steadily for a while, then shrugs. "Simple. There's an official call for offers for all public projects. The offer is posted in the newspaper and different building companies hand in their proposals to the municipal council. Of course, the mayor also sees the prices that the others are bidding. And afterwards, he puts in the bid for Lemasson Enterprises."

"Which is lower than the other bids?"

"Doesn't matter. He can bid the same price as the others or he can quote lower or, if he feels like it, he can quote higher. Just so long as the price he's asking is appropriate to the job. Then at the council meeting, everyone votes on which offer to accept. But the mayor doesn't vote, of course. He can't because he's one of the bidders. He can't even be present in the room. So he leaves. Waits outside."

"I know how this story ends," I say. "When the mayor comes back into the room after the vote, he finds out — big surprise — he and his company have gotten the job. Always. Am I right?"

"You going to be spreading what I say all around town?" Pierre asks suspiciously. "Because I wouldn't like that. I have a business here. I don't need any trouble."

"No spreading," I say, and mean it. "I never spread. I gather."

"I'm not going to stay in this place forever, of course," says Pierre. "I'm going to be moving on soon. Going to get out of the area. It's a lousy business, running a village café and restaurant. You work eighteen hours a day, six days of the week. This is no life. I don't see my kids, I have no family life."

"I know that."

"So this is between the two of us, what I'm telling you."

"Whom would I tell it to? Here in the village, I mean. I reckon everyone but me knows what's going on anyway. And no one gives a shit. Am I right?"

"You're right. And it happens everywhere, in every village. Because, think about it — who's on the municipal council here in Épineux? Pouttier the electrician, Tribhou the carpenter, Hautbois the roofer, Berthereau the cabinetmaker, Paillard the plumber and Pouvreau who sells building material. And all of them are going to profit from a local job. The mayor is going to call them in and give them work when he needs them. He's a builder, Lemasson. He does the foundations, the walls, the building. The others do the rest. Work is going to stay in the village if he gets the bid. Next month or next year, everyone is going to have a job. They'd never be stupid enough to vote against their own interests, would they?"

"Never," I agree. "Even if another offer was better or another company was more competent."

"Never. And it's not just for the work, either. If they didn't vote for the mayor's company, they'd be signing their own death warrants, socially speaking, here in the village. They'd be ostracized. They'd suddenly find that the tax department was looking at their accounts more closely, for example, or their work methods were being inspected. You ever see an inspector around here examining the work that's been done? Never. Those people who profit, all live here in the village. Break the vote and there's no more work here. No work, no taxes paid, and the village and the inhabitants are a lot poorer."

"And there are twelve members on the town council, right? And all the mayor needs is a majority vote and that means, since he can't vote, six are guaranteed beforehand."

"Exactly."

"And how do those guys get voted onto the municipal council?"

"That's what's so amusing. In France, you can put up your own name as an electoral candidate. For example, if you want to be president of the Republic, you need around five hundred signatures from people who will vote for you. But if you want to be mayor, you don't even need that. You just say you are a candidate. And then once someone has made it clear he's a candidate for village mayor, he goes around being friendly to everyone. The usual campaign stuff, making promises here and there. And don't forget, the candidates can make promises because the people who want to be mayor all have a little power. One can repair something for you cheap, for example. Or one is a guy who can bring work and money into the village. And then there are the other guys, those who want to be on the municipal council. These are usually big farmers or successful businessmen or craftsmen, and everyone votes for them because they're big shots in a village. The peasants, they vote for them because they think that these big shots are smarter than they are. And the big shots also have wives who vote for them. And they have their employees who vote for them, and the employee's wives vote for them. And so do their cousins and nephews and nieces and parents. So they get in."

"And Didier? What role did he play? Was he on the council?"

"Not allowed. If you're employed by the village, you can't be on the council. But he would be present at council meetings, of course."

"And he'd know everything that was going on."

"Right."

I scratch my head, the classic gesture for stirring up thoughts. "So when Didier was alive, the mayor needed to count on him to keep his mouth shut about any doubtful practices. But since Didier was angry with the mayor, he couldn't be trusted any longer. Couldn't be counted on."

"Definitely couldn't be counted on. And he tended to be very vocal about what he didn't like, too."

"And he just might have been in the mood to stir up trouble. Because the mayor had humiliated him in front of everyone when he made that comment about the stupid water wheel. Lemasson called him a nobody. A broom pusher. And I was told that the mayor punished him by not giving him a raise in salary, but that he did give one to the others who work for the village. So then, Didier wanted revenge. A vicious circle, it was."

"Possible," says Pierre.

"And Didier could have made problems for Lemasson. Simply because the mayor is profiting from the housing development and the social housing that's being added to it. And he profited from building the town hall. And he profited from building the community hall, and the bridge, and everything else. And he'll keep on profiting. And Didier knew that it was illegal."

Pierre looks at me as if I'm a half-clever kid who's just worked out that the alphabet exists but isn't yet sure what you use it for. "So?"

"So ..." I stop. Then deflate. "Oh, I see. If everyone in the whole village knows that this is happening, if it's just normal practice everywhere, what could Didier actually do about it?"

"Nothing. In principle, he could get in touch with the prefecture and demand that they do an investigation. But they probably wouldn't do it. Lemasson is a popular figure; he's friends with all those important guys. And he keeps everyone in the village happy and in money and jobs."

"But Didier was also a popular figure. Everyone knew him. He went from house to house; he had contacts all throughout the village. So I guess he could blacken Lemasson's name so that people wouldn't vote for him next time. Not that that would change anything, probably. Not with all his friends still on the council."

Pierre yawns noisily, looks at his watch. He's going to throw me out of here in less than a second.

"Hold on," I say, because I have to test the information Tim gave me. "What if Didier found out that there was some kind of fraud? What if he discovered that the mayor was using cheaper materials than the ones he was billing for? Then he'd really have a case against the mayor, wouldn't he?"

"He would," says Pierre, soberly.

"So the best solution would be for the mayor — or someone else who's profiting from the deceit — to bop Didier off. Better dead and silent as the tomb, than alive and kiss and tell, huh? What do you think?"

"What do I think? I think it's possible. But what do I know? Am I a detective, or do I run a restaurant and bar? And to tell the truth, I just can't picture the mayor calling up Didier on the phone, asking him if he happened to be in his bath at the moment, then waltzing through the village with his wife's hair dryer in his hand. Can you?" And making clear these are his final words, Pierre picks up a set of keys and moves towards the door of the café.

"Out on my ear," I say as I step into the night and head towards the square and home. And ponder. What if Didier's death had nothing to do with his sexual excesses? What if he had been a hero, of sorts? I look down at Werewolf. "Hey," I say. "What if I've been barking up the wrong tree?"

Werewolf ignores me. He knows perfectly well I know absolutely nothing about barking up any kind of tree. To illustrate the point, he lifts his left leg against a cement planter (courtesy of Lemasson Enterprises).

40

THE MAN WHO MOST OFTEN LOOKS INTO A HORSE'S — OR CHICKEN'S — mouth is, of course, Jean-Paul. On Monday, I call him. "Time to meet," I say. "This evening. In Derval. In the Café des Sports. It's a big enough town. No one knows us. No one will remember seeing us together." But as far as I'm concerned, the thrill of playing our old game of hide-and-seek has worn wafer thin; there's no thrill in it. He'll go along with it though. Most likely.

I can sense Jean-Paul's hesitation. Scared puppy, I think ungraciously. I don't think I like him very much any more. Love is uncontrollable, fleeting. Here in the morning, gone this afternoon. For it to endure, it needs nurturing.

"What time?" he asks with about as much enthusiasm as a man on his way to be guillotined.

"Doesn't matter to me."

"Seven," he says. Very reluctantly. An attitude that would have been crushing to me only a few weeks ago.

I forget about dressing carefully. This is no lover's tryst; the raw material is just going to have to work its charm.

The café is crowded. A lot of *babas cool*, ex-hippie types in their sixties, are sitting around, trying to look all-knowing and disillusioned. Werewolf and I have to wait for half an hour before Jean-Paul deigns to arrive, and it would be very hard to miss his furtive little glances — left, right, behind, in front — as he slinks his way through the forest of tables and chairs. Paranoia doesn't warm the cockles of my heart. This is the same guy who once made it pitter-patter? Really? This is the person for whom I have been racing about, trying to squeeze out the truth behind Didier's death?

"Tell me what you know," Jean-Paul mumbles, as he nervously jerks out a chair at the corner table where I'm sitting. He doesn't need to mumble. We're too far away from the *babas* to be overheard. Not that they're paying attention to either Jean-Paul or me. Not that they're in the least bit curious. Too busy, they are, working on their own image.

"Did the police come to see you?" I ask.

His face turns a rather unattractive yellowish-white. "Police?"

"Not Chantal either?"

"No." He swallows. Drums up a fake smile for the waiter who has come to take his order, drops the smile as soon as he's gone. Looks hunted. "Have you heard anything about the police wanting to talk to us?"

"No," I say calmly. "But you told me you were worried that they'd find Chantal's letters, so I was just wondering. I mean, Didier really did do a lot of sleeping around. Chantal was just one of a lot."

Jean-Paul's mouth twists bitterly. He reaches up, rubs his jaw with his right hand. As if he's got a bad toothache, suddenly. "Which other women did he sleep with?"

"Oh, farmer's wives, perhaps the hairdresser. That English woman, Fiona, who lived out in the cottage just outside the village. And maybe he blackmailed most of them. Maybe."

"How do you know all this?" He looks at me strangely. As if he's noticed I'm an unappealing sort of witch with the nasty talent of casting evil spells.

I shrug. "I don't know anything. As I said, maybe he was blackmailing everyone, maybe he wasn't. What seems certain, though, is that Didier was destructive and vengeful. And so I conclude that if he tried to blackmail Chantal, he might have done the same with the other women in his life."

"How did you get your information?"

"Easy. By listening to village slander."

"Oh." He closes his eyes for a minute as if he's truly weary.

"But you can rest easy. Chantal's name doesn't come up at all. Not even once. So you might be safe. Especially if you destroyed all the letters she wrote to Didier."

"So we're off the hook. For the time being, at least," says Jean-Paul.

"Yeah," I say, watching him closely. "If it's true what you told me."

"If what's true?" He's looking all sharp-eyed now. Not weary anymore. "What's that supposed to mean?"

"That Didier tried to blackmail Chantal."

"What the hell are you getting at?"

"I'll let you know in just a minute. But for right now, I have another question. Are you sleeping with Nicole Malabry?"

"Nicole Malabry?" He sounds surprised. But not very surprised. Just uncomfortable. Very, very uncomfortable. "Why are you asking me this?"

"Are you?" I wonder if I sound jealous. But I haven't forgotten the view of Nicole, elegant in orange silk, made up to perfection, going into his office.

"No, I'm not. I like her. And she's made it fairly obvious she likes me. She's a nice woman. Attractive. But I don't sleep with every woman I find attractive. Is this why you wanted to meet with me? This is what this is all about?" He's trying to sound angry but not quite managing the act.

"Change of direction again," I say. "Let's chat about the Malabrys. Tell me about their intensive chicken farm. As the veterinarian in the area, you know all about it, don't you?"

Jean-Paul is staring at me, wide-eyed with wariness. He waits silently until the waiter slaps down a little cup of espresso coffee on the table and goes away again. "Give me a break," he mutters. "What the hell do the Malabrys have to do with this?"

"That's what I'm trying to find out. This is called following a hunch. That's what you wanted me to try and do, right? Get to the bottom of things. Work out if anyone was going to charge you with murder. As far as my own life goes, I have nothing to lose. I don't have a reputation to protect, and no one in the whole wide world would accuse me of paying Didier's ticket to the nether regions."

He sighs. Looks resigned. Wastes a great amount of time unwrapping a little packet of sugar, stirring in two cubes, watching his own hand moving the spoon. "What exactly do you want to know?" he says finally.

"Everything about the intensive chicken business. How Malabry's farm works."

"There's nothing unusual going on at Malabry's. It's standard practice. Everyone does it. It's what the broiler chicken business is all about."

"So tell me," I say. "And stop sounding so defensive. If you think it's just normal business, what's going on up there, then you should at least have the strength of your own convictions."

"Okay, okay." He shrugs. "You're right. It's not pretty. I don't think you want to hear this. You're a softie. I don't want to offend your sensibilities with ice-cold veterinary shop talk."

"Test me," I say. "I don't really believe everything in life is cute and cuddly."

He shrugs again. Stares into the coffee cup for a while. "Broilers are bought as chicks and stuffed into the chicken houses. Sometimes seventy-five thousand live in sheds that are meant for far less than that number. But the one thing that counts is rapid weight gain, and broilers are those races of chickens that grow the fastest. But even that's not fast enough for the industry. Chickens only have forty-two days to reach maximum size before being carted off to the slaughter house, so they have to be fed massive amounts of growth promoters like avilamycin."

"And that works."

"It certainly does. It works so well that many of the birds can't even support their own weight. Around eighty percent of them have broken bones, skeletal defects and leg problems. The ones that are severely crippled die of starvation and thirst because they can't reach food or water. Others move around by using their wings to drag themselves along the floor."

"Like crutches."

He nods. "That's not all. Because there are so many stuffed together, the units can't be cleaned, and that means the birds spend their lives on wet, dirty, ammonia-sodden litter. They get breast blisters, hock burns, foot lesions, ulceration, and can go blind. They also have heart attacks, respiratory diseases, fatty liver and kidney syndrome plus a whole panoply of bacterial and viral infections. They die like flies in summer because the sheds aren't adequately ventilated, but because of the overcrowding, most of the dead birds can't even be taken out. That's how bacteria spread; that's why there are so many outbreaks of salmonella and campylobacter."

"Delicious. That's what people eat?"

"The farmers try and reduce the risk of disease with antibiotics, but everyone knows that antibiotics weaken our ability to coexist with microbes."

"Everyone knows. Vets and farmers alike?"

"The information has been out there for a long time."

"But everyone ignores it. And all this is normal?"

"Perfectly normal, acceptable, intensive farm practice in all so-called civilized countries, all over the world." Jean-Paul clacks his tiny coffee cup down into his saucer.

"And there's no official protest. No one says anything. Not the mayor, who probably knows, not the state inspectors. Only Didier dared say anything."

Jean-Paul looks at me with faint amusement. "Why would anyone else protest? These are the farming rules. Most people aren't tree huggers like you or Didier. *Of course*, everyone keeps their mouths shut. Malabry's farm brings in money to the village. In professional taxes."

"Right," I say. "Of course, there's another aspect to the story, isn't there? An aspect that's just a tiny bit unsavoury. Didier did say that up at Malabry's, the overcrowding is worse than on normal intensive farms. And that they are abusive in the amount of antibiotics they use. But stuff like that pays off, doesn't it. The Malabrys drive a Mercedes, they have big-time credit cards, wear chic clothes."

"So?"

"Okay. Fine. So I'm a tree hugger. But it does seem a little unjust. The Malabrys are doing very well financially. And other farmers whose methods are a bit doubtful are also doing well, right? And since everyone wants to go on doing well, they're willing and able to grease a few palms in the village, just so no one calls attention to their methods. And that means everyone on the municipal council gets a little raise. Not a lot, just a little."

"Possible," says Jean-Paul, but he's looking down at the table top, not at me.

"Say, four percent?"

The tabletop is fascinating, evidently. The fake wood swirls in the brown plastic have really nabbed Jean-Paul's attention.

"Come on, kid. Cat got your tongue?" I prod.

"Say, four percent," he says, finally. "It's possible."

"And everyone is satisfied."

"Communism, of a sort," he mumbles. "Back-scratching. Everyone takes care of everyone else in the village."

"It's also called bribing everyone."

"Also," admits Jean-Paul. "But it's often a two-way street, you know. If a farmer who's on the municipal council wants the road to his farm improved and the mayor knows he can count on him to vote for his company, the farmer gets his road. Little things like that go on all the time."

"Do you get bribed, too? You must." I mean, while I'm at it, why not show him I'm condemning him, too?

"I remember when I first started out in practice," he begins, almost dreamily. "I had gone out to a farm where there were around a hundred cows. I was there to take the blood tests that indicated the cattle were healthy before slaughter. The farmer presented me with ten cows to test. Not a hundred. So I asked him where the other cows were. And he said to me, 'Oh, all you need to do is test these ten. Take enough blood to put it into lots of vials. No one will know. That's what the previous vet did all the time.' And he looked at me, laughed and handed me a wad of bills."

"Did you take it?"

Jean-Paul swings a look that could kill in my direction. "Always ready to think the worst of me? No, I didn't. I'd risk my career in a situation like that. What if something went wrong, if there was something wrong with the herd? No way I'd do that, especially then in my younger, more idealistic days." He smiles wryly. "But other vets did and do. They take bribes, they play the game."

"And Nicole and Bernard Malabry never have to worry if their farm isn't up to standard, that their chickens are living in horrendous conditions. That they die like flies. You don't say anything. And the mayor doesn't bother sending in an inspector." I lean back in my chair, try to look casual.

Jean-Paul is resigned. "Look, local veterinarians have nothing to do with the intensive chicken farms, not Malabry's farm nor any other. Vets never get into those places. They are controlled from beginning to end by name brand companies. For example, you've heard of Poulets Saint-Demain, right? It's a popular label. Their broiler chickens are in every supermarket, and they run ads showing pretty white hens pecking around in a big green field filled with white daisies, yellow dandelions and red campion. Saint-Demain claims it produces a quality product. But all big name brand companies are the same. They're the ones who deliver the chicks to the battery farms. They're the ones who send in their own technicians to see how the chicks are raised. Those technicians aren't veterinarians. They don't care about animal welfare. All they want to know is if the birds are reaching maximum size. If they aren't, the dose of growth promoter is increased. And it's these same companies that pick the birds up and take them to the slaughterhouses. That's how it works, these days. So even if I opened my mouth, questioned the whole process, I'd be ignored."

"And you would also be *persona non grata*. Because you might be cutting into everyone's private supplementary income."

"Precisely."

"Did Didier threaten the Malabrys?"

"I got the impression that he did. The Malabrys hinted at it one evening when we were having dinner together, although I'm not certain what he could have done to stop their operation. Didier always did have a tendency to push things too far." The faint derisive curl of Jean-Paul's mouth lets me know exactly what he thinks of that. But then again, he's hardly going to be indulgent towards his wife's ex-lover.

"Which would be a good reason for the Malabrys to get rid of him. He was probably out for vengeance anyway because the mayor humiliated him in public. And Didier wasn't the kind of guy who would take humiliation lying down. So he would have been more than happy to expose everyone."

"So what do you want to do? Arrest the Malabrys?"

I lean over, reach for his coffee spoon, toy with it. "Of course not. I don't even know if they are the guilty ones. I might never know. And this conversation is just between the two of us, right? I don't fancy being electrocuted in my bathtub, then bloating up and ponging. Even if it is the village fashion, these days."

He reaches over, squeezes my hand, the one that's holding the spoon. "You did a great job. I didn't think you'd delve into things like this. Just to get me off the hook. You're wonderful."

I wonder if he really thinks I'll believe that his little gesture of tenderness and sweet words are sincere. They aren't; I know that by now. "Jean-Paul, you didn't think I'd find out about all of this stuff, did you? I mean, when you asked me to snoop around, you thought that I'd never learn about the farms, right? Or about the bribery. You thought I'd just stick to the bed-hopping sort of gossip. That I wasn't really clever enough to go too far. That's what I meant when I said I wasn't sure I believed you about Didier trying to blackmail Chantal. Could be you tried to put me on a false trail. What you really wanted to know was if anyone was associating your name with the Malabrys, linking you with Didier's death. Tell me I'm right."

He shrugs. It's confirmation of something, I suppose. But he decides, very wisely, not to answer.

"In the end, it's the poor chickens I feel awful about," I say. "Those guys are innocent. But at least their slaughterhouse death means the end of an absolutely atrocious life."

"Almost," says Jean-Paul, resigned.

I stare at him. "Almost what?"

"When it's time for broilers to be transported to the slaughterhouse, gangs of catchers are sent in. They have weak bones anyway, the birds, because of all the growth promoters and lack of room they've had to move around in. But because of the way they're handled by the catchers — they're grabbed by their legs and shoved into the crates — they suffer from dislocated hips, broken wings and legs. When they arrive at the slaughterhouse, they're hung upside-down and dragged through an electrically charged water bath. The bath is supposed to stun them before they get to an automatic neck cutter. But technicians claim that high current causes carcass damage, so many aren't stunned at all. And because they aren't all the same size anyway, many chickens — say a quarter of them — are horribly mutilated by the neck cutter but still alive when they enter a scalding tank that makes plucking easier." Jean-Paul raises his hands in a vague gesture of resignation. "So you see, it's a system that has little to do with vets and with alleviating animal suffering."

"What a lovely world," I say. "Quite an advance from the old days of mixed farming. Bring on the new. You eat chicken, by the way?"

He's looking uncomfortable again. "Doesn't everyone?"

"Does Nicole Malabry like kinky sex?"

He starts at the sudden change of topic. "Does what?"

"You heard me. Some of the village gossips have her linked with Didier. People saw her going into his house several times. She wasn't very discreet about it either. I mean, what did she think? That people imagined she was such a chic city lady, she'd never stoop to screwing a mere village employee? But just imagine how fantastic the game was! Not just any old Lady Chatterley and her lover, that story. Nicole and hubby are running a scummy business, and she knows very well that Didier is violently opposed to what they're doing. It's playing with fire, all right. Imagine what would happen if hubby found out. What would he do? I mean, his wife is sleeping with the arch-enemy. And then, just to top things off, Nicole starts having it off with the local vet, too. That's what I mean by kinky. Adding danger and manipulation to just plain bad behaviour."

"And what keeps the little idea that I'm screwing Nicole in your head? More village gossip?" His eyes have narrowed, are angry.

"No. Just observation. Seeing a perfectly primped Nicole Malabry waltzing into your office. Hearing your wife, Chantal, saying that you find Nicole just adorable. Me not believing your story about why you couldn't come to see me."

"Fine." Jean-Paul stands up, gets ready to run.

"So does she? And what kind of pillow talk do you have?"

"You're sick, you know that. Sick." He pushes his way through the café, passes the motionless *babas*, stirs up the dust that's been settling on them for hours, slams the door.

"A perverse personality, that's what I have," I say to Werewolf, who is busy scratching one ear with his hind paw.

41

"WHAT HAPPENED TO THE CHICKENS?" I ASK MONSIEUR DOUSPIS over a violent blare of electronic beeps signalling the correct answer has been given to another idiotic question posed by a well-loved, grinning television moderator.

Monsieur Douspis looks at me uncomprehendingly. "What chickens?"

"Didier's chickens."

"Oh. Those." He grins, glances slyly over at Madame Douspis who is peeling an onion with her sharp little paring knife. She snorts.

"Eaten," she says mildly.

"What?"

"Didier isn't there to take care of them, so we ate them all. Me, Monsieur Vadepied, Madame Filoche, Madame Pierrefonds, Madame Filoche, Monsieur Pouttier. We shared them out. Even the mayor had a few. He said we could do it. Didn't belong to anyone anymore."

"They were all killed? But they were special chickens!" I am appalled. "Didier selected them. They were special breeds! I would have taken care of them forever. They could have lived with me!"

"Tough, some of them were. Tough as old rubber. Can't let chickens get old like he did. Have to cook them for ages. Tough and stringy. Not even worth the effort of cooking them, some. In the supermarket, you get birds that are soft. Not like those old hens of Didier's. Bred to be eaten, chickens are. They're meant for eating, animals. We don't get sentimental about things like that the way you foreigners do. You people from the country of Québec."

42

Fontenay-le-Léger doesn't seem to have budged one single inch into the present since I was here last Thursday. The fifteen-odd houses are still slumbering around the closed church; the sky is still grey. Although it's six days later, Marie-Jeanne's oval-shaped form is still behind the bar of her café; she is still wearing the same puce jacket, the same purple bagging trousers and cheap fake jewels; she is still wiping glasses with the same grubby towel. The only difference is that the waterlogged customer has been replaced by Loïc, Marie-Jeanne's man. An unshaven, stringy, grey-tinged person, he's busy shoving the end of a meaty-smelling baguette into his gob.

"Good stuff," he says and grins widely, revealing an unappealing mouthful of half-chewed mush.

"What is it?"

"*Rillettes*. Marie-Jeanne makes her own."

"Oh," I say, then decide that I should seem interested about this local speciality even if I'm not. I turn to Marie-Jeanne with an amazed look. "You make your own? Really? How interesting. What exactly goes into that?"

"Pork," she answers reluctantly. She doesn't really want me here. She doesn't like other women talking to Loïc, her prized possession. She thinks I just might be nurturing the secret desire to snag him out of her clutches and into mine. "Cousin of mine kills three pigs: one for him, one for his daughter, one for us. Cut out the leg, roasts, make head cheese out of the head, eat the ears separately, deep fried, put the brains in butter. All the rest is ground up and turned into *rillettes*. All the fat. Sometimes twenty kilos of fat in a pig."

"You like *rillettes*?" asks Loïc.

"I might," I say, not wishing to offend, although, to be frank, the very thought of the stuff is awful to me. "It's just that I don't eat meat, you see."

Loïc looks smug, suddenly, as if he's in on a secret. "Don't have pigs in your country, do you? Don't eat pork over there. Forbidden to eat pork, right?"

"Where's that?" I ask, confused. "In Canada?"

"Canada. Country where you come from."

"Of course there are pigs in Canada."

"Not allowed to with your religion and all. Like Algeria. Morocco."

"Oh. I see what you mean. Well, uh, Canada's not an Islamic country. Not the last time I looked, anyway."

Loïc's mouth makes a little moue. He's letting me know he doesn't believe a word of it.

"Lots of French people in Canada, you know. Just like here." It's the only reasonable argument I can come up with.

"Not like France just the same. Speak with an accent, you do. Like people from England."

"Because English is my first language. I come from the province of Ontario, not Québec," I say in an attempt to simplify things.

"Québec *is* Canada." Loïc looks at me with pity, as if there's a lot I don't understand.

I decide to give up. Another war I'll never win in my lifetime. "Actually, it's not pigs I want to talk about, but chickens. We were talking about Didier when I was here last, remember, Marie-Jeanne? And Didier was really enthusiastic about raising rare breeds of chickens as a hobby. Do you know how he got interested in that?"

Marie-Jeanne looks at me as if I should know the answer already. "Because of Marsan. Was Monsieur Marsan's hobby."

"Monsieur Marsan? Who in heaven's name is he?"

Marie-Jeanne wings a secret look in Loïc's direction, as if asking for permission to gossip. But Loïc, intent on his chow, isn't looking her way. So she finishes wiping the glass, puts down the limp, greyish towel, gets into gear. "Marsan took care of Didier when he was a kid. Took him into his own house. Fed him, dressed him, made sure he went to school, did his homework. Nice man. I didn't like his wife much. Interfering bitch, always wanting to gossip, blacken people's name. But he was nice enough. Took charge of Didier or he'd have been spending the nights in the fields, avoiding that drunken mother of his. Have ended up in the streets or prison, maybe, if he didn't get a little love and attention from someone. That's what Marsan gave him. Marsan also raised chickens, specialty chickens. Got Didier interested. Gave him something to care about, something to take care of. That's how Didier learned responsibility, got the job as *garde champêtre*."

"He certainly sounds like a good man, Marsan," I agree enthusiastically. This is a new, fresh, juicy lead to follow. "I'd love to meet him. Where does he live?"

"In the cemetery."

"You mean he's dead?"

"Ten years."

"And his wife?"

"Eight years."

"So I can't go talk to them."

"Not without a Ouija board, you can't."

"Did they have any kids of their own?"

"One. Daughter. Raised with Didier, but thought she was something, she did. Better than everyone else in the village. Should have seen how she carried on. Makeup, fancy clothes — you'd have thought she grew up in the Château de Versailles, not on a little farm, modest as you get. Modest isn't the word, even. Dirt poor, just a few acres to scratch out. But the way she carried on! No one good enough for her around here. Spoiled rotten by her mother, if you ask me. Silly ideas put into her head."

"And where is this daughter at the moment?"

"Gone."

"To the cemetery, too?"

Marie-Jeanne snickers. "Village cemetery too good for her. No, left for the big city, Nicole did."

"Paris?"

"No. Bourges. And of course, Didier didn't get a cent when the farm was sold."

"Why should Didier have gotten any money for the farm? He wasn't a Marsan. He was just treated nicely by them."

"Might have been a Marsan. According to people around here, he might. Said Marsan was probably his father. Looked like him, too. A lot. Didier's mum screwing around with everyone when she was in her cups. Men being what they are, taking every woman who offers herself. Then Didier being taken in by the Marsans like he was their kid. Taught all about chickens."

"And the daughter never came back?"

"Came back here, all right. Only to bury her parents, sell the farm and run with the cash, greedy, rich bitch."

"Not all that rich," I temper. "I mean, selling a modest little dirt-scratching farm doesn't exactly turn anyone into a millionaire."

Marie-Jeanne's jaw juts. "English buying up everything hereabouts. Paying top prices. Pay anything anyone asks. Just to invade our country. Don't leave anything for the locals to live in. Should send them all back to where they came from. All of them."

"Except the spleen," says Loïc, suddenly animated by some deep, secret thought.

Marie-Jeanne and I turn to stare at him.

"Don't use the spleen in *rillettes*," he says, nodding. "Feed that to the dog. But the lungs go in all right. Good stuff."

"Oh. Right. Well, thanks for the information." I get off the bar stool I'm perched on, determined to begin moving in the direction of the door and away from the meaty smell, just in case Loïc insists I have a taste. And suddenly stop. Bourges? Marie-Jeanne said Nicole Marsan had gone to Bourges? It's not such a very big place, Bourges. It's not the main destination of everyone in the country. "The daughter. Marsan's daughter, Nicole. Did she learn about chickens, too?"

Marie-Jeanne shrugs. "Had to. Marsan being so big on them like that. But you couldn't interest Nicole Marsan in that kind of thing. Not her. Wanted to be a city lady. Wanted to learn to be a secretary in Bourges, go work in an office. Marry well. That was her style."

It's too much of a coincidence. It really is. "Do you know if she came ever back to this area to live?"

Loïc looks blank. Marie-Jeanne smirks. "Wouldn't show up here in Fontenay-le-Léger, the little hussy; made too many enemies. Wouldn't want to be associated with a small-time place like this. And then leaving home like that, never coming back once to see her parents, not even her mother when her father died. Only interested in getting her hands on the money for the farm when both of them were pushing up daisies. Anyone from here ever saw her again, they'd give her a piece of their mind."

"Do you know the chicken farmers in Épineux-le-Rainsouin? The Malabrys? Nicole and Bernard?"

Marie-Jeanne's smirk is still in place. "Folk from Épineux don't bother coming here to this village. Too small for them. Not quite good enough. Think they're all living in paradise, folk in Épineux do."

"But you'd recognize Nicole if you saw her again?"

"People don't change that much. Not even when they're covered in fancy clothes. Knew Nicole like I know the back of my hand. I'd recognize her, of course."

Good reason for Nicole Malabry *née* Marsan not showing up at Didier's funeral. Especially since she had known him very well indeed. Well enough to pay him visits in his pink cement house.

43

On Thursday afternoon, I walk out of the centre of Épineux-le-Rainsouin, where the old medieval houses are laid out in a spiral pattern with the church as the centre. Beyond the village boundary lie strips of arable land and pasture, once surrounded by hedges, high trees and swampland. The major agricultural product of this region was hemp, used for the cottage linen industry. It was arduous work growing hemp: plants had to be pulled out of the ground by hand, tied into bales, left to dry, untied again and spread out to bleach in the sun. With homemade tools (now long-vanished), it was spun into linen thread in farm kitchens, then woven into clothing. It was coarse cloth, indeed, and when roads improved, softer quality cloth arrived, bringing local hemp production to a close. In the twentieth century, wetlands were finally drained, and the fields, oddly shaped after centuries of being divided amongst heirs, were redistributed and their size increased by the destruction of trees and hedges. But wetlands filter water; trees prevent flooding and reduce runoff. The disappearance of both resulted in an increase in soil pollution and the depletion of groundwater. Modern farmers, eager to benefit from European Community subsidies, plant vast fields of thirsty corn in ground that is now hard and dry, and the resulting crop is shrivelled, stunted, useless. Farmers are compensated by the government.

Builders of housing developments do not respect traditional village patterns. Our own housing development in Épineux-le-Rainsouin, built in a former apple orchard, also required the destruction of a coppice of mixed wood and several kilometres of hedges. The earth has been gouged out. A little hill, once here, has been levelled. Deep open ditches have been dug to cope with the rush of spring water and sludge. Cement covers pathways, roads, fields, buries a once gentle little stream.

Here the new houses are squat, graceless, untraditional structures, covered in yellow cement, possessing PVC roll-down shutters, PVC windows and PVC doors. Each is surrounded by a chainlink fence. There is no tree in sight; none of the new inhabitants wish to plant any. Where houses are still under construction, I see that their walls are made of cinder block, not brick. Thin planks of wood stand naked against the sky, waiting for imitation slate. As Werewolf and I pass, a white PVC door opens. It is our mayor, Monsieur Aimable Lemasson, who stands there, watching me, witnessing my curiosity. I raise my hand, wave a friendly greeting. He merely nods in return, his face wearing an inscrutable expression. He continues to watch me as I move further down the housing development, down to where the empty streets are already paved and ready to welcome the other squat, graceless houses that will be built along them.

Only once do I look back, pretending to adjust Werewolf's leash. Lemasson is still there. Still staring at me. I hope I look like a nice lady and not a very nosy one, one who links people together, who knows who talks to whom, how information is passed on from village employees to chicken farmers to veterinarians. Just a mild foreign lady out walking her dog, admiring the new buildings of the village housing development.

44

AT ELEVEN ON SATURDAY MORNING, WEREWOLF AND I ARE OUT ENJOYING the early morning warmth in my jungle of a back garden and debating which varieties of tomatoes I will plant this year, when I hear the telephone ringing in the house. Racing like mad, I throw myself down the garden steps into the courtyard, run into the hallway and make a wild grab for the receiver.

"Hello?" I gasp.

"Get over here. Now!" I instantly recognize the soft, endearing snarl. It belongs to Jean-Paul, my lover (or is it ex-lover?). Nothing warms the cockles of one's heart more than sweet words.

"Over where?" I ask, stupefied by the commanding tone.

"My house. I'm at home. Chantal is here with me."

"Right," I say sarcastically (the stupor is wearing off). "Yes, sir. On the double, sir. Your wish is my command, Prince. Just give me a little hint; is this a formal invitation? Full regalia or just tie and tux?"

He slams down the phone. Charming.

Well, well. I have half a mind to go back to the garden and continue contemplating tomatoes. What's all the fuss about? What exactly have I done wrong? What happened to politeness? Where has the gratitude of yesteryear gone? Not that I'm scared or worried. Just nonplussed, and not a little vexed. Also, almost as innocent as a daisy in an early spring field, although, unlike the daisy, curious as hell. I guess Chantal told him that I was prying, prodding information out of her about their anniversary celebration. I knew he wouldn't like that.

I tell Werewolf I'll be back soon; hopefully, the reunited couple doesn't have the intention of knocking me off and burying me under the yellow cowbells pushing up their heads along the riverbank. But just to insure my chances of survival, I glance into Madame Douspis's window, wriggle my fingers in greeting. "Morning," I call.

She swings the window open. "Going to Pierre's for your coffee as usual?" she asks.

"Nope. Just taking a stroll over to see the vet and his wife."

She looks surprised. I am doing something unpredictable. This will soon be a news bulletin of great worth, shared first with her husband, then with Mesdames Filoche and Beauducel. She's dying to ask me for details about this chic invitation, of course, but I merely give an airy little wave, head down the road towards the former convent where Jean-Paul and Chantal live.

"Finally getting a foot in the manse door," I muse aloud. Even when I talk to myself, I can be sarcastic.

Just south of the village, the old convent is well-hidden behind high hedges. Only the high, pointed, red-tiled roof, mottled by moss and poking up behind a cluster of elms, chestnut trees and poplars tells you it's there at all. And of course, the forbidding-looking iron gate, now standing open at the gravel driveway that passes stone stables. The grey granite walls of the house are surrounded by multicoloured rose bushes; the window trim is deep red. A pathway leads to a massive wooden door with an old knocker that looks as though it knew the hand of one of Louis XIII's lackeys. In other words, it's quite a set-up Jean-Paul and Chantal have.

Jean-Paul answers the door, thin-lipped, white-faced, as hostile as an arrogant old aristocrat receiving a miserable, no-status serf. No cheery hello, no affectionate peck on the cheek. No secret flash-of-desire eye contact. He simply ushers me in, precedes me down a long corridor and into a living room.

The room is luxurious, to say the least. Huge, old-fashioned windows give out to the lush vegetation of a traditional back garden, one typical of an old religious institution. There are cushy-looking sofas, bookshelves in dark wood, and a huge stone carved fireplace that dates from the sixteenth century, at least. The floor is elegant patterned wood parquet, waxed to a perfect gloss, and the tables and chairs must have been kicking around in the old days when Marie-Antoinette was playing shepherdess and Louis XVI was fooling around with his hobby, making locks. The walls have the ancient golden hue of unpainted chalk and sand; the beams are honey-coloured and glowing.

The whole scene is an eye-opener for me. A revelation, to say the least. It's life having a good chuckle at my expense. Did I really and truly think that Jean-Paul was ever going to leave all this for me? Have I really been fooling myself for so long? Really? Well, even if I have, I can be excused. I just didn't have all the elements at my disposal. I had never seen this setting. This is what's important to a man like Jean-Paul. My house with its dark passage, the rooms of an old, cheap village hotel — all of that is fine for a dalliance. But this is what he has worked for all these years. This is what he wants.

Chantal is slumped into a corner of a sofa. Despite her tan — or perhaps because of it — she's a rather sickly orange colour. Her dyed, bright blonde hair looks dried out, dead. Jean-Paul sits down beside her, motions me into an armchair opposite. This way, they can both stare at me. I stare right back in a cold fish, undaunted way. They both look awful, cushy surroundings, big-time consumer goods, swanky antique folderols, or no.

"You rang?" I say facetiously, while raising my eyebrows in a stab at insolence. I'm not overly fond of high drama. Especially when I'm the only one on stage who hasn't yet read the script.

Jean-Paul doesn't even bother answering. Instead, he reaches over to one of the dark wood side tables beside the sofa (probably seventeenth-century), picks up a piece of paper, and shoves it over in my direction.

I take it, look at it curiously. It's a letter. Undated, brief, to the point. And like all such disgusting epistles, unsigned. It's not even whimsical, filled with colourful cut-out letters from newspapers and magazines, but a neat computer printout. It states that the sender is in possession of letters — love letters, to be exact. Letters written by Chantal to Didier. That if Chantal wishes to get these letters back, she should send the amount of two thousand euros (cash, of course) to the following address: Thomas Fredon, La Basse Chauvière, Launay. In other words, to my old address. The letter was written by Thomas? Thomas? My Thomas? My old love? The one who died on a rainy night? The one we buried on a sunny, hot afternoon in August?

There is a warning. Chantal's letters are in a safe place with a third party, and if there is any hitch, they will be made public.

I look at the vile thing, read it over and over. My brain, temporarily on holiday break, can't be relied on to make connections, so I read the letter until I have all the crummy wording down by heart. How could Thomas have written this? I wonder crazily. Thomas is dead. Has been dead all these years. Unless he isn't. And if he isn't, why is he blackmailing Chantal? Why hasn't he contacted me? As I said, I'm not making any connections. There's only confusion mixing itself up with a sort of ecstasy. Something on the line of: "Oh, so Thomas isn't dead after all. Isn't that nice? Perhaps we can even meet for dinner. And I wonder who it was we put in his coffin."

Then I look over at Chantal and Jean-Paul. He is looking at me with stony-faced dislike. She still looks defeated, like a Michelin tire with a puncture. Seeing them snaps me out of my reverie. At least it does that much.

"I don't understand," I say finally. "I really don't. I mean, Thomas died, didn't he?"

Neither Jean-Paul nor Chantal speak for a moment. They keep on staring. Then Jean-Paul says, "The name rang a bell. I thought about it for a while. Thomas Fredon. La Basse Chauvière. And then I remembered what you told me, your story about where you lived before you came here. The man you lived with. The one you met in Canada. The ethnologist. And I knew it was you."

"Knew what? Was me? Who?" I say slowly, separating each word as though I'm talking to someone who has just learnt the language. Then comprehension leaks in, slowly like water from a blocked tap. "Of course, Thomas is dead," I say, speaking more to myself than to these two nasty characters perched on their expensive sofa just in front of me. I lean forward, rattle the letter in the air, incredulous. "Let me get this straight. You think I wrote this thing?"

"Yes," says Jean-Paul, simulating perfectly the voice and look of a big wheel in the Inquisition.

"I can't believe you actually just said that. I mean, you think I'm the sort of person who would blackmail someone? You think I'd do something like this?" I get the distinct feeling that I'm sounding like a victim all of a sudden. Injustice does that; it turns one into a protesting, jabbering idiot.

He continues to look at me with self-righteous arrogance. Then relapses into bitterness and even maudlin sentimentality. "I trusted you. You said you would help us. You said you were on our side and I believed you. You said you would help clear this mess up. That's why I confided in you about our problem. And this is what you do." Now he's the one playing victim. I'll bet anything he hasn't told Chantal he's been my lover for the last few years.

"Well, shit," I say. Which is neither elegant nor eloquent. But I'm getting angry. Really angry. Finally. "I mean you are joking, aren't you?" I squint at him. No, he's not joking. Not at all. "Are you really that stupid? Do you really think that I'm that stupid? That I would go around digging up information about what's going on in this village so I can cover my tracks? That I murdered Didier so I could get my dirty paws on his letters and blackmail Chantal?"

Jean-Paul doesn't answer. Just keeps on looking wounded and sorry for himself. So I go on, "Look, you were the one who told me you refused to let Didier blackmail you, right? And now you think I'm crazy enough to write you an anonymous letter and try the same trick? And not only that, I'm so crazy that I leave a trail a hundred kilometres wide so you would know it was me? Because I have this mad desire to be caught and punished for my evil deeds?"

I stand up. I'm just about furious enough to break the place up — gilt, plush, irreplaceable antiques and all. Not that I would, of course. I'm basically a good, respectful *bourgeoise* at heart despite certain cranky aspects of my character and lifestyle. "Well, I'll be on my way. Have a nice afternoon, the two of you. And remember, it's cash I want. I don't accept cheques or credit cards. Too much cheating with that kind of stuff, these days."

I walk towards the door, forbidding myself to tag a string of insults onto the cheerio.

"Wait," Jean-Paul calls out just as I am about to fade into the hallway.

I stop for a split second. Half turn. "Fuck off," I say. I hate him. I hate the two of them. And as for their cushy interior and their showcase marriage, they can have all of it. Just get me out of here.

"I'm sorry," he says, suddenly. Surprisingly.

"Don't go, please," calls Chantal plaintively. "We're sorry. Really, we are."

"Sorry about what?"

"Look, if we've got it wrong …"

"You *have* got it wrong," I spit, deeply distrusting this sudden and wishy-washy change of heart.

"Then let's talk," says Jean-Paul quickly. "Please. I said I'm sorry. We both did. Please. Come back. Let's work this out." He's actually pleading.

I can't believe this situation. First they're going to chop me into animal chow; the next minute, I'm as welcome as perfumed, wild strawberries in winter. "Talk what out?" I'm still at the door, just dying to get the hell out of here. Get out of this whole situation. It has nothing to do with me, after all. I want my peace and quiet. Finally. To hell with bad building and corruption and blackmail and crummy friendships and payoffs and dead chickens.

"Let's talk about what's going on. Let's try and understand this. Together." Jean-Paul looks as if he's ready to cry. Chantal's eyes are already watering with, no doubt, a great big dose of self-pity.

I sigh, then relent. Turn fully around, lean against the door jamb with a definite feeling of defeat. I'm as much involved in this as they are, like it or not. They've managed to hook me. And the blackmailer is, after all, using my old address and the address and name of my dead love.

We all stare at each other in silence for a while.

"You *did* live at La Basse Chauvière, didn't you?" Jean-Paul finally asks.

"I did."

"Who lives there now?"

"No one. The place is abandoned, windows smashed in, door hanging ajar. No one lives there, aside from the mice, rats, frogs, toads, voles, spiders and snakes. The place can't be bought or sold because of miles of family debts and wars between Thomas's children. The lawyers are making a bundle on the job. The law suits will end eventually, although not before the year 2030, I reckon."

"Do you get mail there?"

"Not me. But Thomas still does. Not real mail; invitations to art exhibitions, concerts, conferences, things like that. Junk mail. Except that he's dead," I add inanely and have the odd, bleak, abandoned feeling that he has now, somehow, managed to die twice.

"Why do his letters still go there?" asks Chantal.

"Because we weren't married," I say, raising my fingers in a hopeless, useless sort of gesture. "And because we weren't married, I can't transfer his mail to my own address. That's the rule at the post office; you can't sign a mail transfer order in place of someone else. Even if they're dead and won't be showing up until a next reincarnation. So I go out there once a month or so, take a peek into the mailbox. Just to see if anything important arrives. I suppose you can call it a sentimental journey because nothing important really does come in. It's just become sort of a habit. A sentimental thing that I do."

"And who knows you do it?"

"Beats me."

"Who knows you lived there?"

"You do, Jean-Paul. I never told anyone else the story. Just you." Which isn't strictly true, I realize. Martine knows. She knows the whole story. But would she blackmail anyone? She could, of course, have mentioned my old address to someone else — to someone like Tim or Fiona or even someone else in the village. But I'm not going to mention Martine's name here, not to Jean-Paul and Chantal. I'll deal with that problem later.

"Sure." Jean-Paul jerks his head back. "So I write letters to Chantal and myself telling me I'm blackmailing us, and I can retrieve my own money at a haunted house."

"Very funny." It is, sort of. "Honestly and truly, I haven't got the faintest idea how to untangle all this information. All I can say is, someone knows an awful lot about quite a bit. And I'd like to know how that someone got their hands on Chantal's letters, too. Whoever it is, is a sincerely nasty piece of work. And if that person also happens to have murdered Didier to get his hands on the letters, then Didier, awful as he might have been, was a furry kitty-cat, in comparison. I guess it's pretty clear that Didier made copies of Chantal's letters before you ripped them up. Or you didn't rip all of them up, after all."

Both Chantal and Jean-Paul look at each other soberly. Look back at me, nod in unison, like a couple of cute springy toys.

"Of course, Didier could also have left the letters, or copies of them, with someone he thought he could trust." I'm thinking, of course, of Tim, but decide to keep that thought to myself, too. For the time being, anyway.

"Possibly," Jean-Paul says. "But don't forget, whoever it is also knows about you and Thomas and La Basse Chauvière."

"Not exactly common knowledge," I say. "It's far enough away, fifty kilometres, down at the southern edge of the *département*."

Jean-Paul stands. "Let's drive out there now. I want to see the place."

I gape at him. "What for? To watch the weeds grow? Believe me, there's no one out there. No one's living there."

"But someone is there to receive the money."

"Look," I say with infinite patience. "First you have to send the money, right? No one is going to be stupid enough to just go and hang around there so they can be caught. Whoever it is will at least wait until the mail arrives."

"So what do you suggest?"

I ponder for a minute or two. "La Basse Chauvière is in a hollow. You can see it from the high road that runs to the east. I remember I used to look over when I was coming from that direction in my car, just to see if the lights were on. To see if Thomas was home yet. From there, you can probably see if the postman's car is driving down the lane. My guess is, whoever is doing the blackmailing has checked that out, too. Whoever it is will be pretty cautious. We can't just go out there and snoop around."

"So what can we do?"

"We'll get a bundle of papers," exclaims Chantal excitedly. "We'll put them in an envelope and send them to La Basse Chauvière on Monday morning. Then we can go out there the next day, on Tuesday; it should arrive by then. We can hide out and pounce on the person who picks up the mail."

I look at her. It sounds like a pretty stupid idea to me, like some boarding school adventure story written for twelve-year-olds. She's already seeing herself in the role of Nancy Drew or Trixie Belden. I mean, come right down to it, would a blackmailer really take the risk of being caught red-handed? Only if he were also pretty dull-witted. But I have to admit it: I can't think of a better solution myself.

"There's an old green lane that I know of, completely overgrown, but we can approach the house from there. It's about a two-kilometre walk from the village of Launay. But if you ask my opinion, this doesn't sound like it's going to work. Why not go to the police, Chantal? They'd be better at tracing things. Taking care of this. Some stuff we just can't do on our own."

"No!" It comes out as a shriek. "Let's try this first. Then if it doesn't work, we can go to the police after. I just don't want them poking around into my private life if I can avoid it."

"There are probably other women in the village who are also being blackmailed," I say, exercising patience. "This might all come out sooner or later, you know."

"I don't care," says Chantal petulantly. "I'm just tired of the whole situation."

"Okay," I say and shrug. "If that's what you want."

"We'll all go out there on Tuesday. What time does the mailman usually arrive?"

"Early. Around nine-thirty. If the letter doesn't get there on Tuesday, we'll go back the next day. Whoever is going to pick it up isn't going to let two thousand euros sit around in a mailbox for days on end. I'll come here in the morning. At around seven. I'll make sure no one sees me. We don't want anyone in the village to know we are driving away together. We don't want whoever it is to get suspicious."

I stop talking, look at the two of them. They are drinking in every word I'm saying. Like it's Moses who's speaking. I decide to do a little fishing of my own. "Tell me. Did Nicole Malabry grow up in this area?"

Both Chantal and Jean-Paul stare at me silently; their faces close up like sterilized jam jars.

"Come on."

"She said something to that effect," says Chantal with great reluctance. "But she asked us not to mention it."

"Fine." And I just can't resist sneaking in a bit of sarcasm. "For this big stakeout we're planning, wear green, both of you. Try and look like shrubs."

45

"Why did you tell Tim about Thomas and me?" I ask Martine on Saturday afternoon. We are under the old apple trees at the bottom of her garden; Martine is hunkered down, pouring apple cider into two mugs. It's not the local homemade cider of earlier times, brewed from sweet apples (for taste), bitter apples (for conservation) and acidic ones (for the golden colour). Collected in baskets when the air had a chilly autumnal snap, apples were heaped in farm courtyards and left to ripen. When the apples were ready, neighbours arrived to help with the pressing, then the pouring of perfumed golden juice into the wooden kegs where it would ferment. Work done, feasting and dancing began. Of course, the opening of the casks months later also called for neighbourly merrymaking, and if the year's brew proved to be particularly good, a barrel was brought to the local café and shared out. Nowadays, cider is an industrial product; it comes in glass or plastic bottles, is purchased in supermarkets. On farms, in gardens and lanes, cider apples are left to rot where they fall, enjoyed only by sleepy, autumn wasps.

Martine settles the cider bottle carefully in the grass, leans back on her heels, stares at me. "What am I supposed to have told Tim?"

"That I once lived in La Basse Chauvière with Thomas. About the accident. About my past." I throw out the accusation calmly, flatly, with no preamble. I have absolutely no real reason for believing she did tell him, of course. But if Chantal's love letters are in his possession and he is the one now trying to blackmail Jean-Paul and Chantal, Tim could only have found out about the La Basse Chauvière from Martine. Okay, I know it doesn't really add up — why would Tim blackmail Chantal — although I suppose he could have a motive that I just haven't figured out yet. And if I confront Martine like this, I figure she'll be too surprised to defend herself.

"What are you getting at?" Her voice is as calm as mine but her eyes have narrowed down to slits.

"Just asking a question."

"About Tim and Fiona? Again?" Her lip curls into a sneer.

"About me, actually. About the confidences we shared, you and I. Confidences that weren't for public consumption. You knew that."

"Let me get this straight. You're accusing me of having told Tim and Fiona or everybody else about your past? You're telling me I did? Not asking me?"

"I suppose so. And I guess that's very rude of me, right? So I'll start again. Did you tell Tim and Fiona or anyone else about Thomas and me?"

"No. No, I don't think I did." She is very angry, I see. Yet still fighting to keep her voice level. "But do let me tell you about yourself, about you and your endless questions. Questions, questions, always questions. Whenever you need to get yourself out of a complicated situation, you ask questions. And you know me: if I can possibly help you, I give you a solution. But the solutions, you don't accept them, do you? You can't. If I explain why Didier's death must have been an accident or suicide, you decide it was murder. If I tell you Didier tried to screw Fiona, you poke around until you get some half-assed proof that she was in love with him. And in the end, you piss me off. Because behind all your apparent openness, behind all your questions, there are other elements. Things you don't talk about, things no one else can know."

"Okay, okay." I wriggle both hands in a placating sort of gesture. I hate it when she goes on like this. "Let's just say that people in the village mentioned that they know about Thomas and me. That either one person, or a whole lot of people, know my former address."

"Which people?" It is an accusatory bark.

"I'd rather not say. Not just now. Can you accept that?"

"No. I don't feel in the mood to do so, quite frankly."

"Oh, come on, Martine."

"Come on? You came to accuse me of giving out private information, didn't you?"

"Yes, yes. You're right, of course."

"And why would I do that? Have you worked that out? Do you

think that it's all I have to talk about to everyone? You and your life?"

"Look, it could have been done in simple conversation. Secrets sometimes manage to just jump out of their hiding places."

"There's no reason for me to let anything about your past just 'jump out.' It's not so interesting, your life. Not to me, anyway. Only to you. It's not really any different than what millions of people have gone through, you know."

"Never said it was ..."

"But you probably think I had a reason to talk about you behind your back, right? And what reason would that be? I'm not jealous of you, I don't envy you, I'm not in competition with you. So I have no score to settle."

"Yes, yes. Okay, okay. I'm sorry. I didn't mean to offend you." I hate people being angry with me. "I do trust you."

"Trust!" She spits out the word. "You trust me. Okay, then, you want to find out who you can't trust? Do you? Well, then, open your eyes. Take a look around you. Take a look at jealous people, envious people. They are victims of their own lack of intelligence. Intelligence gives you the power to have distance from your primary emotions. But stupid people, they're incapable of distance. They pass their lives slamming their noses against the glass, frustrated, eaten up, angry. Victims."

She lifts her cup, takes a long gulp of cider. Then slaps the cup onto the grass, stands up and storms into her house.

46

On Tuesday morning, I see that Chantal and Jean-Paul, amazingly enough, have taken my suggestion seriously. She's wearing a green silk blouse, green-brown designer jeans and nifty, polished brown shoes that almost look like walking boots aside from the fact that they are too expensive and chic to be scratched. Her whole outfit looks surprisingly new; she has obviously bought it for the occasion, unable to resist turning personal drama into a fashion statement. Jean-Paul is kitted out in brownish trousers (to look like a tree trunk, I suppose) and a sycamore-green designer T-shirt. He is also sporting a camouflage hunting jacket. Does he hunt? I never asked him if he did and don't now either. I don't want to be totally disgusted by the man. Not today, anyway. Still, it takes no great stretch of the imagination to picture him trudging over fields, high-powered rifle in hand, intent on blasting the life out of small songbirds, lovely pheasants, cooing pigeons, white doves, fuzzy bunnies, leaping hares, Donald Duck and Bambi's mother.

We head south in Jean-Paul's BMW, avoiding Épineux-le-Rainsouin, driving through tiny country lanes to Launay, where we park the car down near the river. We cross the village on foot, then turn left into the grassy, green lane. I feel a strange pang of sadness. I haven't been near this path in years, but once I walked it every morning, back in the old days, the days when I lived in La Basse Chauvière. Even then, I used to drink my morning coffee in the village. But the café in Launay has since closed down (it never was prosperous), and surely no one in the village remembers me now.

The green lane is far less choked by vegetation than I remember it to have been. Walkers must come through these days; anxious to attract tourists, the local government continues to clear many of the remaining old footpaths. I only hope our blackmailer hasn't decided to take the same route. Just before we reach La Basse Chauvière, I push my way through a scraggly break in the hedge and clamber into a field, closely followed by Chantal and Jean-Paul, good little lambs that they are.

"We'll sit here and wait," I whisper. "Just on the other side of this field is the house. The mail van has to come down the gravel road you can see over the top of the hedge, just there. We can hear it, too, from here. Once it's gone, all we have to do is wait and see who comes along to pick up the letter."

So we sit still in the grass, wait without speaking, nerves taut, trying to wriggle our ears in all directions, Werewolf style, and pick up sounds, eyes scanning the weeds searching for movement like soldiers in an old war film. From time to time, we check our watches, resign ourselves to wait just a little while longer. And then to wait some more. But by ten-thirty, it's pretty clear that waiting isn't going to hatch eggs.

"Let's go," I say finally. "There's no mail arriving today."

So we snake our way back through the hedge, trudge back into the village of Launay.

"We'll do this again tomorrow," says Chantal, as she picks out a few leaves from her hair. "It has to get there tomorrow, the envelope I sent. It has to."

I have my doubts this will work — it just seems too easy — but I don't bother voicing them. It's worth a try, anyway.

47

ON WEDNESDAY MORNING, WE GO BACK TO THE FIELD, HIDE BEHIND
the hedge, watch butterflies and bees flit amongst wild flowers ... and
wait in vain for the postal van. Come back again today, Thursday. The
sky has turned a dull, velvet grey, and the grass feels less itchy than it
does under the dazzling sun. Our "stakeout" is more comfortable, but
again, the mail van does not come bumping down the road. Again, no
one, other than those ever-busy insects, passes. It starts drizzling before
we dejectedly make our way back to Launay.

"What went wrong?" wails Chantal when we are sitting in the
BMW. She turns around in her seat to look at me in the back seat. "The
letter should have arrived already."

"Should have," I agree. "But didn't." I'm thinking hard.

"We'll have to come back tomorrow. See if it gets here then."

Jean-Paul sighs. He can't keep making up excuses for why he isn't
out seeing to cows, pigs, sheep and hens every morning. Still, he can't
in good conscience let me and Chantal go out there alone. How can we
tackle a dangerous lunatic if he isn't around to defend us? I wonder if
he is armed, if he has a little gun tucked neatly into the pocket of his
hunting jacket, but I don't care to ask that either.

"What if the mail has been transferred on to somewhere else?" asks
Jean-Paul.

"That's exactly what must have happened," I say. "Only I don't know
how it could have been done. I wasn't allowed to transfer Thomas's mail
to my own address. I wonder how someone else managed it."

I decide it's time I pay a visit to the post office.

48

"YOU HAVE TO HAVE AN *ORDRE DE RÉEXPÉDITION*," SAYS THE BROWN-HAIRED lady behind the counter. She is peering at me with certain suspicion, as if I'm planning something highly illegal. I do have, after all, a thick accent. And what's this foreigner doing, asking about the French post, about sending letters to another address?

"And how do I get one of those?"

"You can ask for a form here in the post office. You fill it in at home, bring it back here, and show me a piece of photo ID. Then a week or two later, your mail goes on to your new address."

"And if I want to have my boyfriend's mail forwarded on, too?"

"No problem. You just note down on the form that the address change is for you and your boyfriend. You put down your name and your boyfriend's; you both sign the form. Then you both come back here, and each one of you presents a piece of ID."

"What if he can't come back with me? What if he's working?"

She looks even more suspicious now. "So bring his ID with you. Get him to sign the form at home first. That way, we can register the change of address even if he can't be here."

I leave the post office. Sit in my car and think for a while. So I could have had Thomas's mail transferred after all. All I'd had to do was fake his signature and use one of his ID cards. Except back then, everyone in the local post office knew him and knew he'd just died. So I couldn't have.

I get out of the car again, go back into the post office. "Look, what if my mail has been transferred without my knowing? What do I do then?"

Now she really is staring at me in an unfriendly way. "If you think that's happened, then give us your name and address and we'll register a complaint." She is even huffy.

"Okay." I wonder how my next question is going to go over. Perhaps she'll push a little emergency button under the counter, the one that rings a bell in a police station. The steel bars above the front door will come crashing down, and ten police cars will pull up, their lights flashing. Who will know I'm in custody? Who will feed Werewolf? "Look, the problem is, it's not really my mail that has been transferred to another address. It's my ex-boyfriend's."

"Well, there's nothing we can do about that," she snaps. She now thinks I'm a stalker trying to get my paws on an ex-boyfriend's mail, get some big-time revenge because he threw me out on my ear and went for a lusher, juicier model.

"It's not what you think," I say. "You see, he's dead."

"That doesn't matter."

"Well, it does in a way. Because he couldn't have arranged to have his mail transferred. He died in an accident."

"What are you trying to say?"

"That his mail was transferred by someone else. A third party. To an unknown address."

"And how do you know this?" she asks through razor-thin lips.

"Because it doesn't come to his address anymore."

"And how do you know that?"

"Because I go and pick it up." I have the dreadful feeling that this was exactly the wrong answer to give. For sure, her fingers will be fumbling around under the counter now, searching for the hidden button.

"That's not legal. Picking up someone else's mail. You don't have the right to do that."

"I know," I say. "I'm just doing him a favour. Honestly. It's a hell of a bother for him to heave himself out of the grave, come and pick it up himself." I turn, get the hell out of the post office and into my car. Very pronto. What if there was a hidden camera somewhere? If so, and if she reports me, my house will be surrounded by submarine cars in no time. Mail theft will be the least of my worries; I'll also probably be charged with Didier's murder. For a foreigner, they might just bring back the guillotine. My execution will take place in front of a roaring crowd, and my head, according to that charming revolutionary tradition, will be snagged up high on a spike of my garden gate.

49

I've reached an impasse. What am I supposed to do with all the information I've gathered? I'm no closer to knowing who, if anyone, killed Didier. But as the expression goes, busy hands are happy hands, so I decide to wash windows at three o'clock, Friday afternoon. This abnormally domestic (for me, anyway) cleaning action causes an uproar on the square. Monsieur Douspis, who has just returned in his car from the pharmacy in Derval, is the first to spot me. "Washing windows, huh?" he calls out. Then smiles with both approval and appreciation.

"Yes. Have to do it every once in a while," I say facetiously. "But only once in a while." Which for me is the truth; certainly I haven't washed windows in at least four or five years. Goodness knows what everyone has been saying behind my back.

At four-twelve (the huge church clock is just across the road, metres away), Monsieur Sauvebœuf and Monsieur Vadepied pass on the way from Monsieur Vadepied's garage. "Washing windows, I see," says Monsieur Sauvebœuf with an approving nod.

"Yes," I say. "Next time planned is sometime in 2015. Can't let things get out of hand, you know."

Both men nod slowly, uncertain as to whether this is meant to be serious or not. Then they continue on over the square.

Monsieur and Madame Voiton pass. City folk, they spend their summers here in Épineux-le-Rainsouin in what was once a village butcher shop that has since been converted into a house of yellow cement by Lemasson Enterprises, with a tidy concrete garden, also created by Lemasson Enterprises.

"Oh, how nice clean windows look," calls Madame Voiton. Monsieur Voiton nods, smiles encouragingly. Werewolf gets up from the sidewalk where he is sunbathing and greets them, knowing they always pat him on the head and occasionally give him cookies.

The young mother renting the house just beside the Sauvebœuf's ambles by, pushing a baby in a stroller. She glances at me, glances away. Young people in the village keep to themselves. They don't bother with hellos or comments to those of us who are older, but converse only with other young couples. Their talk concerns babies or the property they wish to purchase in the new housing development.

Monsieur Vadepied crosses the square again, going in the opposite direction without Monsieur Sauvebœuf. He is now heading back to his garage to fetch something of great importance: a hammer, a nail, a screwdriver. He waves.

Madame Sauvebœuf comes by as I'm tackling the glass in the old front door. "My husband said you were washing the windows," she says, her malicious little half-smile playing, as ever it does, across her lips.

"Good news travels fast," I say.

"So I said to myself, well, I'll go and have a look."

"And so you did."

"It's nice to have clean windows. We were all wondering if you felt the same way." So my windows have indeed been a fascinating subject of conversation after all. "In the old days when this was a hotel, there was no running water. We didn't have water in our houses either then, you know. Not like today. Cleaning and washing was a real task, but we did it all the same. We had to go fetch it at the pump, over there on the corner. We had a yoke around our necks and tin pails suspended on either side. Water didn't get here into the houses until after the war."

"I know," I say. "And there were no toilets in the village either until 1988."

"We had outhouses," says Madame Sauvebœuf, nodding wisely (and ever smiling). "Our outhouse was all the way down the road. We used a bucket in the night and carried it down to the outhouse to be emptied in the morning. And this hotel and the old hotel that Madame Filoche used to run in the building that is now the village café, well, the servants had to carry the waste buckets down to the river and dump them there. But still, when your place was still a hotel, café and restaurant, and there were no modern conveniences, the windows were always kept nice and clean."

"I suppose they were," I say, mildly enough, although old country inns were rarely places of great salubrity. A stay in one often meant discomfort and misery for travellers already fatigued by a journey in a horse-drawn *diligence* over potholed, muddy roads, and preyed on by brigands and bands of the impoverished. There were some hotels, rare enough, where tasty soup boiled on the hob, where juicy hams hung from the beams, where lamps glowed, where a huge cut of meat or delicate songbirds grilled on the fire. Where cheery men ate, drank and played cards at the tables, where dogs and cats scrabbled for scraps on the floor, where clocks chimed and utensils glowed.

But the countryside was sparse with such happy spots and far more generous with those that were a traveller's bane: inns where one rubbed shoulders with the lowest of peddlers, with noisy brigands, wandering priests, or impoverished tattered cranks who, paint box and crayons in hand, roamed for pleasure. In these dreary hostels, there was either little to eat or victuals that were rotten and stinking. One retired, bone-weary and hungry, to a bed whose linen was rarely changed and whose huge feathered quilts and mass of pillows were a happy home to those more despised creatures of the insect world. Victor Hugo wrote of these malodorous inns where soup was thin, but the dishes greasy:

Oh diabolic foul inn, hotel of fleas
Where the skin, in the morning, is covered with red bites
Where the kitchen stinks, where one sleeps uncomfortably
Where one hears the travelling salesmen sing all night

Avoiding argument, I squeeze out my sponge under Madame Sauvebœuf's watchful eye, begin on another pane.

"When you're finished here, you can tackle a few of those," she says. Her malicious smile has spread across her face in ripples of venomous delight.

"What? Where?" I ask in mild confusion.

"Your next door neighbour's, that's where. Could do with a wash, they could, but she's too lazy for the job, never getting out of bed the whole day long. Hear her television going all the time. Drinks, too. Shameful behaviour. Men coming in and out all the time."

I wonder if Christelle can hear what Madame Sauvebœuf is saying.

She has a voice that pierces like an electric drill, and she's not even making a faint stab at discretion. She wants to be heard, I decide. She hates Christelle. But Christelle's windows are closed as usual. She must be downstairs by now, I think. Not upstairs in her bedroom. Not at this hour, surely.

As I look up, I register for the very first time — although I've been seeing it for years — how close Christelle's upstairs bedroom window is to the window of my office at the end of the house. A little over an arm's length away, in fact. Close enough for us to shake hands with each other, almost. Close enough for her to hand me a cigarette. Almost. Because, as I mentioned, her house was once part of my hotel, and up there, the upstairs rooms (and their windows) followed each other along the long corridor, a corridor blocked for at least a century and a half by a stone wall. Big windows, they are. Elegant, even. One after another: a long line of windows.

I drop my sponge back into the bucket. Keep on staring.

Very, very close indeed, her window and mine, says the little itch of a voice that creeps up from my subconscious from time to time. Close enough that someone standing right where you are now, someone wanting to throw stones at Christelle's window, could hit yours instead. Someone who had had just a little too much to drink in Pierre's bar. Someone who wanted to contact Christelle but knows she only answers her door when she is certain who's out there, someone who knows she almost never answers her mobile phone because she has debts everywhere.

Didier? Didier and Christelle? Why would Didier want to visit Christelle at night? No, the question has to be posed the other way around. Why wouldn't Didier want to visit Christelle at night? Christelle, with her golden skin, her long, wavy dark hair, her slanting eyes. Christelle always ready to "receive" male admirers. And Didier, always ready for a new female conquest.

50

I PICK UP THE BUCKET, ABANDON THE WINDOWS, COME INTO THE HOUSE
and think. I think of waylaying the mailman who delivers to La Basse
Chauvière. A bad idea. If he's as suspicious as the woman in the post
office, I'll be charged with mail theft — at the very least. I think about
how easy it would have been to have had Thomas's mail transferred to
my address years ago. Really easy. A forged signature is a child's game
when you come right down to it. I open a bottle of Muscadet (Château
des Grandes Noelles), go sit in the courtyard with Werewolf.

Think about how I always opened a bottle of red wine in the days
when Jean-Paul came to visit. Always red wine back then, although I
prefer white. About how I used to feel in the days when Jean-Paul would
come to visit. About how I used to feel about him. About how quickly
feelings and illusions disappear. About romance in general, about the
plight of single women. Me, in particular. Christelle, in particular.

And I look over the courtyard. I look at the wooden gate that has
always been open — still is — although it is unlikely that Jean-Paul
will be walking through it again. And I realize my error: corruption
is endemic, therefore acceptable. Because this is so, no one had to kill
Didier to prevent him stirring up trouble; they only had to give him the
feeling that he was more than a broom pusher. That he was important.
Important enough to be given a four percent raise like everyone else.
But another person — one who is mocked unrecognized and resentful,
a perpetual victim — wouldn't she also dream of triumph? Of love?
And when opportunity comes trotting in, take a grab at the brass ring?

I go upstairs, turn on my computer, go on the Internet. Search for
the official site of the French post office. Find it. Then search under
"change of address."

And in the end, it, too, is as easy as making mud pies. You fill in an online form, send it to the post office. By regular mail, they send a reply with a code of confirmation to your home address (in this case La Basse Chauvière) to ensure that the address you sent in is a valid one. Then all you have to do is go out to La Basse Chauvière and wait. Once the code has been delivered, you go back home, reconnect to the post office site, enter the code, validate the change of address request.

No ID needed.

It's a perfect solution. For a while, anyway. Only for a while. In the end, you screw up. And some people just can't help screwing up. Some people have a natural talent for it. People like Christelle. People with character flaws. People who are jealous. People who are, as Martine said, incapable of distance. Who pass their lives slamming their nose against the glass, frustrated, eaten up, angry. Who think of themselves as victims.

The night Didier had thrown stones at the window, no, it really hadn't been me he wanted to see. If it had been, he would have knocked at my door. But Didier had meant to reach Christelle's window. And he had missed because he was too drunk to aim properly. And my vanity had led me astray. Vanity, one of my little character flaws.

I keep on thinking. Of the right-of-way that leads through Christelle's courtyard to my back gate. Of the gate and back door to my house that are always unlocked. Who could pass through without the neighbours noticing? Jean-Paul. But he arrived at night when the streets were dark, the shutters down. He took no risks, Jean-Paul, made sure no one could see him. But one person — only one — could come anytime, even during the day, when I wasn't home. Only one person ran no risk of being seen. One person only could come into my house, come into my office, go through my papers, find out all about me. Find out about Thomas, La Basse Chauvière. One person, so well known to Werewolf that he wouldn't even bark. Wouldn't even mind.

It all ties together: Didier and Christelle. They must have known each other well. Very well. Two people looking out for the main chance. Only Christelle doesn't know that Chantal refused to be blackmailed by Didier. And she doesn't know that Jean-Paul is my lover, that he confides in me. She can't possibly imagine he would show me a letter, a letter addressed to my old address, to Thomas's old address: La Basse Chauvière.

And Christelle, she tells lies. So many lies, you don't know where the truth is. Plans to make big money? Cash that will be rolling in soon? Computer courses? Computers? Printers? The Internet? I didn't believe her for a minute. Didn't believe she could actually work hard at something, could even be good at it. And I was wrong.

51

IT IS DARK WHEN I PUSH OPEN THE WOODEN GATE THAT LEADS TO Christelle's courtyard and the right-of-way. I knock, using the usual code: three taps, then two. I am angry, a self-righteous feeling born of betrayal.

She isn't looking at me when she opens the door, cigarette in hand, but has her eyes glued to the blaring television and yet another of those well-loved television clones who is making coy jokes and drumming up audience hysteria for the washer dryer combo machine to be won by answering a sub-culture question. I sit down at the table, pick up the tin box of cigarettes, flick it open, take one, light it. I do not offer thirty *centimes*.

"Zidane," Christelle bellows over frenzied screams, electronic bleeps and nasal giggles from a bloated, purple, cartoon character.

"What?"

"Zidane. That's the correct answer. Guy up there just won the washer dryer machine." The right answer is flashing in fluorescent red above the cartoon head: Zidane, it is.

"How's secretarial work on the Internet going?" I ask.

Christelle doesn't bother answering. Does she know the game is up? Can she sense it? Was my tone just too supercilious? Is she thinking of new lies or a way to hedge? Perhaps her feeling of power is so great at the moment that I have become a cockroach: innocuous, irritating, but nothing that can't be managed with poison.

"Or have I got it wrong?" I ask coolly. "Perhaps it's not setting up a secretarial business you are interested in. Only a little postal fraud and blackmail."

She's still ignoring me, lifting fag to mouth, inhaling deeply. The smoke curls past the paint-by-number impressionists towards the ugly plywood covering the old ceiling beams. What a cheap, shabby room this is. A sagging armchair is pushed against the wall; the table and chairs are things other people left behind, undesired, when moving house. A few battered pots and pans sit on an ugly brick kitchen counter. There is no personal touch anywhere, nothing that describes a life, indicates preference. It is merely a loveless, soulless space.

"Doo-waa beep-beep-beep, doo-waa beep-beep-beep, doo-waa beep-beep-beep," chimes a female vocal group, while giggling babies play with plastic blocks on furry rugs in a detergent commercial.

I reach across the table, pick up the remote control, click off the television. Now there is only blessed silence, the first I've ever known in Christelle's house. But she keeps her eyes screwed to the dead screen, as if there's still something to watch up there, something of utmost importance.

"In the end, Didier was your lover. Or one of your lovers."

She ignores me, of course. But she isn't denying I'm right, either. So I battle on. "There you were, the two of you, both with the same idea: using sex to get your hands on cash. It's not prostitution, is it? That's something nobler because prostitutes are social workers of a kind: they alleviate frustration and loneliness. But people like you and Didier, you have to make people your victims. Only you are a little worse than he was. You don't stop at murder."

Christelle punches out her cigarette although there's really no need; it's only a burnt-out stub between her fingers. She reaches for the metal box, takes out another, lights it. Turns finally to me, her eyes cold, neutral. "You'd better leave now. Visiting time is over."

"While I'm still alive?"

She sneers. "You think I'm that stupid? You think I'm going to kill you? And then what? Bury you in the courtyard? You think you're so important? You can't prove anything. No one can."

"That's why Didier was in his bath, wasn't it. He was in his bath because you were there. He thought he had nothing to fear from you. He thought he could trust you. You were his lover of the moment. The girl next door, so to speak. But he was wrong. You were the one who brought the hair dryer. You were the one who chucked it in."

"He was a blackmailer. You feeling sorry for a blackmailer?"

"What are you?"

"He was a shit," spits Christelle. As if this is all the reason she needs.

"Maybe he was a shit to you. Maybe. And maybe he was a blackmailer. But you can't know that, can you?"

"Can't I?" She smiles, proud, certain.

"Okay. Maybe he was. If so, how do you know?"

"Easy," she says. "Easy as pie. All you have to be is curious. You should know all about that. You're the one goes around asking questions. Your problem is that you aren't smart enough to ask the right questions, come up with the right answers. I am."

"So how did you find out? Did he tell you? Did he brag about it? And when he did, you agreed that blackmail was a really cute idea. Then you thought it out and decided that there would be more money in it for you if you did it alone. Is that how it went?"

She curls her lip. "He never even knew I found out he blackmailed people. He never had the faintest idea. He never would have told me either. He didn't care about me enough to do something like that. He probably never cared about anyone. You know, in the beginning I really liked him. I thought he was my kind of person. That we had something going for the two of us: both of us stuck in this crappy village, both of us with bigger ideas than anyone else. I thought we could do things together, have a future. But little by little, I realized what he was. I heard things. I know lots of men, married men. They come to me, they tell me stories. About their wives. About Didier going after them. I listen; I keep my eyes open. I know things, more than all the people put together here in this dead-end hole. And a hell of a lot more than you, too. Who do you think you are, going around, playing at being interested in everyone and everything? Asking questions all the time and never telling anyone about yourself? And nobody even minds. You come here whenever you want, just come into my house, take cigarettes, pose your nosy questions. And whenever I come to your house, you can't wait to get rid of me. You think I'm not good enough for you, not good enough to talk to you on your territory."

"Are you referring to your shitty, drunken visits in the middle of the night? The ones that take place at three or four in the morning?

When you can hardly stand?"

"Fuck you. No matter what you do in this shithole of a village, everybody likes you. Goody-goody. I'm not good enough for you to listen to me, but there you go, blah-blah-blahing to everyone else, and everyone thinks you're just great. The Canadian goody-goody who's so interested in French traditions. And what about me? What do they think about me? I know. Don't think I can't hear what everyone says. Don't think I'm deaf."

"And that's what happened with Didier, right? You realized he would never love you. And that mattered to you. A lot."

She stares at me with hatred. "I heard him that night, the night he threw stones at your window. I heard him." She flares her nose. "He was hot, Didier. He had to sleep with everyone. He was crazy. His prick was always hard, and he didn't care where he stuck it. There weren't enough women in the whole world for him. He had to have them all. Even you. He always made fun of you. Sneered at you behind your back, just the way he sneered at everyone else. And then he goes and throws stones at your window. He lied to me. He wanted to sleep with you, too. He had to have everyone."

"He didn't," I say. I'm feeling sorry for her, almost. She's got it all wrong. She must have suffered at what she thought was Didier's defection. "He wasn't at all interested in me, Christelle. He was throwing stones at your window that night. Not mine. But he was drunk, so he missed and hit mine instead. And you thought he had come to see me."

"I watched you, the two of you. Crossing the square together. Going into Didier's house. He should have been with me that night. I was waiting for him. But no, he changes his mind. Decides to spend the night with you instead. That shit."

"You saw us crossing the square and going to Didier's house," I confirm, "and you decided we were going to spend the night together. And because of that, you made plans. You decided to kill him as soon as possible and then take over the job of blackmailing his ex-lovers. Was that the way it went?"

"I planned everything out," she nods proudly in confirmation.

"Except you got things wrong. That night, I was in Didier's house for maybe five minutes. Then I left. But you weren't watching anymore, were you? You had already decided that I was the enemy. The rival."

Christelle digests this information for a minute or two. Then shrugs it off. It just isn't important enough. Not any more, anyway. So what? So she did get it wrong. There was no romance between me and Didier. She doesn't care about unimportant details like that now.

"So, how did you find out he was blackmailing people if he didn't tell you?" I ask patiently. "Did you go through his papers? Find love letters that women sent him? Is that how?"

She smiles smugly. "I didn't need letters."

"You didn't?"

She lights another cigarette, shoves it between her lips. Gets up, goes to the cupboard, pulls out a bottle of wine, pours a glass. Then looking over at me with smug content, raises the glass in a toast of congratulations. To herself, of course.

I watch her, think: Why didn't she need letters? If there had been letters in Didier's house, the police would have found them, wouldn't they? They would have started asking questions in the village. But perhaps even Didier didn't have the originals. Hadn't Jean-Paul and Chantal destroyed the letters Chantal had sent him? But Christelle still knew about them. Could use them for blackmail.

"I think I know what happened," I say. "Didier had copies of the letters on his computer. I'm right, aren't I?"

She sits, still looking triumphant. Takes another swig of wine.

"And you made copies of them. Deleted them from his computer, downloaded them into your new laptop." I'm only guessing, of course, but it feels right.

"Photos, too," Christelle says gleefully. She's so proud of herself, she can't even be bothered denying anything. No, she feels like bragging now. She must figure it's time someone recognized how clever she really is.

"Photos? There were photos?"

"Stupid what women will do. You should see the photo collection he had on his computer; looks like a porno site. The oh-so-good village women, the wonderful respectable housewives, with their asses in the air. Thinking they were the ultimate fantasy. Incredible. Didier, he had himself covered every step of the way. Women like to be photographed,

I learnt that from my mother. I watched her making herself up, dressing up, doing everything she could so people would take her picture. All women are the same. Especially when they're too old and ugly to be seen in the nude and a young lover tells them they are beautiful. You should see them, the photos. You should read the letters. Laugh? You want to be sick."

"Or sad, maybe. How about sympathy?" But I'm talking to the plasterboard walls, to the table and chairs, to the paint-by-number Van Goghs, Cézannes, Monets.

"But I was just a little bit smarter than Didier, wasn't I? He would never have stuck with me. He would have dumped me, too, just like he dumped everyone. He didn't know how smart I am. He didn't know I'm great with computers. He didn't know that while he was sleeping, I would find out what he was up to. When he was away in dreamland, I just went into his office, turned on his computer and had a look. It's a dog-eat-dog world and I wanted to know things. I wanted to know what he was up to, who the other women in his life were. If he belonged to a chat group. Things like that are important when you have a relationship with someone. Have to look out for your future. See where things are going to go."

"And you went through my papers, too. No big risk. You could go in and out of my house anytime I wasn't there. Maybe you were looking for something incriminating? Perhaps you wanted to see if you could find out if something was going on between me and Didier? A romance, a relationship. But all you found of interest was my old address."

"Your fault," she says, and she means it. "Your fault. When people have secrets, it attracts my attention. You always asked me my life, my past. But you never talked about yourself. I never knew a thing about you. So I had to find out, didn't I? I have to know who you really are."

I take another cigarette from the box. Light it. "When I ask questions, it's not to blackmail people. That's the difference. I don't kill people either. And by the way, how do you know Didier actually did blackmail all those women? Perhaps he only tried it once or twice, then decided the game was too dangerous. Perhaps he only kept that stuff because he got a voyeur's kick out of looking at it. What proof do you have?"

Christelle doesn't answer. She's bored.

"Think about it, Christelle. Didier didn't wear flashy clothes. The house he lived in is municipal housing. He didn't pay rent. He didn't even own a car; he just used the village van to drive around in. He didn't travel, didn't even eat big expensive meals in the restaurant. I don't know if he had a big lump sum in the bank, but if he did, the police just might have noticed and wondered where it came from."

Christelle reaches for the remote control, clicks the television back on. The audience is screaming with enthusiasm. The right answer flashes up on the screen: Claude François, the French singer electrocuted in the bathtub in 1978.

"Did Didier have Internet access?"

Christelle glances at me briefly, then turns back to the television screen. "Yeah. So what?"

So what? From Didier's computer, Christelle wouldn't have to worry about going on the Internet, contacting the post office. Even the post office couldn't trace her. The e-mail address that came up was his.

Her face is stony. She doesn't even bother asking me how I worked the whole thing out. She isn't the least bit interested.

52

At five in the morning, the telephone rings. Christelle, I think in my half-asleep state. She'll make up some reason to see me because she can't walk into my house anymore. The back gate is firmly latched on my side; the back door is locked. She needs an excuse. She has to get rid of me. Dog-eat-dog.

I pick up the phone. The voice belongs to Madame Douspis. She is shouting, "Come. Come quickly. My husband is unconscious. Come. Come."

I throw on a sweater and a pair of jeans, am out the door in a flash. But already I can see an ambulance in the dark street and Monsieur Douspis being carried out the front door on a stretcher. Madame Douspis is standing in the lit doorway on her wobbly legs. Behind her, poking their heads out from the hallway, are Madame Filoche and Madame Beauducel in their bathrobes. She must have called them, too; it's another social event, in a way. But no one is speaking; this is a scene out of a silent movie.

The ambulance doors slam shut and it drives away, wheels whirring on the rain-wet road, tail lights streaking through the village street.

"What happened?" I ask.

Madame Douspis wrings her hands. "It was an attack," she says. "He got up to go to the bathroom and fell on the floor." Tears start rolling down her cheeks. "They say he might die."

"Do you want me to take you to the hospital in my car?"

Madame Douspis shakes her head. "I'll wait here. They told me to wait here. I'll wait here until they call me. They'll tell me to come." She pokes at a tear with her gnarled forefingertip. "Strange. Strange. Who falls on the floor? Who? He does. Not me. I'm the one who is sick, not him. It's very, very strange."

We go into the house, sit down around the plastic table. Madame Filoche fumbles around in the tiny back kitchen, prepares coffee. We sit until the village square fills with morning light, wait for the phone to ring.

"He'll be all right," says Madame Beauducel. "I can feel it in my bones. He'll be all right. He'll come through."

"He'll be fine," says Madame Filoche. "Men are tough. They come through. He was in good health. He'll come through. My husband died like that. In the middle of the night. Stood up, keeled right over. Dead."

"My husband was sick for years," says Madame Beauducel. "Doctors couldn't do a thing for him. It's not easy being a widow."

"I'm the one has to take all the pills," says Madame Douspis. "Who will take me to the bathroom in the night? Who will drive to the *pharmacie* and pick up my prescriptions? I'm the one has to be taken care of. I'm the one who is seriously ill. I'm the one who is in danger. I'm the one who should be taken to the hospital. I'm the one the doctors should be treating." She stops, looks defiantly at all of us, as if she's jealous of her husband.

53

CHRISTELLE'S CAR IS NOT OUTSIDE HER HOUSE. WHERE HAS SHE GONE? I go into my courtyard, unlock and open the wooden gate, take the right-of-way to her door. I don't bother knocking with my usual three taps, then two. There's no point to it.

The door is ajar. She is not here. There is garbage strewn everywhere. The television is gone, the paint-by-number impressionists, too. But the sagging armchair, the forget-me-quick table and chairs are still in position. I go upstairs to her bedroom. There's no computer here, no scanner, no printer. Nothing remains except odd bits of clothing scattered over the floor, rejects in a hasty departure. Empty hangers dangle in a cheap armoire covered with flocked, blue wallpaper.

She's gone away and won't be back. With her is the laptop computer; on it are the love letters written to Didier. And the photos. Surely she won't try blackmailing anyone again, will she? Surely she knows the game is up? Even she can't screw up that much. Or can she?

54

I TELEPHONE JEAN-PAUL AT HIS OFFICE ON MONDAY AFTERNOON. "COME to my house. This evening when you leave work. We have to talk. And when you come, knock on the front door. Like a normal person does. Like everyone else."

On the other end of the phone, he is silent. Then — perhaps it's the tone of my voice, definite, unaffectionate and certainly not pleading — he agrees. "Six-thirty. You have any news?"

But I ignore his question. "Six-thirty," I confirm.

He isn't late. Right on time, he knocks. On the front door. Like everyone else.

"Come in, come in. Sit," I say, as friendly as friendly can be, my right hand waving airily in the direction of the sofa. I have a strange and heady feeling that this is a fine hour in my life, although I'm not certain what I am about to say to this lover of mine, this handsome, grey-haired man who is looking, at the moment, wary, nervous, pinched.

An open bottle of white wine (the wine I like; not red, the wine he likes) sits on the low table just between fireplace and sofa. I pour out two glasses. "It's okay now," I say as I hand one to Jean-Paul. "At least I know who the latest blackmailer is. And because I know the whole story, because I've worked it out, you might be protected. Perhaps she'll stop now that I know everything." And I tell him. About the letter we sent, the one that never arrived at La Basse Chauvière. About all the village women who loved Didier. About Christelle who loved him, too. Once. Didier's perfect mate, in a way.

Jean-Paul listens, drinks the wine, doesn't ask questions. Soon I see his wariness dropping off, giving way to the usual old confident complacency. He becomes the familiar man I have loved these last years, the man whose lip corners quirk naturally upward, as if a good joke is in the offing, or as if a fool, one worthy of being sneered at, has entered upon the scene. He carefully places his glass down on the wooden tabletop, rubs his forehead with his balled fist, as if emerging from deep mist into a world of sunlight and green pastures. "Thank God," he whispers.

"Thank God what?" I ask.

"Thank God, we can live in peace again. Finally."

"Who? Who can live in peace?"

"We. Us." He looks over at me, meets my eyes. But his look is an amused one. As if he thinks I don't quite understand what this is all about. "We can live in peace. You. Me. Everyone in the village. All the women who were stupid enough to fall for that creep, Didier. All of us."

"All except the chickens, of course. And what about telling the police?"

"Police? What the hell do the police have to do with this? If they had been doing their job correctly in the first place, if they had even taken an interest in what Didier was up to in the beginning, then we wouldn't even have had this problem. Now it's over. We don't have to drag the police into this. Chantal and I don't want to get involved in scandal."

"And Christelle? What about Christelle?"

He shrugs as if the very name is nothing more than an annoyance. "What about her?"

"She killed Didier. She murdered him. Took a life. Doesn't that count for anything?"

"He was a blackmailing little shit," says Jean-Paul, and I see that the hint of a smile has quite vanished again, has flattened out to a thin line of rage. "And a blackmailing little shit like Didier deserves whatever shitty end he gets."

"Oh? Oh, really? Let's not forget Christelle is also a blackmailing shit. She's probably been trying to blackmail half the women in the village. Think of the misery she's already caused. You want her to get away with this? What if she doesn't stop? What if she continues to try and blackmail everyone?"

Jean-Paul merely shrugs. His rage has already vanished. Didier is dead. That's all that matters. Didier slept with his wife, with the fine and lovely Chantal, and for that heinous crime, he has been punished by death. "Christelle won't try it again. She knows you know the whole story now, that she can be arrested for murder. She'll keep her mouth shut, all right. And if she doesn't, I'll ferret her out. Make sure she stops. Don't you worry about that. What's important is we can live in peace again. You. Me. The two of us. Just like before."

He means it. He's being sincere. Jean-Paul is not a man who doubts his charm. His smile is back again, and his eyes have slanted into a warm intensity of desire. He's raising his hand, wriggling his index finger in a gesture that means "come closer, come here, come to me, come sit over here with me." He says, "I want to touch you. I love you."

"No," I say gently, smiling, too, shaking my head. "Sorry. No more you and me. Finished, all of that."

He stares at me for a minute, drops the hand. Is he surprised? Really? It's not easy to tell. Now he shrugs. The look in his eyes, the warm look of a lover, dies. "I thought so."

"You haven't actually been very noble. Or even nice to me."

"Are you joking? Don't you understand what my position was? I might have been charged with murder if Chantal's letters had been found. Look at things from my side for once. I have everything to lose if people know about us. About you and me. Don't you understand any of this? My position here in the village, my reputation, my business, everything would go down the drain."

"Because you have a mistress? You know that's not true. You know it. Even if you left Chantal, divorced her, no one would care. These things happen. Everyone has the morals of alley cats, it seems to me. People divorce all the time. All that happens is that people have something new to gossip about for a while."

"You can't know that there wouldn't be repercussions," he says, but he sounds rather feeble and knows he does. He even looks slightly embarrassed.

"It didn't really mean that much to you, what we shared," I say, although some part of me still hopes he'll protest, say something that will show me it really does matter to him, that all of what went on between us was true and sincere, that it was love. Yet I know by now there's not a chance I'd start again, try to drum up once more all the old feelings I had for him.

"So it's finished, you and me? You really mean that? That's your final word?" His tone is curt.

"Over," I confirm. "Over … is the final word."

He stares silently for a minute, then stands. "I'm sorry," he says coolly. "I'm sorry you feel this way." It's the most he's going to give.

I nod. Then shrug. I really don't care, after all.

He walks towards the door. I follow him. Werewolf follows us both. Jean-Paul stops. Turns. Looks anxious, suddenly. "You won't tell anyone about us, will you? I mean, what we had together, it will remain our secret, won't it? You won't tell anyone in the village?"

I almost feel like laughing. I almost feel delighted. "My hero," I say, finally permitting myself a little bit of sarcasm. "A real hero. Right to the end."

He looks confused. Perhaps he's merely wondering if there is something he can recapture. Dignity, for example? But it's too late already. Already the confusion is being swept away by annoyance. He turns his back on me, opens the door, vanishes into the dusky evening street.

I close the door, turn the lock. "All's well that ends well," I say to Werewolf. He looks bored; he's not really into Shakespeare.

55

On Tuesday morning, Madame Douspis tells us all she does not feel in need of company. She has locked the door, lets none of us in, not me, not Madame Filoche, not Madame Beauducel.

"I want to be alone for a while," she says to all of us. "Such a relief to be on one's own, finally. Don't have to cook. Don't have to think of a menu for the day. This is my little holiday. All for me."

We must respect her wish. We can see her in her leaf-green chair, ever at her post. When we pass on the way to the bakery, we wave. She waves back. According to the hospital doctors, Monsieur Douspis is recovering slowly. He will not be returning home soon, for he will have to undergo a long convalescence in a home. He will have to take many pills for the rest of his life, follow a strict diet. Perhaps, finally, he will require as much care as Madame Douspis.

"It's not right," says Madame Filoche. "It's not right, her ignoring us like this. She needs us. That's not friendship, locking us out like this."

"She's even sleeping in that chair of hers," says Madame Beauducel. "I'll bet she is. She probably doesn't even go near her bed. Who takes her to the bathroom? That's what I want to know. Is she eating properly? It's not right. I tell you, it's not right."

"Doesn't like it when we ask about her husband," says Madame Filoche. "If you ask me, I'd say she's jealous. We're all asking about him and not her, for once."

56

OUR GENDARMERIE IS IN DERVAL IN A HIDEOUS BLOCK OF A BUILDING
now standing in the spot formerly occupied by the sixteenth-century
Hôtel du Cheval Blanc. Once a major stop on the east-west road, the
Cheval Blanc was a lodging of quality frequented by nobles, court
agents, priests, monks and mendicant friars, who would spend the night
in beds, on barn straw, or even on inn tables. But by the twentieth
century, improved roads and motorized vehicles allowed for speedier
travel on to more exciting places; it was no longer essential to stop in
Derval, a town of little importance. The old, grey stone Hôtel du Cheval
Blanc with its small-paned windows, quarry-tiled floors and huge fireplace became just another local café, and then vanished altogether in
1973, replaced by cement and cinder block.

I push the buzzer near the steel door of the gendarmerie. There is
a few minutes hesitation; no doubt, I'm being observed by cameras.
Do I look dangerous? Threatening? Then there is an answering buzz
indicating the door has been unlatched.

A young gendarme stands at a counter. Other voices come from a
room off to the left.

"Can I help you?" The man isn't smiling or welcoming, of course.
He probably reckons I am just another cranky, older woman coming to
complain about the neighbour's cat eating my geraniums.

"It's about the death in Épineux-le-Rainsouin. The death of the
garde champêtre, Didier Blot."

The gendarme looks bored. Vaguely attentive, but bored
nonetheless.

"Apparently, it has been decided that the death was accidental or
that it was suicide," I continue, hoping that, at least, he'll confirm. But
he doesn't. He merely waits. "In fact, it was murder. My neighbour,

Christelle Moisson, killed him. She was in his house. He was her lover. And she threw the hair dryer into the bath."

Another gendarme has appeared. He stands in the doorway of the back room, observes me with doubt. "How do you know?"

"She told me."

"And why would she do a thing like that, murder someone?"

"Because she wanted to use love letters he received from women he had slept with so she could blackmail them. She thought it would be the perfect way to make money."

"Where are the letters?"

"The letters were copied onto his computer. My neighbour found them, copied them onto her own laptop computer, then deleted them from his. At least, that's what I think happened."

"And you have proof? Proof he was blackmailing people? Or that she was? You know anyone who is willing to substantiate this? To come and make a deposition?"

"No," I admit. "But if you asked around, perhaps some women in the village would be willing to talk. Especially if they have been blackmailed since Didier's death. And you could find Christelle, look at her computer."

The gendarme at the counter turns, looks at the second gendarme standing in the doorway. He shrugs. The man in the doorway shrugs. "We did ask around in the village. Nobody mentioned anything to us about blackmail. And if we have no complaints, there's no reason to investigate anything. We can't just go on hearsay. On just your word."

The other gendarme looks like he's quashing a knowing smile. "Why would your neighbour admit she killed someone? Why tell you? It sounds a little far-fetched, doesn't it?"

"I accused her first. She used an old address of mine to receive the blackmail money. She put in a change of address on the Internet. Then she admitted everything."

He cocks an eyebrow, as if he wants to make it clear he really does know he's talking to just a foreign biddy, a vicious one who adores gossip and scandal and blackening the reputations of good local people. "She received mail that was sent to you?"

"Well, no, not to me. Mail belonging to a man who is dead." I'm beginning to feel miserable.

"And she received his mail in her own name?"

"I doubt it," I say, thinking about that shadowy figure, Thierry, the lover who constantly cropped up in Christelle's stories. Perhaps he really exists.

Both men shrug again. I'm boring them silly. "Are you certain there was an address change?"

"No, I guess not. But I think there was one. A letter I sent didn't arrive." There's no point in bringing Chantal and Jean-Paul into the story. I definitely know they'll deny everything anyway.

"So the letter you sent could simply have gotten lost?" The gendarme thinks I'm a fool.

"We could send another one. See if it arrives? You could check with the post office. I can't because I have no authority to do something like that."

"And your neighbour, the one who you claim killed Didier Blot, why would she involve you?"

"She didn't really. She just needed my old address. Also, she thought I was sleeping with Didier. He was her ex-boyfriend, you see."

"You were rivals." His eyes have that all-knowing glint.

"Not at all," I say hotly. "She imagined we were rivals."

"And is she younger than you, your neighbour?"

I look from one man to the other. What's the point of continuing? I can see which way the wind is blowing. He thinks I'm eaten up by jealousy because my pretty toy boy left me and went on to some succulent, youthful *poupée*. The gendarme at the counter takes a step backwards. His tone is flat. "According to your mayor, Monsieur Lemasson, Didier Blot was seriously depressed. He was afraid of losing his job. That sounds to us like reason enough to commit suicide. Happens all the time. But thank you very much, Madame. We'll look into what you said."

I know they won't.

57

Early Thursday morning, six days after Monsieur Douspis was taken to the hospital, the weekly cleaning lady finds Madame Douspis still in her chair at the window, but dead.

"She obviously hadn't been taking her medication," the doctor says later. "Those pills kept her alive. And she needed her insulin."

Mesdames Filoche and Beauducel show little emotion at her passing. Instead, they seem to be happy that they were right.

"She wanted to be sicker than her husband. She wanted to be in danger," says Madame Filoche. "It was a competition between them. She had always been sicker than he was and now, he was the one who was winning. She couldn't stand that. She didn't mean to die, I'm sure of that. She only wanted to be worse off than he was."

Madame Beauducel nods smugly, her almost lipless mouth clamped firmly shut. She has always been a woman of few words.

58

Monsieur Douspis returns from the nursing home in Derval at
the end of August. He is twenty kilos lighter and healthier-looking than
any of us has ever seen him. He says he has no intention of leaving his
house; his meals will be delivered by the meals-on-wheels service. But he
misses his wife. Life is difficult without her. He hates being on his own.
Madame Filoche and Madame Beauducel no longer come to visit him
now that Madame Douspis is dead. I think it strange; they still all need
each other for companionship, after all.

His four children came to the village on the weekend. "We don't
care whether or not he wants to remain in the house alone," announced
his eldest daughter. "We are taking matters into our own hands. We will
put the house up for sale and arrange for our father to be transferred to
a home, up in the north, near Lille. That way he can be cared for."

"I'll die if they send me there," Monsieur Douspis says to me. "Three
months, I'll last, in a place like that. I want to stay here. I'm fine here.
In my own house."

59

"Why has everyone abandoned him like this?" I ask Monsieur Vadepied. I'm sitting at his plastic table surrounded by his wife's doll and teddy bear collection. The canaries, still alive and well, are chirping madly over the television game show.

"He's an old goat, that's why," says Monsieur Vadepied.

Madame Vadepied nods, an evil smile on her face. "Madame Filoche went to visit him when he came home. The first thing he said to her was that he wanted to take her to bed. Is that a way to act? Old goat, he is."

"Well, he's a widower now," I say, determined to defend the man. "A single man. And Madame Filoche is a widow. So why not? They'd make a cute couple. Life might be better for them if they were together. Besides, what's wrong with suggesting they go to bed? What's wrong with being a goat?" I'm hoping, of course, that the Vadepieds will come out with a few juicy details about animal husbandry.

But Monsieur Vadepied only snorts.

"Shouldn't be thinking about things like that at his age," says Madame Vadepied. "Gave it up thirty years ago, we did. Told my husband I wasn't having any more of it. Not right, otherwise."

"Oh," I say, slightly embarrassed.

"Children of his want to sell the house. Get it over with. Sauvebœuf says he saw a young couple with two children visiting. Came with the notary. Want to buy. Talking about renovating. Modernizing. We need that in this village: new people, children, new ideas."

60

PIERRE HAS DECIDED THAT HE AND HIS FAMILY WILL LEAVE THE RESTAU-
rant before the year is out, move east to Alsace where tourism brings
in more money. It is not certain that a new proprietor will take over
the business; running a bar and restaurant in a small village is a losing
proposition these days.

Madame Filoche no longer visits anyone. She stays at her post
behind the opaque curtains at her window, observes us all, but is rarely
to be seen. I catch a glimpse of Madame Houdusse in the evening when
she comes down the road, passes behind the *lavoir* and goes to visit
Madame Beauducel. I do not know what the subjects of gossip are, for
I am not invited to participate.

Didier's job has been taken over by a young man with a wife and
new baby. He is not talkative or forthcoming. His wife is just a teensy
bit snobbish; she has the position of wife of a *garde champêtre*, after all.

The village is changing; I am old enough to dislike change. I miss
the mornings at the Douspis's house; I will miss Pierre.

And when I think about it, I realize I even miss Christelle.

61

THE MAIN SQUARE OF ÉPINEUX-LE-RAINSOUIN IS NOT ATTRACTIVE; THERE are no trees, there is no grass, no horse manure. There are no longer bumpy cobblestones on the road, and no chicken coops or bric-a-brac line the sidewalks. There are no benches where people can sit and talk of subjects of interest: who is sleeping with whom, who is pregnant with whose baby. To inspire village pride, five more cement planters have been installed by Lemasson Enterprises; next spring, tidy geraniums and other domesticated forms of vegetation will grow in them.

Épineux-le-Rainsouin is a place one drives through on the way to somewhere else. And driving through, one asks, "Who would want to live in a dead end like this?"

People live here because this is where they were born. Others arrive, are unable, forever after, to escape the sticky flypaper attraction of a village they have made their home. Yet a village is a microcosm and the mettle of greater places — New York, Budapest, Montreal, Brussels, Lahore, Stockholm, or Tel Aviv — can be measured by small events taking place here. We too have domestic violence, theft, corruption, adultery and murder.

Small-time, you say? Why, the great of the world could not exist without us. We point the way.